BEAU,
LEE,
THE BOMB,
&
ME

BEAU, LEE, THE BOMB, & ME

MARY McKINLEY

KENSINGTON PUBLISHING CORP.
www.kensingtonbooks.com

KTEEN BOOKS are published by

Kensington Publishing Corp.
119 West 40th Street
New York, NY 10018

All Kensington titles, imprints, and distributed lines are available at special quantity discounts for bulk purchases for sales promotion, premiums, fundraising, educational, or institutional use.

Special book excerpts or customized printings can also be created to fit specific needs. For details, write or phone the office of the Kensington Special Sales Manager: Attn. Special Sales Department. Kensington Publishing Corp., 119 West 40th Street, New York, NY 10018. Phone: 1-800-221-2647.

Kensington and the KTeen logo Reg. U.S. Pat. & TM Off.

eISBN-13: 978-1-61773-256-0
eISBN-10: 1-61773-256-7
First Kensington Electronic Edition: November 2014

ISBN-13: 978-1-61773-255-3
ISBN-10: 1-61773-255-9
First Kensington Trade Paperback Printing: November 2014

10 9 8 7 6 5 4 3 2 1

Printed in the United States of America

For John, who found me when I was lost

BEAU,
LEE,
THE BOMB,
&
ME

In early October, about a month after school started—right before it gets really crappy weather-wise in Seattle—is when I remember Beau blowing in.

And I must say, I wasn't at all upset that he'd transferred to our school.

I thought, *Good; fresh meat.*

Because I knew he would be tormented for the entire time he was at Baboon High.

Like I am. All day . . . every day.

The first time I saw Beau he was wearing a deep blue shirt that matched his eyes. He was tall and skinny, with wavy dark hair and a nice face, a lot like John Lennon from the Beatles.

He'd come from a high school in another state and was tan. He hadn't got the memo about not wearing bright colors in Seattle. If you don't have on some variation of rusty black, you aren't part of the team.

I must have been staring because we made eye contact, and he nodded and kind of bobbed his chin, like "hello," which was more human kindness than I'd been shown in this freaking hole for years.

I was so shocked I stopped, and it must have showed on my face because he tilted his head questioningly as he walked by. I looked away and headed toward my classroom, but I was so off my game/perturbed by our little encounter that I didn't even hear the hissing and catcalls directed my way by the geniuses right away, till they knocked my backpack off my shoulder and a bunch of crap went flying. When I crouched down to grab my stuff, they stomped on it and shoved by me, hard, till I unbalanced and fell through the threshold of my classroom, on my ass.

Like I said, I am tormented every day of my life here. Every. Day.

And why? Good question! But is there a good answer?

Yes! Turns out: I'm fair game. . . .

For I am Rusty, the Un-chosen. I am Rusty, the Shunned.

For real. They hate me. See, I'm extremely smart. And that's not good, but that's not all. . . .

I'm also extremely fat.

And not just muffin-top-chub-club . . .

Oh no, *no*, my friends; I mean I stopped weighing after I hit two hundred and thirty pounds. I don't even know what I weigh. I'm sixteen years old and I reflect on death nearly every day.

And the death that I reflect on is mine. Because I hate my life. Sometimes I actually *daydream,* for hours here in my room, about just what I'd do . . . about the stress and the mess and how to deal . . .

Not so much that I feel bad about how I look, because they don't even know I lift weights and underneath the fat I'm very strong, but because of the way I feel about the constant verbal and borderline physical abuse—just to *stop the noise*. To shut them up, finally, y'know? Just shut 'em down. Show them that they can't fire me 'cuz I already quit. Like: Hey, here's proof that I don't care about being excluded; screw you all, I'll exclude myself! Who needs a bunch of friends, anyway . . . ? I'll show you . . .

Then I stop. Deep down inside my mainspring hasn't broken. So far, anyway.

I'll know when I implode.

But in my own defense: Why is it always at my expense? *Any* regular person would be hammered down eventually by the intense contempt, followed by some *stupid* stab at humor. And seriously, if these guys had just one good line, just *one* killing joke, even just one little funny bone in their whole amoeba bodies. . . . But alas, no, and still there's never a letup. It's all day; it's moronic and it's unrelenting. You walk down the hall and people make barnyard noises, grunting and oinking in a pretty fair display of both their gift for comedy and their parents' degree of relation, which I do my duty to ignore. Bless their feeble little hearts. . . .

And ignore it I do. See, I've learned the path of least resistance. A good day is when they just yell out things and laugh like hyenas, like they have the least clue what it is to be witty or clever or anything but an extreme waste of space. Always the dull tools, always a lot of them together, *always*. They do this because they are pack animals, and cowards.

And I have come to expect this. You see, I am not a stupid girl; oh no, quite the opposite. I am very suspicious of sudden goodwill. I have been fooled by that one before. Back when I still had hope. Back in the day, when I was young and my heart was pure . . .

The popular girls in sixth grade are suddenly my friends! Wow, great; my life is going to get better now that we are getting older and maybe they won't make fun of me anymore, or at least just not so much.

So: my first slumber party! I even get to buy new pajamas! We talked about it endlessly at school that week; I was included and I was suddenly happy! I didn't know what I had been missing, this companionship of my peers, and to find it filled a deep chasm in my heart.

Oh, my, I'm sure you know where this is going . . . I'll just say it.

They ditched me.

I called—the girl said, come over, they were all there and going for pizza as soon as I got there. So I had my mom, who was so excited that I was finally getting friends, drive me across town to this girl's house, and, *because my mom is fat too,* I told her to drop me off three doors down because I didn't want them to see her being all fat, and maybe make fun of me anew— so this is all my own crappy karma coming back on me—but she drove off and I knocked on the door, and of course they were gone. Her dad and little brother were there; they had no idea anyone else was supposed to show up; her mom had taken them somewhere, probably the mall, but maybe the other mall. I sat down at his insistence, and he called, but she didn't pick up, neither his wife *nor* his evil freaking daughter.

Her little brother just stared at me out of the corner of his eye and snickered. His dad frowned at him, but he was laughing too; you could see it in his eyes. I shrugged, said oops, my bad—I must have gotten the wrong day or something, and I live just a little way away so I'll just be on my way.

He didn't offer a ride.

I walked the whole way home. I was crying so hard my nose was dripping freely in front of me as I lurched alone along the side of the dark road, like some zombie in a stupid indie film, crying aloud in my humiliation, keening, screaming, stupid/ stupid/stupid, gagging, staggering, staggered by my gullibility, stopping to bend over to catch my jagged breath . . . wondering *why* had they done it, wondering what had *I done* to deserve this? This is fair because they find me so ugly I don't count? *They* decide? Freaking low-rent morons! Terrible loser brats who grow up into terrible loser adults!

And yet they got away with it. It was soon, in fact, considered *hilarious.*

I cried myself hoarse because I could. They lived outside the city, and the road I was walking on was quiet and lonesome.

Because I didn't exercise in those days I was winded when I got back to my part of the town, which was only like five miles, but I was slow, to say the least. I had exhausted myself by this time, for the present anyway, and I felt dull-eyed and sullen. Also I didn't know what to tell my mom. When she saw me, she looked so disappointed it was like it was *her* party that failed.

My poor mama, who is too good for this world . . . she should have been a nun. She thought about it for a long time. She loves Jesus and being Catholic and rescuing stray cats and dogs and being a nurse, which she gave up for us kids "till the baby is in high school." The baby—who was then in fifth grade—the only boy, also fat, also messed with, is my little brother Paul. We are the fat family, and my dad has taken off for parts unknown. . . . Actually that's not true; he lives in Alaska and sends money. He just doesn't come down much. This I must admit.

Anyway, I pulled myself together and went in and told my mom I had what's-her-face's mom give me a ride home because I felt sick. Which was very true indeed. I felt gut punched and nauseous and shamed. And by that time I looked it.

That night was the first time I thought about killing myself. I was twelve.

The funny thing is I really can't remember her last name anymore. Her family moved in eighth grade, and I hope she is as happy as she deserves to be; that, in fact, she is an ex-con living with neck-tattoo remorse, in an unheated trailer with bedbugs. Her first name was Kris, and she thought she was *much* prettier than she actually was. She wore her dishwater blond hair very long, but it was extremely frizzy and damaged, completely lacking shine. And she was so stupid it was almost endearing, watching her try to flounder along when it was her turn to read aloud; it was like a wiener dog in deep snow, her nasal whine woofing out words hesitantly, like an ESL student, her jackass friends braying out their valuable encouragement.

I tell you, I despair of this generation. . . .

When I get home from school that evening, I get on Facebook and read my messages. I have friends in Scotland who are a little older than me and with whom I chat almost every day. Thank gawd for the cyber buddies. There are two girls I talk to every time I'm online: Sharon (aka Shazzie) and Winnie. Winnie is a nurse, and Shazzie is majoring in English, or "reads" English, as they say over there, when they mean "study" English. I crack them up. They think I'm "a right wheeze," as they say! I don't have any profile pics of my actual face; I either use *The Simpsons'* cartoons, Prince Harry, or I have this picture of Tina Fey (with her mouth wide open and her eyes bugging out) that I post on occasion. I also learned that to friend anyone who friended me from school was exhibiting very poor judgment. I stupidly did when they asked, so dimly excited once again that maybe . . .

But no . . . I ended up unfriending them when it became clear that all they wanted to do was post pics of the tortured Orcas of horrible, *horrible* SeaWorld and tag them "Rusty Winters" and send them to each other. The people from school who "friended" me were seriously *not*, but oh, the butt-clenching humor they spawned! I know that Facebook is no longer groovy for the teen set and I'm all yay, not a moment too soon! Let my lil' peers do Snapchat and Twitter and whatevs, I'll be fine if they drift away into the huge ocean of social media and are never heard of again; *I* won't miss them.

So I ended up friends with some of my mom's younger nursing student friends who are freshmen, and then one had friends in the UK; then I struck up a friendship with this one nurse (Winnie) and her friend Shazzie, both truly awesome young women in their early twenties in Glasgow, and their friends friended me and, well, you know. Now we talk every day.

I sit down at the screen that is my portal, like Narnia, and mosey onto Facebook. Now I'm in Scotland. Just like that. It's late over here in the UK.

"How was your day?" I see on my wall. "How are your new classes going? xx."

That's Shaz. She puts kisses but no hugs at the end of her posts, thus: *xxx,* but no *xox.* Winnie too. It's a Brit thing.

"Great!!!!" I write back. "Apparently I look like a garbage can! What do you call it? A rubbish bin? They mistook me for one today. Super fun!!!!!!! ☹ x."

"What?!! How did they mistake you for a rubbish bin, Ry? xx."

" 'Cuz they are stupid. I was, like, why are they sharpening their pencils so much, and then after the bell I stood up and all this pencil shaving fell out of my hair & clothes. xx."

"Very stupid!! Ugggghhh! Did the wee rotters get in trouble? xx."

"NO!!!!!!! ☹ x."

"That's mental, Rylee! Why?!! Tell your mum!!!!"

"I have. Over other things. She yelled."

"Good on her—& you!! How is it now?"

"It didn't help except now they make fun of her TOO. It SUCKS ☹ ☹   ☹!!!!!!!"

"Poor YOU! ☹ I HATE your bloody school! xxx."

"ME TOO! I SODDING BLOODY HATE MY BEASTLY SCHOOL!!!!!"

Which sounds so poser, when I say it like the Brits do. But I recharge. I really do. Sharon is awesome. I post again:

"Lol! Thanks, Shazzie! That helps!! I feel better! xxx."

"Never fear! One of these days I'll meet you in Glasgow for chai! Winnie too! ☺ xx."

"And scones! Count on it!!! I'll be there with bells on! ☺ xx."

How demented is my life that someone I consider about my closest friend in the world lives on the other side of the earth and could walk right by me and not know me? Or worse. Shaz and Winnie asked me to post a picture of myself, but I am too cautious a young woman by now. If they laughed or something I don't know what I'd do. I don't think I could stand it.

I don't even think they would—it's just I won't risk it anymore.

But that's par now; it's just one of many things I won't risk—like driving to school regularly. I learned to avoid risks a lot. I got my license and am in the process of saving for my own car. My mom's is a minivan, and it's a toss-up which is worse, driving that to school or riding the bus. I usually opt for the bus; they keyed "soooy" into the side of the van the first (and last) time I drove it to school. I'm *thinking* it was meant to be a hog call. But, hey, it could be a soy lover with a drawl. . . .

You see, I can still jest. Smiley face. Ha-ha-ha. Lol.

That afternoon, New Dude Beau rode the same bus as me. Moving through the menagerie, amid the inevitable chorus of oinking and lowing and barking and other noises the swill feel necessary to utter when first I draw near; I spot an empty seat, thank gawd, and squeeze in.

Luckily it's a seat neither too far nor too close to the front. . . . I pull out my book. I always have a book. It makes for a huge "no trespassing" wall, (and also reading is fundamental, right?) I can stare right through the red faces trying to hurt me.

My mom says, "Ignore them!" She says, "*They're* the ones oinking like pigs." She says I need to "grow a thicker skin." Sometimes I come home and I go straight to my room and I feel like I can't even get to the bed before I lose strength and fall. I would grow a thicker skin if I knew how. She says, "Stand up to them," that I'm smarter than all of them put together. Which is true, but when I stood up for myself in middle school, it only increased the cruelties, all very cat and mouse; oh well, if she's not quite dead yet—let us mess with her some more, even.

So instead I grew thicker books. I've read *The Grapes of Wrath* twice, then *Gone with the Wind.* Then *Uncle Tom's Cabin,* then *Anna Karenina.* I've read all of Jane Austen and most of Charles Dickens. I love *David Copperfield.* No, not the magician.

Jeez, look it up. . . .

But today was different. New Guy got on my bus. He hadn't been there in the morning, so it was unexpected. The extremely loud rabbling and noise stopped for a second when he got on. Then grew immediately back to its usual deafening roar. New Guy walked by me and sat about three quarters of the way back, which, if you're not part of the acknowledged too-cool-for-school group of academics that ride that region of the bus, is just askin' fer trubble, partner.

Which came . . . I wasn't reading: I was listening while pretending to read, something at which I have grown expert. I watched from the corner of my eye. They started low and slow, just kind of testing the waters. . . .

I hadn't heard the dawn of the chorus in a long time. I listen, fascinated.

"Hey, Blue Shirt! Hey—what do you think this is, the Gay Pride Parade?"

And of course—the fatal mistake: Turning calmly and look-ing at them, he says, like a normal human:

"Yeah, my name is Beau. Hi." He pronounced it "Bow," like "bow and arrow."

And with that he sealed his fate with the baboon colony.

He has that androgynous way of speaking that some guys do. It's just the way they talk. Whether they are gay or not.

The pack circled, smelling blood. One hyena alone cannot take down the prey, but an entire craven pack. . . .

They explode into laughter, which, as they say, is only one letter away from slaughter, and it's *on*.

"*Oh my gawd! Aahhhhahahaha! Wait—it's a fag reality show! Ahhhhh! Are you effin' kidding me? No effin' way!*"

Only they're not saying "effin'."

Beau turns back around, but he's in throwing proximity, and so small but increasingly large and heavy things start to be thrown at him. They're up to pencils, which, as I well know, freaking *hurt,* when he turns back around. Narrowly avoiding one in the eye, he says:

"Why are you doing this?"

I'm shaken. He is so *calm.*

And of course, the monkeys went bananas! They were so happy to have something else to take their minds off the freak-ing tragedy of being themselves! They howl and grunt, and I'm sure if they knew how to dress themselves, they would have flung their own poo, but thank gawd for buttons, right?

So goes the entire bus ride. Beau turns back around and ig-nores them, and I'm feeling amazed that we were almost to my stop without one comment about me from the douche bag pa-trol. I'm actually a little verklempt that someone else has taken the heat, but, while grateful, I'm not about to make one peep to save him in case the attention of the pack is diverted back to me again. If they could just tag team one of us every *other* day, it would be such a blessed relief.

When it's Beau's stop, I watch with great interest. If the hyena pack gets off the bus with him, someone should call the cops.

Beau gets off, and they look after him with great interest. It was grunt-discussed whether they should "effin' follow him," but they wanted to get over to one of the suck-up middle hyena's house before his spawners arrived home and drink up the beer laid in for Skidmark Fest, or whatever these grubby little dorks do. They saw *me* looking, however, and thus was Beau forgotten.

See, I would have thought that Beau's handsome face and skinniness would have protected him.

But no! Apparently even the *perception* of gayness outweighs good looks. At least it does at Baboon High, my alma mater. Even with the girls. I watch him getting "bumped" in the halls. I watch him being "accidentally" smashed into the lockers. He was too smart, I noticed, to *ever* drink at a water fountain.

I respected that.

I don't have much info about gay people. I'd never thought about it except on *Will & Grace* reruns and *Project Runway*. . . . Oh, wait—there's also *South Park* and the gay cable station that has hilarious stand-up, but I'm not sure any of that is real helpful. I never really cared one way or the other. I don't know any gay people.

I see news stories though. I realize it's one of the things people are still prejudiced about.

I know my mom thinks it's a sin, but even though she's very Catholic—whoops, I mean, *we're* Catholic—she's very kind. She says, "If people didn't have those feelings deep, deep down, they couldn't possibly *want* to do 'those things,' so it wasn't a choice, and so other people shouldn't be mean." And she likes Pope Francis a lot; he is chiller about just about everything.

But she also insists that "they shouldn't ever act on their feelings." *Ever.*

Just pray it away. *Forever.*

We had that conversation after watching that English comedian, Eddie Izzard, on TV.

But first: I've *always* gone to Mass with my mom. When I was little, I always took the whole Adam and Eve, and Noah, and Cain and Abel, and the sacraments, and "Esau was a hairy man" as the unquestioned truth.

Till last year when I got confirmed.

It was when I read about the early church, as instructed, that I grew somewhat agitated and continued investigating. I felt like I was being conned. There were no good answers for any of my questions. And believe me, with all the reflection I do on death, I have a *lot* of questions.

This, and time, is creating in me an irritated skepticism instead of unblinking acceptance.

So I guess I've made my own creed. I say: Love Is The Answer . . . We Can Work It Out.

My mom rolls her eyes. She says it's just my "teenage rebellion."

Then I parrot back something she tells me a lot:
We shall see. . . .

A couple of weeks into the school year it's time for homecoming.

I'm a junior finally, so homecoming is a big deal apparently. Just kidding. I know it is. I've watched the hype for two years now, and "my, oh my!" is all I got to say. Hope their team wins. Whatever. At least it comes in autumn, my favorite time of year. In spite of the fact that's when school starts.

I like the *valor* of autumn. I compare the leaves to the "noble six hundred" in the poem "The Charge of the Light Brigade"— beautiful and doomed.

I know . . . I'm so emo. But look it up anyway, you guys; it's freaking powerful.

The classes have all become texting central. Thirty-eight kids to a classroom enables them to get away with a lot. All the girls at my table are studying this week is fashion.

The pictures of little dresses they send each other on their phones are cute. I can see them on their screens out of the corner of my eye.

They all look like *Teeny Skeeze!*

That's my new line of fashion, btw: "Teeny Skeeze." Kind of a reverse take on that "kinder-whore" fashion look (where big girls dress up like oddly skanky little girls), this is where *actual* little girls learn it's their *job* to be judged on their butts, not brains, and *looks* alone are the *most* important.

Where our motto is:

"You're Never Too Young to Feel Fat!"

Potty-training thongs and diaper-compatible skinny jeans starting in toddler size eighteen months. Wonderbra onesies. Sledgehammer teething toys.

What do you think?

I think I'll be *rich!*

When I get home, my mom is on the computer. Which she always is now. It's a pain. Now that Mom is hogging the computer more and more, I would love to get a smartphone.

But I don't need the extra expense, which Mom said I have to pay for if I want one.

Also, I keep thinking if I wait a little longer, smartphones will be made by people with a safe workplace! I got totally freaked out when I saw all that stuff about workers jumping off buildings because it's so horrible making smartphones. Why does it have to be like that? I want a smartphone so much! But one made by people in proper conditions! I *know* it will cost more. I don't care if it costs more! It's worth it! Why is it so impossible?!

Whenever I say this I have been shot down in flames on Facebook with people screaming at me in all caps, telling me everything I own comes with suicide nets attached, but I say you gotta say it! If you don't speak up, it won't be heard! If you don't strive, it won't exist! Right?

You *know* I'm right!

Think about it! What if Thomas Jefferson and C-Note Franklin had just sat on the couch, dipping snuff and playing *Grand Theft Horse Buggy VII* and telling each other "Nah, screw it, sounds way too complicated . . . never gonna happen"?

What then, I ask you?

Anyway, Mom went back to school for a refresher course so she can return to being a registered nurse now that Paul is in high school, just like she planned. The upside is she looks happy. The downside is now she takes over the computer and I don't.

I go see what Paul is watching on TV.

"Whatcha watching?" I sit down on the couch beside him.

He answers without moving his eyes from the screen, in a hypnotic trance.

"This old lady. She, um . . . like goes and watches monkeys in Africa and then names them and knows what people do."

I crack up.

"Dude! You are so funny! Don't you know who that is? That is *Jane Goodall,* and she is a huge scientist and totally famous and those aren't monkeys! They're *chimps,* one of our closest living relatives! In fact, I think we go to school with some of them!"

Paul is awesome, but he is *so* not into knowing about things like anthropology. He is into Bruce Lee movies. He recently started a karate class, which is somewhat similar. He likes it a lot.

We sit and watch the "monkeys," which are actually quite troubling. Right off the bat, Dr. Jane says the big chimps are mean so we leave them strictly alone. But the little chimps that are orphans! Their mothers were poached for "bush meat," which I'd never heard of. But they frequently don't kill the babies. They sell them and the Jane Goodall Institute goes and buys them in the market and puts them on, like, a training reserve and teaches them to be righteous chimps and then go live on this chimp island.

As I listen, the caretakers of the baby chimps are teaching them things like how to be afraid of snakes. You'd think they would know that by instinct, but no. So the caregivers learn the panic yell from tapes of real chimps and then they put the baby chimps by a rubber snake, all coiled up like it's real, and yell the panic yell—more and more panicky as the babies get closer, till the baby chimps are freaked out by association and run off when they see a snake.

Their mothers would be so proud.

When it goes to commercial, Paul turns and looks at me.

"Do you think that's true?"

"What?"

"That we came from apes."

"Dude, yes! We're primates. We're all hominoids. One happy family. We're apes *now*."

"Dude, seriously. You know what I mean."

"I am serious, but I won't belabor the point. Here's what I think: Could you understand the warning in that yell? When the teachers amped it up, when the chimp babies got closer to the snake—didn't it freak you out too? That the danger was getting closer? It freaked me out totally. I think we used to speak that language; we just forgot all that stuff when we didn't need it anymore."

"Mom doesn't."

"What—speak chimp language?"

"Har. No, you know what I mean. Come from apes."

"I know. It's weird; she's a nurse, which is essentially a scientist."

"She says, 'I didn't come from any old slime!' "

"Dude, I *know*." I shake my head.

"Well, so what do *you* think?" Paul's face is troubled.

"Paul, I just said what I think. At least what I think I think. For now. I reserve the right to rethink this for pretty much my entire life. I think the question we're asking is: What do *you* think?" I look at him when I ask. I'm kind of wondering why we are talking about this; it's not really like Paul.

I remember I started to worry a lot about the big things when I started feeling depressed, when I got so lonely I echoed with emptiness. Hopefully Paul is not starting to feel low too.

"I don't know. I want to go to heaven." He sounds so young, like a little kid.

"Oh, dude, you too? I know, same here. That is the worst thing about thinking a lot. Having to continue when you start asking questions . . . Scary."

"Because then, where *do* you go? Like, do you even believe in God anymore, Ry?" He looks at me like he used to, like when I was older and wiser, instead of older and without a clue, like now. Since I don't know the answers anymore, I try to divert him.

"Paul, is everything okay? Are you cool? Is school okay?" His tone is so bleak and familiar it makes me anxious. But he nods.

"Yeah, I'm okay. I'm not bummed, if that's what you're asking. I just think about stuff more than I used to . . . and mostly what I think about is 'Where do you go when you die?' "

Whew. Well, in that case, join the crowd. I shrug. Limbo, where it's like Christmas every day? That was the company line for the unbaptized. At least it used to be. I always thought limbo sounded way better than heaven did, actually. I vaguely dreaded the whole heaven deal, what with the "saints and angels, on high, singing one unending hymn of praise" thing. Unending praise sounds lame. And now I'm also apprehensive that there's *nothing*. . . .

"Dude, I know. Listen, you may as well believe in heaven if it makes you feel bad not to," I say helplessly. That sounds random, even to me. Sadly, I got nothin'.

"I wish I just *could*. I think about this twenty-four-seven." He looks a little hollow-eyed.

"Same. Why though? Are you going to do confirmation in spring?" He also could put it off a year.

Paul eyes me slowly.

"I don't even think I want to." He looks at me guiltily. "If it's not *real*."

I look back with a wide, surprised face.

Now, this is not going to sit well with our beloved mother. Not one little bit. The only thing she really gets excited about is getting to Mass. *On time*. It's what makes her tick.

I shrug and grimace. Whatever. It's real to Mom.

"Dunno, bro. You are gonna get a '*talkin' to*'!" I make an uh-oh face.

"I know . . . I even feel guilty saying it to you. I feel like if I'm wrong I'm going to get struck by lightning."

"Omg, dude! That is *exactly* what the 'powers that be' always want people to think. It helps control the population. The population controls itself and allows the leaders to treat them like sh—"

"Don't start! This isn't about politics! This is about eternity!"

"By Calvin Klein?" I'm goofing, just trying to cheer him up. It hurts to see him all deflated and depressed. I bop him softly with a pillow. Right on the head.

"Whatever . . . be serious. It sucks when you get like this."

I dial it down. He's right. It sucks when I get like this.

"Okay . . . I'm sorry. Listen, I was all freaked out about it last year. I still am, so I joke. But if you do get confirmed, I researched a bunch of stuff last year—and I think there has been a cover-up! And a smear campaign! There *were* women priests in the early church. Lots! And Mary Magdalene was *never* a prostitute! Also, the Council of Nicaea was a freaking loony bin; omg, Paul—they were fistfighting! Santa Claus got his *nose* broken! And do not get me started on the priest scandals!" Even though I *am* starting.

"Rusty! *Stop!*" Paul moans. I stop and then continue more calmly.

"Okay, okay, I'm not . . . but I guess you have to examine things for yourself when you start growing up. It's just part of the process. It's no fun. In fact, it totally sucks . . . and you will *aggravate your ma.*" I shake my head. "Seriously. No upside till you decide."

Jane Goodall comes back on, and Paul returns his attention to the show. He blows out his cheeks in a huge sigh. The screen shows these huge chimps grooming each other. We hear that the young males who don't usually hang out together start to groom each other before they go looking to randomly find and kill another chimp. Great. Even the chimps are douche bags.

I can't take any more tragedy, either chimp or human, so I bail.

The next morning the air is crisp and the sun is low in the southeast. You can see your breath. I love the first two weeks of October: Indian summer. Then it descends into awful and remains awful for about six months. Then pretty crappy for another three. Yay Seattle!

I stand at the bus stop. I always get there first; it's less noticeable. That way I am like part of the scenery, just reading my book, when the others arrive.

The new kid is next to show up.

Which makes no sense. Yesterday he'd gotten off two stops before me.

He's early too.

I watch him from the corner of my eye. I am not going to say anything, but I feel benevolent toward him because of the chin thing in the hall.

I fake read.

He just sits on this low fence and looks around. He looks at me.

I ignore him with all my concentration.

"What are you reading?"

I really am unsure how to react at this point. He seems like he is asking me a question, and since there are no other people around I think, *Well, maybe . . .* But I am very careful—in fact, quite suspicious. I take my time before I look up.

When I do, I carefully mark my place in the book before I deliberately close it and look at him. I'm waiting for the crap to start flipping, but he just looks at me quizzically.

"What?" I look at him belligerently, with my game face.

"I said: 'What are you reading?' "

"*Life of Pi,*" I say grudgingly.

His face lights up.

"I read that! It's gross about the tiger."

"What's gross?" I am only in the beginning. I haven't seen the movie.

"Well, they run low on—wait, I don't want to spoil anything for you."

Which is so totally nice, I am disarmed. People usually go out of their *way* to spoil things for me. I can feel myself turning red.

"Oh. Okay. Um . . . thanks . . . duh duh duh . . . I'm a moron!!" (Okay; I did not really say the last part, but seriously, I got no skills when someone is kind to me. I practically tear up.)

My face is now a tomato, both in color and contour, and I

can feel my forehead starting to sweat. He's okay though and starts to pull his own paperback out of his backpack.

"Have you read this?" He holds it up. I look to see what he has.

It's *Heavier Than Heaven* by Charles R. Cross. There is a picture of Kurt Cobain on the cover. Yes! *Nirvana*!

"Oh! I *have* read that! In Alaska when I went to see my dad! I—" Stop abruptly. TMI.

But New Dude Beau merely looks encouraging.

"Sweet. Where in Alaska?"

"Uh, well, Anchorage. Then to Kodiak."

"Seriously? Kodiak Island? I've heard of it. Have you ever seen one of those bears? The big ones?"

"Yes, but only on a scope a mile away. Also this taxidermy one, which was gigantic."

"A scope? A scope like a telescope?"

"A scope like a rifle scope."

"You have a rifle?" He looks a little askance. I try to explain.

"No. Yes. Well, in Alaska. But not a rifle . . . I mean, I can't *own* it till I'm twenty-one, but I have a handgun. My dad does though; he has a gun collection, like tons of guns. He hunts and fishes and such. He got me one when I was born, a '.38 special.' I've shot it a bunch—up there, when I went to visit once. But he's given my brother about ten guns and rifles . . . at least."

For some reason this totally annoys me. I don't even like guns. I do, however, want nine random other things from my dad—so it's *fair*.

"Whoa. That's like my dad. Only in Kansas."

"Where in Kansas?"

"Near Salina?"

"Far from the crazy hippies and liberals?"

"Exactly." He nods quite seriously. "My dad hates all those 'ass-wipes.' "

"I think my dad kind of likes them. In Alaska everyone con-

siders themselves this rugged individualist—at least back in the
'70s, what with the legal pot and all."

"*What?* Weed was legal in the *'70s?* Seriously?"

"In Alaska. Yeah."

New Dude Beau looks at me. "Wow. What happened?"

I sigh and nod knowingly.

"I know . . ." Even though I don't. I've never smoked pot.

New Dude Beau looks at me.

"By the way—hi. My name is Beau."

Which I know, but I get all flustered again.

"Rylee Winters. Also known as Rusty." Like I'm going to
sell him a car or something. Why don't I just add "put 'er there,
fella!" and stick my hand out like a *total* freaking mutant. Jeez,
I make myself cringe.

He doesn't appear to notice.

"Cool. You're the third girl Riley I've known."

"How many guy Rileys?"

"Um . . . like, eighty?"

We both nod and smile.

"I know, right?" I say. I had an Uncle Riley.

And then the baboon boys arrive.

I've been sitting on this low stone wall, and Beau has been
standing over by the bus sign. The alpha baboon and his two
trusty baboon aides swagger down the street from the cul-de-
sac they live in. They have trickily dressed in human clothing,
entirely saggin'.

So gangsta! My favorite part is when these lil' butt-itches
scrawl "Straight Outta Compton" or "Pimps Up, Hos Down"
or some other twaddle on their little monkey bags. *As if!* They
would be eaten by toddlers and house cats in South Central
LA! *And* they sound like idiots!

Spare me from lily-white posing posers shipped in from the
burbs.

As am I—lily-white—but not a poser. I live right here in inner city Seattle and go to their crappy schools. But I don't claim any "street cred," as these young folks say nowadays.

Beau, once again, looks really calm and doesn't do or say anything. The worst of the jerks comes up to him.

"Hey, douche! Where's your gay shirt? Get it dirty?"

Beau doesn't even answer. He just looks at him and shrugs. Sort of smiles and shakes his head like, "Really?"

"Where is it, *faggot?*"

"Dude, why are you even acting like this?"

" 'Cause I hate effin' fags, that's why. Fag."

"But you don't know anything about me. Why are you just assuming?"

"You have a fag face and wear fag clothes and sound like a fag. That's why. Fag."

To my utter amazement, Beau doesn't look intimidated or afraid or angry or in any way pissed off. He keeps his eyes on the boy, whose mother named him Nick, but for whom I have other names, and shrugs like, "Sucks to be you then."

Nick isn't as assured now because usually kids get all one way or the other when he starts. He is such a *silly* bully. He moved here in the third grade and has been wasting the air of my town ever since.

He's used to kids freaking out, bursting into tears, and running off so he can chase them etc. when he starts his little mandrill-power displays.

None of which Beau did. So Nick escalated. He got up into Beau's personal face space and was so close he could almost touch him. He was a little taller and put his face menacingly into Beau's.

Beau looked disgusted and turned his face, and then Nick shoved him.

Backward on his butt. Hard.

Beau was up almost before he was down. Before anyone else could even move.

"Leave me alone, dude. You don't even know my name. I don't even know yours." Beau moved away. Nick just ran at him, and then I saw the most wonderful thing I had seen in a long time.

Beau caught Nick's hand and did something that *stopped him and forced him to his knees.*

It was stellar, though I couldn't really see what he did. One minute Nick is going to punch Beau's face and the next he is kneeling in front of him, moaning in contrition.

Well, maybe not contrition, but he's on his knees and moaning.

It's beyond awesome, and I'm standing amazed and excited, euphoric that I'm actually enthusiastic! Woo!

Beau drops Nick's hand and stands there, waiting. Nick looks at his hand and gets to his feet. Puts it in his armpit.

I notice his two friends are not jumping in. Good to know who's got your back.

Red-face Nick rushes him again like he's going to strangle him, and this time Beau takes a step to him, grabs his hand again, and down goes Nick—*down* goes Nick! I almost cheer!

I tell you, *mis amigos,* it is regal.

As the bus pulls up and Nick stands up again, dirty wet knees making him look like the loser he was, and is, and will always be, he gives one clown-fish stink-eye to Beau as he gets on the bus and hisses:

"It's *on,* faggot."

Have you ever heard the saying, "The enemy of my enemy is my friend"?

There's something to that.

I was liking Beau just for himself when we talked, but now I liked Beau for being awesome and kicking the butt of this jerk who has been making my life miserable for oh-so-many years.

I was glad when I saw I had three classes with him, one of which was English, still my fave . . . as my English teacher used to be, as well. Mr. Adkins, my English teacher, my hero, the most popular teacher at the school. *Pitter-pat.* That was my lil' heart when I thought about him.

But now that's changed. Now I know a little story about my English teacher.

My only "friend," Leonie Caitiff, who, I'm pretty sure, is only my friend because we were assigned the same table, told me about it when we were sitting in art class together.

Thus, Mr. Adkins used to be my favorite teacher.

Past tense.

I broke up with him in my heart when I found out he seduced Leonie.

I know. It's bad.

Now, I'm going to tell you a sad and messed-up story about the grown man who @$%*!!^ the crazy little sophomore while he was her teacher in high school. Ready?

Reread above sentence.

'Cause that is pretty much the story. Unfortunately not that big a news flash.

Leonie was not quite fifteen when she started having sex with him.

I know. I said it was bad.

They "fell in love," you see. She told me.

Like I said, Leonie Caitiff speaks to me because we were assigned to sit at the same table in art class. She started talking to me after about a week of busting on me to seem cooler in front of the other kids, which stopped when she realized it didn't help.

I understood. She is rejected by the cool kids 'cuz she has a really scandalous reputation; she got boobs in fourth grade and because she's wild and does stuff with guys . . . on the freaking bus.

Which so doesn't help. The boys want her, but they mock her.

They call her "Turbo-Ho" or "Turbo" for short. They laugh at her. But that doesn't seem to matter to her. She has this huge, sad need for male approval, does Leonie Caitiff.

And believe me, she gets good grades in English.

I look up from my art when she scurries in and sits down. Cartooning is our art elective this quarter. Art class is downstairs in the school basement, beside the home ec kitchen, and the whole classroom smells like cookies today. It reminds me I like cookies, which is something other people like to remind me of as well.

Leonie is rushed. She makes it in the nick of time, as the bell rings.

"Did you get my text?" She sits down and starts brushing her huge mane of hair.

She is very pretty. She is full of color; her blue-green eyes and long curly red-gold hair complement her paper-white skin and tons of pale gold freckles. Her hair is what red hair should look like. She smokes a lot so her teeth are a little more colorful than they should be, and nobody has taught the wee thing how to apply makeup so it doesn't look trashy, thus her lipstick's a maroon slash of color that clashes with her hair, but all in all she is strikingly good looking.

"No." I look over at her. "My phone is off."

"Why?"

"Um . . . 'cuz I already know what it would say?"

"Whatever. I just got a text from *him*." She starts scrabbling through her gigantic bag for her phone.

"Awesome! What does *he* want? To correct your paper? How appropriate! That's wonderful!" She can't even hear my sarcasm.

"He wants to meet here on Saturday. Then go somewhere."

"Leonie! No!"

"Rusty! Yes!"

A wadded-up piece of paper rolls across my freshly inked caption. Of course Leonie has to unwad it and read the message: "T—ride home bus 34." She looks over at the pig trough that threw it, hoping it's this one guy she thinks is cute. She nods at him, smiling.

"*Leonie Caitiff!* That is disgusting!" I feel like smacking her. "They don't even *like* you!"

She looks at me then, hurt and hip deep in denial.

"Yes, they *do!*"

"No, they *don't!* They call you T and Turbo and throw things at you. They're *horrible!*"

"You just don't understand, Rusty, because you're a virgin. You just can't get it." She says the word *virgin* smirking, like it means ax murderer or baby eater or something.

"I *do* get when someone is being disrespected, which you totally are," I hiss back.

The guys at the other table are oinking in delight. They aren't even all assigned to the same table, but our teacher is a small dude and doesn't want to mess with them. He ignores the noise. I feel my anger, which is the only thing that I ever feel reliably, begin to rise. I swallow it down. I return to my ink.

New Dude Beau comes into art class. He gives the teacher a note, and the teacher gestures him to our table. It is the only one that doesn't already have four people at it, but I think *Great—now we are officially the freak table,* and wait for the assault of "things butt-wipes throw at freaks" to begin raining down on us.

Leonie looks up, and I see her eyes get dark . . . oh, boy, here we go. She smiles.

"*Hi*. Are you at our table?"

"Yeah. Hi. I'm Beau." He's still standing, hesitating. The class is in chaos, as usual, so no one even much notices yet, though the first bell has rung.

Then the second one rings. The din decreases a decibel. He sits down.

"I'm Leonie." She starts twiddling her hair, a sure sign with that one.

"Hi."

"Do you need some paper? I have another pen. . . ." She leans over to push these things across the table to him in a way that you can totally see down her shirt. He looks away quickly.

"Thanks."

I look over at him. He starts digging around like there is something *so* interesting in his backpack, but I notice that the tips of his ears are bright red.

Ole Leonie strikes again. I go back to my lettering. Capital letter *A*. Capital letter *A*.

I like cartooning class. Mr. J plays old rock from when he was a teenager. Today we hear *The Dark Side of the Moon* by Pink Floyd. Yesterday it was The Police. The day before: AC/DC. Before that: "Space Oddity."

My favorite so far is Talking Heads' "Once in a Lifetime." I like how David Byrne chops.

Plus, his suit in the video looks like something SpongeBob would wear to traffic court.

I said that to Mr. J and he cracked up. He said I have the makings of a disaffected hipster. I had no idea what he meant, but I smiled anyway because it was good to hear someone offering an unvicious opinion about what I have the makings of.

Mr. J also said if I did become one, to promise never to get my face tattooed or shave my eyebrows or pierce my eyelids. He was goofing, but I totally agreed.

I don't need to go out of my way to find *dis*-affection. I have it around me here by the ton.

So Leonie continues to chat up Beau. He starts by giving her monosyllabic answers, but she is so sweet (when she wants to be) that he can't resist for long. Neither could I when she started talking to me.

She gathers the intelligence that Beau will be seventeen in May, that "Beau" is not short for anything else; that his last name is Gales; he just moved here from the Midwest; he was born there; that he likes his mom and his stepdad, who live here, but doesn't like his dad at all, who lives there; that he is *probably* more of a dog person that a cat person, though he doesn't have any pets right now; that his favorite color is iridescence; and his middle name is John.

Good work, Detective Nosy McNoserson. I think you have captured our man.

We return to our cartooning. I don't like to talk while I caption because it makes me spell things wrong, which is an automatic fail. Leonie can hardly even hold the pen because she has big old fingernails like the ladies down at the DMV.

She never gets better than a C plus. Probably because Mr. J is happily married.

See, I think mean thoughts, but I'm not really mean. I don't mean to be mean. I'm just not that surprised by meanness, deep down. If it's not messed up one way, it'll be messed up some other way.

I feel we live in messed-up times. Everyone laughs at personal pain, no matter how heartless. People casually watch torture on TV shows and aren't even freaked.

Whatever . . . welcome to the new Dark Ages.

I feel offended and empty a lot. I feel empty the most, empty and totally lonely. Stranded. Stuck here in Stoopidville, goin' to Baboon High.

Today the unthinkable happened.

I have been eating lunch by myself for my entire life. When we even share the same lunch period, Leonie always sits with the doofs, just yukkin' it up, like a hyena. It's so typical.

I myself have also developed a routine: I sit down. I unwrap my stuff and open a book. Then I put on my headphones and read through lunch. I am not available to anything except physical contact; sounds and sights cannot affect me. I have my armor on.

And so that's exactly what I was doing when Beau came up to one of the empty seats around me in the otherwise crowded to overflowing cafeteria and sat down.

I looked up in panic.

"You probably don't want to do that." I looked at him in confusion and a little anger. He was just going to make us (read: me) a target.

He didn't budge. He just looked at me.

"Why?" He didn't seem to understand.

"If you sit here, they will say things." I was trying to talk without moving my mouth, like a spy or something. I didn't want to draw any attention.

"So?" He just shook his head and looked at me in resignation. "If I *don't* sit here, they will still say things." He shrugged. "They're a plague of frogs. What are you reading now?"

I looked down at my book quickly. I could feel an incredulous smile coming on.

The truth will set you free.

I ate lunch with someone today.

And just like that, we start hanging out together. I can use my mom's car almost whenever I want it, and as long as it has as much gas in it when I bring it back blah-blah and be careful blah-blah, then I can use it.

So now: We rollin' in the minivan!

Beau has a lot of stories. He's done a lot of things I haven't, among which are drinking beer and smoking pot. He tried it in Kansas.

He says it's not a big deal.

I disagree.

Leonie agrees.

She, of course, has been drunk a lot. She also smokes pot a lot because I smell it on her at school. No matter how much I dog her on it.

I'm not going to deal with drugs or sex right now in my life. I am the smartest person I know, and I don't think either will help me memorize or learn, which is what I do best. Luckily, the guys of Baboon High do not seem bummed about me passing on sex. They appear to be bearing up stoically.

However, I do plan on investigating everything when I go to college. See what all the fuss is about. When I'm older and have a bunch of friends.

Someday . . .

I will have my own place and a lot of buddies and classmates, and we will sit up all night, talking and drinking beer and passing joints, discussing things like infinity and the middle class and protesting for change, like I see people do on TV, only more peacefully, hopefully. And maybe I'll meet some singular guy and we'll hit it off. . . .

Optimistically, this is how it will work, even in community college, which is where I'm headed. At least for the first couple of years. Then we'll see.

We've been able to save a lot, Mom and me, almost enough for the whole first year, which I think is pretty good. I have it in my bank account. I don't know what I'll choose for a major yet. I will need further calculation.

The next day after school Beau, Leonie, and I go down to Lake Washington and sit on the picnic tables. The water is blue, and the breeze is light so it's perfect. It stays about seventy degrees in October till it gets rainy and wet. Then we "fall back" an hour into standard time and it gets dark and cold till *late* spring. It also occasionally snows, which is ghastly for us, though other parts of the country find us pants-wetting funny because we'll abandon our cars if, like, more than twenty flakes fall from the sky.

It's beautiful now because of the late Indian summer, all warm with red and gold leaves. We sit enjoying the aquamarine water's reflection of the clouds. We throw sticks at the Canadian geese flock when they keep waddling over to beg from us. We are not fans. They honk and crap everywhere. Like *everywhere.*

Leonie lights up a cig. Blue smoke wafts. Beau looks at her.

"How much are smokes these days?"

She looks at him like he's going to give her grief for smoking, which is exactly what he is going to do.

"A lot."

"Like ten dollars?"

"Not quite."

"But a good way to spend your money, huh? Like almost three hundred bucks a month?"

Leonie looks shocked, and I see her doing mental arithmetic. Beau goes on.

"How much in a year . . . let's see . . . bring down the zero . . . wow—about the same as buying a sports car!"

Leonie looks cranky.

"Well, it's not my fault."

We both just look at her. She knows she's being feeble but keeps on.

"My mom smokes. I just take hers. It's my mom's fault."

Which statistically is true. Smoker moms make smoker kids.

However, we are here to rebel against *our parents,* I think. Which I mention.

It feels good to be on the side where *I'm* not the one getting picked on.

Leonie looks at me like *"Et tu, Brute?"* But I'm not being mean; I just think smoking is gross and it makes her teeth yellow. Oh yeah—and you *die.*

She shifts so she's not looking at us and goes on smoking. Beau looks at me and shrugs.

"It's not like we'll give up on you, Lee," he sings to her back. "So you may as well quit."

"I can't hear you. I'm looking at the water." She tosses her shiny hair over her shoulder. It catches the wind and rises, shimmering. I think of that song about the sun floating on a breeze.

Her hair is so pretty that I touch it lightly. The curly waves fall past her waist and sparkle golden red in the sun. She can't feel my touch through the weight of her mane. Beau regards us, smiling, but then turns his head sharply. I, too, pause and focus.

He's gone tense, watching and listening. I look to see what he sees.

And here they come. They're still a little way away on the cobbled lake path. There are a bunch of them, and I know they don't see us yet because they're just using their normal deafening grunts, not the special menacing deafening grunts they save for Beau.

"Let's go," I say. Beau nods without taking his eyes off them.

We get up to leave, but then Leonie catches sight of them.

"Oh look—those guys are from school!" She starts to wave.

I snatch down her hand and hiss at her.

"*Stop!* Do you want him to get beat up?"

"They won't. They're nice!" She looks at me distractedly. I hiss at Leo a lot.

"No, they're *not!* They are not nice to you, though you don't seem to realize it, or to me and especially not to Beau. Now let's get gone!" I take her arm. She comes with me reluctantly. We melt back into the brush at the side of the lake and cut back safely to the van.

Homecoming came and went, and I didn't go and never will and will always wonder about it, so as to have the worst of both worlds. I won't go to prom either.

But the empty part of me will always wonder. . . .

Oh well; stow that with everything else I have shut down.

It abruptly got dark and cold and wet for winter, like it does here, and we all buttoned up for the rain and wind. Winter coat season and I'm finishing my new one just in time.

I sometimes sew my own clothes. I'm good with mechanical things and also I got so fat after the divorce it became necessary. Luckily I've recently shed a few pounds so I can just wear sweats and hoodies again. It's my uniform: gray sweats and T-shirts and hoodies, usually with the hood up. But I still make my own coats. It's way cheaper than trying to find a long coat in my size. I always ace home ec, and when I was a freshman I sewed everybody's projects till I realized it didn't help; they were still vile to me and I was a tool for sewing for free. So I made some business cards and put them in fabric stores for when someone wanted something made. It's good money, only kind of hit and miss. I'm going to start a real business when I turn eighteen. I can create just about anything.

The coat I designed this year is like the guy's in *The Man from Snowy River*, which was an image that came up when I googled "long black coat": a man wearing a mid-calf-length black coat with a short cape for the rain. Only I am going to put a hood on my mine also. I'm also going to line it with cinnamon-brown satin because my third-grade teacher once said that was a good color on me. She said it went with my hair (which is uncontrollable and wiry and rust-colored, hence my nickname) and eyes (which are dark brown to the point of coal black). My teacher's name was Ms. Said and I loved her.

It will be very warm and also a very big wall between me and them. A wall against the world. . . .

Except for maybe Beau and Leonie.

And my mom and Paul.

I never see Paul these days because he has turned into the Karate Kid. He is at the dojo four or five nights a week. He's moved up a belt color to yellow, which apparently is pretty fast. He says he wants to be a black belt. I say, "Kick on wich yer bad self, bro!"

Same with Mom; she is getting her refresher course nursing certification so she's all updated and then she'll be working a part-time job, afternoons till six, as a charge nurse. She says she will go to full-time RN next year, but for now this is good.

She looks so happy. She actually looks younger.

I'm the only grim one stuck here. I stay in my room and brood. I'm too furious to cry.

Frequently I watch TV to kill time, though I always get disgusted and pissed off. Everything is based on being spiteful; everyone is getting crappy random tricks played on them, and the more traumatizing the punking, the better! Or they try to do some idiot stunt and annihilate themselves and we laugh till we wheeze! Is our society losing its grip? As long as someone ends up bleeding and dazed we salivate and howl! Meanness passes for humor.

But *why?*

Mr. J says we are a jaded generation because of 9/11. We grew up in the shadow of sneak attacks and war, and it has made us expect the worst.

I agree. We have and we do, but that can't be the excuse for being vicious our whole lives, can it? We have to try again! We have to get our trust back.

And omg, you guys, when I compare what passes for entertainment now to the art and music that came before us, I *seize*.

We (APs) translated *Julius Caesar* from Middle English last year . . . and I can just see them doing that in five hundred years with some of our immortal twenty-first century verse: "Yo, Big Bootie Bitch, Twerk Dat Bubble Butt All Up in My Grill— Ain't Axin' Twyz, Yo."

Yay, our epoch! I'm so proud of the *art* we're making!

And yes, my friends, I do understand that I really am a delicate flower child. A lil' orchid of sensitivity, tiptoeing through the tulips in a cattle rancher coat. . . .

But seriously, what's so funny about peace, love, and understanding?

Anyway, I'm still sitting at my desk in my room when I hear some noise and know Paul is home. I go out to see him before he goes to his karate school, his dojo: his home away from home.

I wander into the kitchen.

"Whatcha doin'?"

"I'm starving! I only have fifteen minutes and then I have to go! There's nothing to eat here!" He's slamming cupboards and the fridge door. I go over and take the bread out of the microwave that we also use as a bread box.

"Here, I'll make you some PB&Js."

"Man, is that all we have? I want some mac and cheese."

"Sorry, bro. We got your PBs or your PB&Js, and that's really about it till one of us goes shopping."

"Which I can't even *do* till Mom takes me for my learner's permit. Or *you*."

I make his sandwich without meeting his accusing stare. It's true; I have been very slow to help him get his permit till I get my car because Mom is already enough competition when I want to use the van.

I am researching a particular model of green car, used, for

which I am at least one thousand bucks short, probably three to four months away from being earned by Winters' Sewing Service.

I stay in the kitchen while he eats and drinks milk from the carton. I tell him to just take it with him, which he does when someone starts honking the horn. It's already dark out, only a little after five o'clock. He grabs his bag and slams the door.

It gets very quiet. I start turning on lights. Mom will be home after a while.

When we come back from Thanksgiving break, Leonie says she has something *really* important to tell us. We wait till art class, where we can talk while we work.

"He says he wants to get *serious*." And as we have discovered, "he" means Mr. Adkins.

I look at Beau. Neither of us will rat her out, because you *can't*, but we have been trying to convince her of how stupid this is on her part and how incredibly immoral on his.

Mr. Adkins. What a douche. She was fourteen when he started asking her to stay after class. I don't know why he hasn't gotten caught. Oh, wait! Yes, I do.

Because nobody tells.

Leonie, of course, won't say anything. I tell her to. I know *I* should, but she would be so betrayed that I just keep justifying not doing anything and try to get her to tell instead.

I know this is wrong. I know I should tell. I *know* I should tell. I *am* going to. I will. But only if I have to. I want *her* to tell. Soon.

"Did you *hear* me? I said: He wants to get serious."

I just look at her. Beau leans in.

"How long have you been seeing him?"

"Forever. We're in love." Leonie stares at him coolly.

"That is insane."

"Beau, you don't know him like I do. We're soul mates."
She begins tracing hearts on her paper intently.

Beau looks at me, and we roll our eyeballs at each other, so
Leonie has to comment.

"Neither of you can possibly understand him . . . or *us*." She
glares at me briefly.

"But if you're soul mates, why are you so secret?" I inquire.
"He should want everyone knowing about you . . . it being so
cool and eternal and all, right?"

Leonie looks sad for a second. Like maybe she's brought
this up too. Absently, she adds jags on the paper that make all
the hearts broken. She sighs.

"He doesn't want to. He says no one would understand.
And you are just proving that. We are like *Twilight*. We're like
Edward and Bella. Everyone is trying to keep us apart."

I try not to barf in my hands. Instead, I offer another theory.

"Or maybe he is doing someone else too. That way you
won't know about each other."

Her face wads up, startled and horrified.

"*NO!*"

The entire class looks at us and we pipe down in a hurry.
Spitballs begin to fly our way.

That. Was. Stupid.

We forgot where we were. In country, as they say when you
are at war. Which we are.

At war.

With losers.

Later that afternoon I'm hanging out with Beau in my room.
"In which Mr. Rochester almost bites it in a fire."

I'm listening to him on speaker with Leo while I do crosswords. He's faking an English accent. He sounds like a Grey
Poupon commercial.

"He does?" Leo's voice sounds genuinely puzzled.

Beau sighs theatrically.

"Omg, Leo, did you or did you not just read that novel?"

"I totally did, but I didn't see where there was a fire."

"Dude, how do you think he got blinded?"

There is silence on the other end for a sec, then:

"Ohhh . . ."

"Did you not get that before?"

"*Yeah* . . . so that totally makes sense now, how she can marry him and everything now—'cuz the crazy wife died in the fire!"

"Yup!"

" 'Kay, lemme go write this! Peace!"

" 'Kay, deuces."

Beau hangs up and looks over at me. He holds his hand over his heart, histrionically.

"She's so special."

I snort-laugh. Hard.

"She is a *very* special girl."

"*Jane Eyre* is *hard!*"

"*Jane Eyre* make brain hurt!"

"Aaahhhhhhh!! Brain! Hurt! Ow!" Beau is rolling on the bed. He's a Gumby.

We are hella funnier than Monty Python!

We continue to chill. It's dark already.

Leonie had a "date" with some tool from school so she couldn't join us. She made it home in spite of wherever random destination she'd ended up at. I'd told her I would give her a ride since I'm daring to drive the minivan again, but no, she wanted to go home with this guy—though, of course, she never made it that far.

So she walked home. And remembered her homework and so on . . .

This, however, is actually a huge improvement. I mentioned

that it would be completely obvious about their little thang if Leo never did any English homework and still got straight As, so she started doing it just to prove me wrong. Hah!

"We bag on her a lot," says Beau.

"We kind of do."

"Too much?"

"Maybe . . . "

"We are going to be so nice to Leonie for the entire rest of the school year and summer!"

"Except for occasionally—when she can't hear!" We cackle.

Bonding! It rules. *I am hanging out with a friend.*

A song we both like is playing and we are distracted. We rattle and hum.

I like how Beau enjoys the old New Wave I play. Retro. It's what I listen to the most.

He rolls off the bed and comes over to my desk and gives me a little shoulder hug as I sit doing crosswords.

I am taken aback. He is so sweet.

"Gotta go."

"Dude, wait one second till my mom comes back from getting Paul and I will run you. It's dark and rainy out."

"I'll be okay, Mommy."

"Seriously. She'll be home really soon."

"Rust, I told my mom I'd be back by now."

"It's like a mile!"

"I'll jog! I'm good!"

I stop nagging, but I'm still worried.

He leaves.

I'm sure he'll be fine.

When I go to school the next morning, Leonie's full of her secret.

"We are going to get engaged!" Her eyes are glittering pinwheels. She's on full tilt.

"No, you're not." I try for the wet blanket. She glares at me. With *ruby* red peepers.

She's very drunk and also high. (Again.) She reeks.

Which makes me add, "Also, I can totally *smell* you, Skunky!"

We are walking in the hall up to where my locker is when we see a disturbance, which in my disturbing school is really saying something. There is a crowd around the principal and the janitor and the school secretary, who are staring at Beau's locker.

"Die Fag" has been spray-painted in red.

Almost as red as Beau's face. He's standing in front of his locker. He looks dazed.

Sadly, I can believe this. It's the way these losers roll. Sneaky and cowardly. I cannot count how many notes have been stuck on me. However, no one has spray-painted my locker.

Beau's locker partner comes up and sees the mess. He's a quiet guy named D'Shawn.

He's not quiet now. He shakes his head.

"Oh, *hell* no! I want a different locker!" He points at Beau. "A different locker partner too! I ain't getting *my* ass kicked!"

The principal just crooks her finger to go with her and they all walk away. Beau doesn't see me or Leonie in the crowd. He goes around the corner with the principal and the others.

Leonie and I stare at each other. Her buzz is harshed.

"This totally sucks!" Her cherry-bombed eyes are wide. "Who do you think did that?"

"Ass-face Nick and his stupid gang, of course." I feel like snapping him like a twig.

The bell rings and we have to go to our classes.

All day long I'm so obsessed with what is happening to Beau I don't get much done. He is gone from second period also, which means we won't know what's up till art class, at the end of the day.

When I get to class Leonie is already there and she has that intense look on her face that means she has forgotten all about Beau and wants to talk about the horrifying Mr. Adkins, or "Ratskin," as I call him now.

"I just told him he has got to let me tell my mom, and we need to go *public* with our relationship."

"That sounds so impressive when you say it like that. I didn't know you were both running for office! Also: That is so *not* going to happen. I don't care what he *tells* you, he is not going to let *you* tell. You aren't even legal! He's committing a crime. He knows that, and he also knows he's a complete creep when it gets out. He's not stupid. Well, he is, but not that way."

"I don't know why you hate him so much now. You used to like him a lot!"

"That's right. I *did*."

"Maybe you wish it was you . . ."

I don't even dignify that with an answer. I do wither her with a look. She tries a different tack.

"It's no big deal . . . it's not like I was a virgin before."

I turn on her then. I have to. I just have had too much.

"Shut *up!* I don't care! That's not the point! He is a douche bag! You're a *kid!* He's in a position of authority and that makes it wrong and despicable!" I spew out words like a wood chipper. "This is a rotten thing he's done!" I'm so manic I'm sputtering.

Lee looks worried by my vehemence.

"What do you mean 'position of authority'?"

"Lee, don't act dumb—because you're not! He's your *teacher!*"

"So? A lot of people go out with their professors!"

He'd obviously told her that.

"They're in college, and even then they *still* aren't supposed to till they graduate!"

"Well, I don't care! We're in love! We're going to get mar-

ried!" Leonie scowls like she's going to cry if I don't let up. So
I do. I shut up and pen my disapproval onto my notebook.
Deeply and repeatedly.

We sit and pretend to study. The second bell rings and still
no Beau.

He isn't at school. He's been sent home.

When class is over, I turn on my phone and there's a text
from Beau. I show Leo and she immediately gets worried. We
blow off the fact we're pissed at each other and head over to his
house after school. He's quiet and his eyes are swollen. Leo and
I stand awkwardly as I try to get him to talk.

"Is Nick going to get suspended?"

Beau just stares at me. He looks miserable and lost. He
shakes his head.

"They don't know he did it. They asked me who I suspected, but of course I didn't have any proof that it was him.
That's always the way, isn't it?"

"We're witnesses."

"Actually not. You didn't *see* him do anything."

We are quiet for a while. It's true. We didn't.

Beau heaves a deep sigh and looks out the window. Then he
gazes back at us.

"It's starting again."

We look at him, waiting.

"The gay thing." He's silent as he covers his eyes. His hand
shakes slightly.

"The what?"

"I started getting harassed, in PE especially, when I started
middle school. I *had* to learn self-defense. I got hit so hard once
it made me puke. I got one million fouls and bloody noses. . . .
I mean, *sixth* grade, and I was already freaked out about sex."
His voice trails off. He scrubs his eyes with the heel of his hand
and sighs erratically. Then he gets a grip and settles.

He regards us from a thousand miles away.

"I try to be cool, just do my thing and not even *look* at anyone, but it doesn't help."

I nod. I so know. It doesn't help. I don't understand why. I will never understand why.

"We have to tell someone about this!" Leonie is disturbed by Beau's apathy.

"Leo, Ms. Blip knows. She doesn't care. She's homophobic."

"What's that?"

I groan, but Beau answers her patiently.

"It means she hates gay people. Literally, it means she fears gay people."

"Yeah, but what for? Why would anybody fear *you?* Plus, you're not even gay, are you?"

Beau looks at both of us. Shrugs and tells.

"Yes. I'm gay."

Leonie looks confused. She squints at him.

"But how? You just seem normal to me."

He laughs bitterly.

"Yeah! I do, don't I?"

"Like how do you even know? Have you ever even kissed a boy?"

Beau is quiet for a minute, and I can tell he hasn't. I wonder if he is considering lying like he would be if he were straight and we asked him if he'd ever kissed a girl.

We all stare at each other, feeling sort of bewildered.

"No, not exactly,". he finally admits grudgingly. "But I know I want to try."

Leonie is quiet for a second, considering.

"Well, so say you're gay. So what? What's the big deal? Who cares, if you're nice?" Leonie cannot seem to make sense of such an unprovoked assault. Her forehead furrows.

I want to get back to the day's events.

"So what did Blip say?"

"She said maybe I should rethink my choice of high school. That maybe I wasn't going to be a 'good fit.' I almost said something snotty and silly back, but I figured it would all become *my* fault if I made a joke or got angry. She said to just go home and think it over . . . like I could do anything else."

Leonie is back and on the march. Her temper's up.

"Well, that's not fair!"

We look at her sympathetically. No, it isn't—that's very true.

"It's not fair! You didn't choose to be gay! Wait—*did* you?"

Beau shakes his head and smiles at her in such a sad way.

"No, honey. And I don't even think of myself as worthy of being singled out. I don't think that's enough reason. I just can't see why being gay is worth so much attention. I mean, jeez, learn to cope."

Which I totally agree with. It does seem like the people who are so worried about it are not thinking for themselves. To which I say:

"They are obediently hating, as instructed. Very docile! Like tame little hater sheep."

I hasten to remind our generation: Obedience denied! It's a phase we're going through, remember? Question authority! Listen to *your* heart!

Beau nods but shrugs.

"Tell them that."

"I will! I'll tell them: Who *cares?* It's nobody's business! Read *Lord of the Flies*! We are always just that far away from anarchy!" I show them an inch with my thumb and finger.

(Paul would say I'm "starting.")

They regard me warily because I've climbed on my soapbox: "Read *This Boy's Life*! Omg! We need to respect each other! Respect our differences! Bad things happen when you don't! It blows my mind that nobody takes advantage of all this stuff! It's like shortcuts!"

Beau and Leo just stare at me. They glance at each other like I've stopped making sense.

"Rusty, nobody reads books at our school, except to not flunk," Beau reminds me gently.

But I've got a full head of steam and can't be shut down.

"I *know!* It's pathetic! But it's right there—bad things happen when people judge each other's personal lives! Obsessing about *anyone's* sex life for very long is just *gross!* It's way more perverted being the person doing the imagining than the person being gay. Yuck! I mean it; go find something to do with yourself! Get a *life.* Get a job!"

Beau and Leo nod. They sigh. They agree it's true.

As long as the balance of power is equal . . . right, Leonie? Because if not, say if you're being taken advantage of, then there is *a problem.* I think this, but do not say it.

We were quiet for a while as we sit and ponder what's bugging us.

The next day is also quite remarkable.

Sitting together, we ride the bus, Beau and I.

Like always, I am afraid to attract attention, but I am getting sick of being so heartless. After all, he's my *friend.* We sit together, asking for trouble merely by our combined presence—the chub chick and the gay guy, in exactly the way I have always sought to avoid.

As we get off the bus, we pick the spit wads and twigs and assorted and accumulated crap out of our clothes and hair. I am so angry I forget to see who was saying what.

I am through with my inaction. It's time to get going.

I turn to Beau.

"Are you going to go see Blip today?"

"No."

"I agree. No point. But we can't just let this pass."

"Plus, she can come get me if she wants to. Anyway, she's not going to do sh—"

"*BEAU!*" It's Leonie. She's running in the hallway. She reaches us and hugs us both.

We stand together. The gang o' misfits. Together we shall pass through the halls!

Together. It's so good to have a tribe. I can hardly recognize my life from how it was. I knew I was empty before. I was hollow and lost, frozen in place and jarringly alone . . . and the loneliness seemed like it would be endless.

I couldn't bear to acknowledge that it was unbearable.

I have never had much to do with Ms. Blip before but now I thoroughly dislike her. I think she is a bigot. She basically refused to guarantee Beau's safety. She said there was no way she could, when people get so "worked up" over the subject.

I know. I was there. She said it in a snarky way. Like she, too, was all worked up over the subject of people being gay.

And disapproved mightily . . .

I thought she was supposed to be neutral, being the principal and in charge of things and all, but apparently not. But she had to address what happened to Beau.

So we had an assembly about "Let's All Get Along," how our school is so diverse and we should all be chill, then the cheerleaders had a bunch of messages, then put their gloves on and did about five hundred clapping routines, then our jazz choir sang for about two hours, which they do anytime they are given a captive audience, during which a bunch of people got their lunch money jacked.

Basically, nothing changed. Beau continued to get talked smack to and shoved around. His stuff kept getting stolen and broken. No response at all . . .

And finally, since the school administration didn't address

the problem effectively, the harassment escalated till the day he got beat up.

It had gotten bad enough that Leonie and I tried to escort him whenever he walked anywhere near school grounds. The irony of girls keeping a boy safe was not lost on us, though I found it more depressing than he did.

But of course the time came when Nick and his troop caught him cutting across the soccer field near the greenbelt. And descended on him like a chimp patrol.

Beau is tough. He put up a good fight, but there were four guys. He did manage to break Nick's nose.

But they messed him up. Pretty bad. He staggered to his house and collapsed, and when his mom saw him, she took him to the hospital. They called us from there.

We got to his house as he was getting back home. He was moving like an old man. The baboon squad had given him a lot of body shots. His left jaw was misshapen, and one eye was swollen shut and dark blue. . . .

Very slowly, we help him into his room. Leonie's crying as we move him to his bed, so slow and stiff like an old dude, but I wasn't. Inside I was an electrical storm.

Projectile hate *radiating*—!

I hear his mom crying in the other room. His stepdad's out, but will be home later.

While Leonie fetched Beau a drink of water, I go to see his mom for a second.

She's standing at the window, looking out at the backyard. They have about twenty bird feeders and hummingbird feeders and suet for squirrels and I don't know what all. Very kind and hospitable.

I walk over to where she's standing. She has the same eyes and the same look in them as Beau.

We just look out the back window and watch it rain.

Eventually she sighs. Takes a shaky breath.

"We're pressing charges." Her voice is a little shaky too.

"Good. I wish I had seen something. I'd testify."

"Yeah, well, those kids chose the *wrong* family." Her soft voice has a certain quality that made me very sure they had.

We're quiet again. Then I hear a tiny squeak and look over and tears are running down her cheeks. She's crying hard but almost silently. She sees me see.

"He's the best guy in the world." Her shoulders shake. "*Why* do these people think they can put their hands on my boy?" Her eyes look kind of frantic. Like confused.

I want so bad to pat her shoulder, but I don't. I just stand. Once again, it's like I'm frozen in place.

I want to cry too, but I can't even nod.

Some friend I am.

When I stagger back to Beau's room, Leonie is on the computer and he's lying on his bed.

"How are you feeling?"

"Sketchy. I don't think these pain pills make me smart."

"It's not about smart right now."

"Yeah . . . mostly my rib . . ."

"Yeah, be careful. What is the difference between cracked and broken?"

"Cracked gets well faster."

"Oh, well. Good."

We are quiet, and we hear his mom in the other room on the phone. She is pissed *off*. We listen in. She has the attention of someone, and it sounds like it's a lawyer or something. We hear the term "school district" several times. She has begun speaking through her teeth. We look at each other.

"Dang." Leonie looks scared. I, however, am impressed by her badassery.

"Your mom is amazing. I would offer a hand, but it doesn't sound like she needs one."

"Yeah." Beau looks worried. "She doesn't need this either. They have other things to deal with."

Beau's stepdad Matt writes for TV, but his show just got canceled. So he is on unemployment. His mom is an interior designer but still building up her business here. I guess she's not getting a lot of work at the moment. None of her clients have spare money to change their color scheme a lot—not *quite* yet, as she puts it. So she's looking for more work.

After a while she hangs up. We hear her knock on Beau's door.

"Beau? Listen, we are pressing charges."

We look at each other. Beau answers while staring at me.

"*No.*"

"*Yes.* Open the door."

"It's open. Just walk in."

She does. His mom's name is Gina. I think I really like her.

"This is just *not* going to happen here. This is *Seattle! South* Seattle!"

"So?" Beau shrugs and looks at her, unimpressed.

"Well, we are better than that here!"

"Really, Mom? Why *is* 'Seattle, South Seattle' so great?"

"Because! We are tolerant! We are incredibly diverse! We are *cool!*"

We all look at her. Then, bitterly, we burst out laughing. It kind of sounds like crying. She looks at us.

"What?! We are!"

"O-*kay*, Mom." Beau looks pained. His tone is patronizing. "I got this."

"You guys, don't be jaded. It's okay to make a difference."

Jaded. That word again.

His mom continues.

"You should call your uncle. He had to figure all this out too, you know. Back in the day."

We look at Beau curiously.

"Okay, Mom. Except, as I told you, they threw my phone in the lake. However, thank you . . . and now, if you could just excuse us, I *got* this." He gives her a hard look. Then winces.

"What?! You can still call Uncle Frankie!" His mom leaves. We look at him. Leonie asks first.

"They threw your *phone* in the lake?!" She is horrified.

"Yeah. Whatever. You can still call me; I have an old one. It's not smart, is all."

She stares at him with so much indignation he is compelled to add, "It's okay. I only know you guys here. I don't care. Besides, the number was still Kansas, and my contract is almost up." He shrugs soothingly as she continues to splutter. "Anyway, Leo, you don't have a smartphone, either . . . or Rusty either. I guess we're old school."

I change the subject.

"Who is Uncle Frankie?"

Beau just shakes his head. Gently. I hand him the water glass again. He sips.

"My mom thinks she can solve the world." He's starting to drift. I help hold the glass.

"Yeah, but who is he?" I bend near his ear. Beau looks blearily at us both. I set the water glass back on the bedside stand.

"Frankie is my dad's older brother. They don't speak. My dad hates him. He's gay."

We sit and digest that information for a while. Beau gets sleepy from the pain pills. He starts to snore gently. Leonie looks at me. She keeps her voice down.

"I think his mom is right. He should call his uncle."

I actually agree with her. Maybe his uncle would know how to stop the harassment.

"We'll work on him," I whisper.

Of course Beau is out of commission for days. Leonie and I stop by and bring him his homework even though he can see what's up on the school website.

His face has gone from dark blue to yellow-green and purple. He spends all his time on the It Gets Better Project website. He's quiet and absentminded. We have to repeat ourselves constantly. He is frequently nonresponsive to my jokes. His eyes are distant and sad.

Watching him, we exchange worried glances, Leonie and I. Beau can't just check out. He will not be allowed to just fade away or do something crazy! We get super paranoid and vigilant. I start checking in with him excessively. He has to stay here! He has to live in this world with us.

If only to make sure it actually gets better.

His mom is going ahead with criminal charges on Nick and two of the other guys for assault and property theft. She is getting a lawyer to sue the school district and Ms. Blip personally.

She is *mad*.

When we close the door to Beau's room, he locks it.

"I'm leaving."

We stand there looking dumbstruck. Which we were, briefly, though Leonie found her voice pretty quick.

"Where?"

"I don't know. Away."

"Did you call your uncle?" I ask. I think this could be a solution. His uncle can help.

"Yes, and I left a message. I might go there."

"When did you leave the message?"

"Yesterday. He hasn't gotten back to me. He probably doesn't remember who I am."

We both stand looking at him. He stands looking out his window. We glance at each other.

Beau is going to run away. Not good.

"Well . . . then . . . but what is your uncle even going to be able to do?"

"*Tell* me things! I'm sure it was worse in the olden days. He's gotta know something."

That part actually sounds okay, but why not just a phone call? Then Leo pipes up.

"Where does your uncle live?"

Beau looks at me like I'm going to laugh at him.

"San Francisco," he says. His good eye squints at me defiantly.

Oh. He only lives in the gayest gay capital of the world. I don't even know how I know this, but I do. I nod in support. Lee sees me and does likewise.

"So I'll go to San Francisco. I can hitchhike," Beau informs us. He shrugs like no big deal. "He's been through a bunch of crap. Maybe he'll know what to do. I'm leaving tonight."

"No!!" Leonie and I are a chorus of horror.

"Why? It's only a few hundred miles. I'll see the ocean."

Thank gawd even Leonie knows enough to splutter with outrage.

"No, Beau! You only take rides with people you *know!*"

He's irritable for the first time.

"See, you guys are *girls*. It's okay for a *guy* to hitchhike. It's not even that far."

"It's so *not* okay!" Again we speak in unison. Screech in unison, more like.

"Yes, it *is!*"

Okay, if Beau is still taking those pain pills this could go on for a while. I distract him.

"Beau, your mom is going to *freak* out."

"No, she won't. I'll leave a note. Besides, Matt'll be here. He's always around. He writes for TV, so he basically lives in front of the computer."

"I would have thought he lived in front of the TV. . . ." Leonie looks puzzled.

"Nah, he hates TV. I've never seen him watch it."

"Weird."

"Yeah, I know . . . not even the shows he writes. Especially not the ones he writes."

I try to redirect them to the subject of not running away.

"*Any* wayssss . . . I don't think a note is fair. I think you could just tell her you need a break and want to see the ocean."

"No, she's all involved in suing everyone she can think of. Which she can't afford to do. She'd just want me to stay. We would have a big fight. I'm just going to leave."

"Beau . . ."

"Rusty, I'm not going to stay here and ruin my mom's life. Especially when she was so cool to me when I came out."

"What did she do when you told her?" I'm very curious about this one.

"Cried at first. But said she loved me just the same. She was just crying because life's made so much harder for gay people. Which, guess what—is true."

"Your mom's *so* cool." I am utterly sincere. His mom is wise.

"Yeah. Some of her designers are gay. She realizes life can go on. So, yeah. She is cool. That's one huge reason I love her and I'm running away."

I am again impressed. He admits to loving his mom. Easily. I nod reflectively.

"But now I think she's mad and she's going to try to make it better all by herself, and if I'm not here, it might take the wind out of her sails a little, you know? She doesn't need to be hiring a lawyer for a million bucks just now." He looks worn out and hollow-eyed.

"You need to rest if you're taking off," I say, buying time.

"Yeah." He nods, exhausted. "I was going to leave tonight, but I might wait another day. My face feels like crap. I stopped taking those pain pills."

"Then I'm going to give you three ibuprofen, and you take a nap, and when you wake up, I will help you write a note, okay?"

"Okay. I'll text you when I wake up."

When we go out of his room, Leonie hisses.

"Why are you helping him?"

I look at her.

"Because I'm going to go with him."

I go back to my house. I have an idea. Maybe a good one.

No one is at home; Paul is at the dojo and Mom is at the hospital. So far so good.

I go into my room. I have a bank account, but I also have money under the mattress.

I know; I'm not exactly one of them there Biz Kid$. I'm not making my money grow like I could because I'm sort of paranoid. But I have $1,723 in twenties and smaller, right here. I smooth them out. When I put them in an envelope, it's so fat it looks gangsta. So I plug in my iron and press the money under a cloth till it looks more respectable. Then I unplug and put the bills back in the envelope. I get a piece of paper. I think for a minute then write:

> *Dear Mom:*
> *Beau and I are going to go visit his uncle in*
> *San Francisco. I am taking the van because it's*
> *an emergency, but I'm leaving you my money.*

*I will send more ASAP, but I looked up the
blue book on our van, which is $1,600 (because
of its mileage), so really you are making
$123.00 on the deal. Please don't be mad, be-
cause this is really important and I will call you
when we get there. I won't pick up though because I don't want to get yelled at. Sorry.
      Love,
      Rylee*

I look at the note. Then I add:

I love you (both) very much.

I stick it in the envelope with the $krilla.

When Beau's text came through, I was ready. I had my extra
sweats and stuff packed and some food and juice and water. I
got my pillow and two sleeping bags we never use and a pillow
I know my mom doesn't really like from the couch and headed
over to his house.

When I get there, Beau is already sitting on his front steps.
When he sees me, he stands up and brings his stuff to the van.
He looks like he feels much better. Way less puffy. I look him
over. He's got the uniform: hoodie and skinny jeans. Bubble
jacket, unzipped.

"You look better. And I like the Clash tee and them fancy
fresh kicks!" He has on his new red and black checkerboard
Vans.

Beau smiles and sticks out one foot, acknowledging their
awesomeness, but then returns abruptly to the business at hand.
He speaks rapidly. He's got a plan.

"I can afford a ticket to Portland, okay? Would you take me
to the bus station? I want to leave tonight. I do feel better."

I take a deep breath.

"Okay. I'm coming with you."

He looks over at me sharply. Doesn't say anything for a while, considering. Then:

"Really?"

"Yes, really. I just gave my mom a bunch of money for the van, and we can drive down the coast. I've only ever been about as far south as Long Beach."

"You'll mess up your grades and attendance and all. Break doesn't start till next week."

"Maybe not. I've nearly got enough credits to graduate right now. But if I do mess up, it won't be for long. I'll just figure it out in community college."

He turns and looks at me.

"Dude, you'd do that for me? I know how important being smart is for you." He smiles at me affectionately.

I'm embarrassed, as always, so I creak out, "No big deal," in the direction of his groovy ruby shoes. I feel myself welling up.

I am made of blubbering blubbery blubber. I nod quickly and, thank gawd, get a text.

It's Leonie. She's coming over.

She's there almost immediately. She's on her skateboard.

"Good . . . I was afraid I'd miss you." She's out of breath. Smoker. She has a lumpy pillowcase.

"I'm coming too." She says it like we are going to respond, "Oh no, you aren't."

We look at each other. Beau shrugs. Laughs.

"Fine!"

I look at her.

"Do you have any money?"

She digs in her pocket.

"I've got thirty-seven bucks and fifty . . . eight cents. I had forty, but I got a small drip."

"Did you bring anything like a sleeping bag or a pillow?"
She looks stricken.

"Oh . . . uh-oh."

"*Dude.*" I sigh. "It's okay."

Beau chimes in.

"What's a drip?" He's not from here. I eyeball Leo.

"Drip coffee. For, like, way too much—when she should be saving it for our trip!"

Leo looks distressed again and starts to deny and defend, but Beau intervenes.

"Never mind! Look, put your stuff in; I'll just get you a pillow from my house."

When he goes in, Leonie looks at me. Like she's filled with a huge prophesy.

"I told him I was leaving and he better make up his mind. And I'm not coming back, either . . . unless he calls." She nods like she thinks she's made progress.

I start to open my mouth to debate her, but I clamp it shut. Not the time.

"Great. Good idea," I manage out the side of my mouth. I put her pillowcase through the open side door of the van.

I'm not going to spin my wheels right now trying to talk her out of this toxic teacher. But maybe if she gets away from him . . .

"Did you tell your mom?"

"Nah. She'll take a while to notice."

I'm always sad when Leonie says things like that. Her mom doesn't seem to be around much, and Leonie never seems to know where she is either, which must *suck*. Poor Leo.

Beau comes back with a pillow and a folded comforter.

"I thought this felt good."

"Ooh! Thanks! It's squishy and perfect. She won't mind?"

"Nah. She can get a billion of them."

Leonie stows her skateboard as she gets in the van. She takes over the short middle bench behind the driver. Beau gets in shotgun.

"Did you leave a note?"

"Yup."

"What'd it say?"

"That I loved her and say hi to Matt and I was going to go talk to my uncle like she suggested."

"Yeah, okay then. That pretty much says it all."

We adjust ourselves for drive time.

"All right! California, here we come!" I start to ease out of the driveway. We go a block.

Leonie leans forward. She is framed in the rearview mirror. She has an idea.

"I'm hungry."

"Leo! Why didn't you eat before you came over?"

"Because! There was, like, *nothing* in my house. Except white wine, which I hate, and some bread in the fridge. I ate the bread."

Beau and I look at each other. We suddenly feel very fortunate.

"Okay. We'll stop before we get going. Let's go to Silver Fork before it closes."

We head to our little greasy spoon, which is what my mom and Paul and I call it. Mom used to bring us there for breakfast sometimes on Saturdays. It reminds me of better days. The food's good.

We are hardly even seated before we have a ton of food and our own pot of coffee, the cute old-school kind, pre Starbucks. We all start hamming. It's like truck stop food, which it probably was, when Rainier was a major train track through Seattle. Now, however, there is I-5, which we will be getting on, southbound for sun, in just a little while.

We grub in silence for a few minutes. Beau stops eating first.

Leonie cleans her plate. Then his. I know she's hungry, but she always eats like a starving dog during lunch, and the only place she ever seems to gain weight is her boobs. She is like Lara-Croft-anime-chick built. It's amazing. It would be totally daunting to hang out with her if I wasn't several light-years from being in the same league, but as it is . . .

I keep eating.

Beau leans back and watches us: Leonie in the booth on his side with me across the table. He looks around idly. I can see his eye is much better.

"This place is like a hundred years old."

"Yeah, maybe. It's always been here. We used to come here on weekends, my mom and brother and I."

"That's nice, to have a place you can come back to like that. Like this."

"Yeah. I guess so."

"What's its name again?"

"Silver Fork." I have toast in my mouth, which I know is rude.

Beau thinks for a minute.

"Wait, isn't that the name of that town?"

"Silver Fork?"

"No, just 'Fork.' You know—where they filmed *Twilight*? I thought that was around here somewhere."

"Oh, *Forks* . . . well, sort of. It's over on the coast. I used to go there for supplies with my dad before he took off. It's really close to this little fishing village we used to stay at by the ocean, called La Push."

Leonie has gotten very interested.

"You guys! We should totally go there first! I've never been!"

I look at her. She wants to go to La Push?

"You want to go to La Push?"

"*No!* To *Forks!*" Her eyes are huge.

"What?! No way!" Is she kidding?

"*Yes!* It would be awesome!"

"Lee, why would we want to go to wet, rainy, awful Forks?"

"Because, Rusty! *Twilight!* Besides, it's not that far."

Beau chimes in. He looks interested in something for the first time in a while.

"Seriously? How far is 'not that far'?"

"Just over to the coast."

"Lee, I'm not from here. How far away is the coast?"

Leonie looks at me helplessly. Because she has No Clue.

"Practically two hundred miles is all!" I say.

She turns to Beau.

"Maybe two hundred miles is all." She gestures dismissively.

He looks from one to the other of us. I can see the wheels turning behind his eyes. At least the good one.

"How long would that take?"

Leonie replies with a vengeance.

"Not long! Maybe an extra day."

"Leonie, that is so not true! It's, like, little logging roads all through the outback. It's through a *rain forest!* It takes all day just to get there. You have to go on a ferry and all kinds of crap."

I am 100 percent not enthused.

But they both look at me and I can tell they want to.

Omg. Freaking *Twilight.* Gross.

Yeah, yeah, I know: I was the only one my age on the planet, in the entire space-time continuum, but I guess I'm (again) a freak of nature because I find *Twilight* and, in fact, all things *Twi-hard* completely wince-worthy. And it's not like I don't get how lethally hot everybody is. It's just: I so *don't care.* They all just seem to flail around, driven hot and bothered to *un-*death by each other.

Especially Bella. I have never seen anyone as bothered as Bella.

And I so can't be. Bothered.

But watching these two, with Beau looking all happy for the first time in a while, I sigh. I try one last feeble attempt at a veto.

"Guys, they don't really live there, you know. Robert Pattinson does *not* have a house in Forks, Washington, and for sure nobody is going to be running around without a shirt on this time of year. After we *finally* get there." I crunch my crust crossly.

They look at each other and laugh. *Twilight*! They are maniacal with delight.

"It's so not far!" Leonie says again. They high-five each other.

I look at Leonie like a Sunday-school teacher. An insanely cranky Sunday-school teacher. "Two hundred miles *is* a very long way. Also, through the Olympic rain forest is about the skinniest winding roads you're gonna find. And it's dark by four in the afternoon. So that's great: It's going to take all night, and when we get there, we are going to be chased, really fast, by vampires and a pack of buck-naked werewolves. Freaking great!"

They stop cackling and look at me with matching pained expressions.

"Rust, just because *you* don't like *Twilight* is no reason to make fun of it to us just because we do," Leonie informs me with feeling. Then she stares right at me.

"Besides, how are you even so sure that the werewolves were buck-naked? *Aha!* You do so like *Twilight*! Rusty, it's okay! We think it's awesome! Edward was hella awesome! They're so cool and tragic! Omg! They were so hella doomed!"

Okay, I knew the werewolves were only half naked. I was

just dogging them. And, in my own defense, I saw a pic of Werewolf Guy online (not on purpose) just last week; it's not like it isn't still everywhere. I don't exactly need to seek it out to absorb it. But I gotta say: doomed or not, nice six-pack.

In response, I roll my eyes at them so far back in my head I remember my mom used to tell me to stop or my face would stick like that.

We finish eating, and I calculate 20 percent for a tip and pay. Another friend on Facebook, Erica, hates people who undertip since she waits tables. She's my mom's friend and also studying to be a registered nurse, which is how she met Mom and friended me.

We get in the van. I have carefully painted over "soooy" with blue fingernail polish that somewhat matches so you can only see it when it glitters. That reminds me of stupid *Twilight* again, because I heard stupid Edward glitters for some stupid reason, so I get all torqued off again. It's like really bad poetry: I'm all torqued and goin' to Forks.

We pull out onto Rainier and get onto I-5 going *north* bound. I know we could get there somehow from town, but I'm going the way my dad always took us. We'll head to Edmonds and catch the ferry to Kingston. After that we'll drive through deep, *deep* forest; like forever, approximately. Then we'll be in beautiful downtown Forks, where they better not blink or they'll miss it, but then we can keep going to La Push, and Beau can see the Pacific Ocean in all its crazy winter glory.

And I will too . . . again. It is *wild*.

I actually start to get a little stoked. I hum while we drive. The hour or whatever it takes to get to Edmonds goes fast.

And, of course, the ferry has just sailed by the time we get there. I get a schedule. There is one more sailing in the wee hours of the a.m.

We settle in and wait.

*   *   *

"Actually, I'm still hungry."

"Leonie Caitiff! No way!" I'm indignant.

"Well, I *am*."

"Omg, Leo, seriously. We just ate, and I don't think there were any IHOPs or anything around. Just get comfy and we'll be on the ferry in a little while. It's only like a half hour ride. You'll be fine."

Unbelievable. If *I'm* not even hungry, how can she be already?

We sit with the iPod playing through the van speakers. My van, my music. Except for Macklemore (Seattle's fave son) and a few others, it's all retro and emo, like David Bowie and Sting and U2, plus other groups I learned from people who were teenagers back in the day. But you'd be surprised how much you can kind of recognize from sampling.

There is a rap on the window and it's a cop. I look at Leo and Beau. Have we been called in already? They look back with wide eyes. I try to be calm and unroll the window.

"What's up? You kids okay? You're out way past your bedtime." His voice is accusing.

I take a deep breath and put on my oldest, most trustworthiest voice.

"No, it's fine, officer. We missed the ferry, and we're just waiting for the next one."

He sticks his face in the window and looks inside at Beau and Leonie, then inhales deeply.

Ha-ha! Nothing to smell! His light is in our faces, and we squint.

"What happened to you?" he asks Beau.

"Fight at school, sir."

"Yeah? What were you fighting about?"

"Um, I guess it was just a difference of opinion, officer," Beau says mildly.

"A difference of opinion, huh . . ." He shines his flashlight around the backseat again. Looks up at the sky and over at the dock. We can see him deciding.

"Okay, listen, get on the ferry and go home. I'll be back to check for you after it sails . . . so don't be here. It's past your bedtime." Which he had just said half a minute ago.

"We will, officer. Thank you for making sure we're okay!" I try to fuel-inject feeling into the words with my best smile. My face practically creaks.

He nods, scowling, then turns and walks off. He swaggers like he's a badass.

I look at Beau, who is as white as a sheet.

"Dude, are you okay?"

He takes a deep and shaky breath. Shakes his head.

"Not keen on cops." He tries to laugh to underplay his wobbles. He looks at his trembling hands. He squeezes them between his knees.

"Why, Beau? What happened?" Leo puts her hand gently on his shoulder.

"When I lived with my dad . . ." He trails off. He looks over at us like his response explains *what* happened instead of *when* it happened. We wait.

When he speaks again, his voice is stronger and calmer.

"Um, I was walking from school last year when I still lived in Kansas and I got jumped by three guys from my school, right on the sidewalk, in midday." He looks at us wearily, though that still explains nothing about cops. We wait.

"So, it was in front of a bunch of houses and someone called the police . . ."

"Good!"

"Yeah, well . . . they came. They broke up the ass kicking I was getting, but then instead of taking those guys in they took *me*."

"To jail?" I'm scandalized.

"No. They drove me around in the backseat through town and basically yelled at me for about two hours while I puked and felt horrible from getting my ass kicked, before bringing me back to my dad and telling him what happened, or at least what *they* said happened."

"Wait. They yelled at *you?*"

"Told me to be a man and man up and act like a man. It was very helpful and instructive." Beau's voice is ancient. I follow his eyes and see the ferry chugging in the distance.

"So . . . what'd your dad do?" I ask tentatively. I'm cold. I'm suddenly sure I can guess.

Beau looks over at me then, with his one good black-and-blue blue eye, suddenly bested and exhausted.

"Well, he listened to the cops and then when they left *he* beat the hell out of me."

We don't say much on the ride over. Actually, we don't say anything the entire ride. We're each disappeared in our thoughts. Like taken hostage by them.

When the ferry docks I take the directions that say Port Angeles, Forks and La Push and we're on the road again.

Driving at night is an extra trip. From Kingston you head northwest and sort of follow the water for a long time. You cross Hood Canal. It's huge. Eventually you get to the Olympic National Park and start driving in the deep woods. I pass a sign that mentions an apple maggot quarantine area, about which I have no clue, so I'm guessing that the apple maggots are all free range. It's super dark. Even the trees somehow look menacing, hungry and dark, coniferous and carnivorous, lining the sides of the road like an unending army. I look in the rearview. Leonie has dozed off. I glance over. Beau is still awake beside me.

"How are you doing?"

"Okay." He stops looking out the passenger side window and instead looks out the windshield, straight ahead.

"I don't think you sound okay." Though I don't know what to do for him.

He looks right at me then.

"Yeah . . . no. I'm not. I'm not okay. I'm freaking sick of telling old *and* new stories about getting my ass handed to me. I'm sick of having to think which way to get to school or home if I'm by myself. I'm sick of using the self-defense I was forced to learn. I'm sick of people and their stupid opinions. I hate school. I freaking hate homophobic jocks and bullies. I want to be at peace, y'know? I just want to feel at *home* somewhere."

I do know. Though I don't get beat up, I am constantly verbally abused. Which isn't as bad but is relentless and it saps my will to live. Seriously.

I say what I hope rather than what I believe.

"Dude, like they say: It gets better. We just have to *hang on* till college. I *know* it will be different in college." This I do believe. It *will* be different there.

"Why is that going to be so different? A lot of kids who killed themselves are in college! Some of them were in universities. Good ones too."

"I know." I got nothing to say to that. They were—and are. The suicides keep happening.

So then, when will it get better?

Beau continues. "Well, why didn't the losers who 'outed' them get in more trouble—like *socially* for the way they acted? Why isn't a storm of outrage and mockery following those guys? That was a horrible thing to do! Why haven't people turned on the haters and like . . . I don't know—kicked them off the Internet and *shunned* them?! I don't know! Why doesn't someone hate on *them* for a while? Why do I always deserve this mess?"

He sounds like he might break down, so he stares out the side window, then takes a deep breath and settles.

We drive in silence for quite a while. We pass Port Angeles without comment or incident and leave the water for deeper woods.

It's very dark in the forest with only our high beams to guide us.

We can hear Leonie shifting and talking in her sleep. I try to hear what she's muttering. Beau turns around and watches her for a minute. She's thrashing around. She laughs in her sleep.

"They're so cute at that age." He untangles the comforter from around her head.

I snort. Beau cracks me up. He pulls her hair out of her mouth.

"I wonder what she's dreaming of."

I stink-eye him. Who else? She dreams of Ratskin.

"Hmmm . . . let me hazard a guess."

"Yeah. Probably." Beau nods, bummed.

"That guy is a criminal."

"You gonna turn him in?" He is making a point.

I'm silent. He's right. I know I should, but somehow I have this idea that it's not my place to turn him in, it's hers. After all, I never got hit on. All I know is what she said and that's called hearsay.

But here is one thing I saw. I saw him standing really close, talking to this hot little freshman, all up in her face one day when I went back into the classroom. I'd forgotten to get my graded reading journal so he wasn't expecting anyone and thought he was alone with her. When I came in, he jumped like twenty feet, which to me is a sign o' guilty intentions, at the very least.

I never told Leonie for several reasons. One: She is the gold medalist of selective hearing; if she doesn't like it, it's not true. Two: Everyone is so quick to tell me every crappy thing they can think up it makes me hesitant to ruin someone else's day (though what if that someone else might be ruining her *life?*). Three: Once again, I don't really have anything more than suspicions. I could see me telling her and her jumping around and telling him and him denying it and her telling him I said so and all kinds of trouble for all of us just radiating out like rays from my own big mouth.

I suddenly realize I can tell Beau though, and I do. While Leonie sleeps the sleep of the innocent, I confess in a whisper her stupid teacher-boyfriend's criminal indiscretions, since he never will. Beau already knew most of it, but now I tell him *every*thing.

Beau listens and has no absolution for Ratskin. The unbruised side of his face registers disgust. It feels so good to rat that loser out! I can feel my shoulders and neck starting to unfreeze. I roll them and sit up straighter. We sit in silence when I finish.

Beau stares at me, and his laugh is quiet and bitter.

"*Wow.*"

"Yeah."

"Wow . . . this is *so* messed up."

"Yeah."

He shakes his head and looks out the window.

"It's like a new installment of the Hurt Patrol." He says this almost under his breath.

"Of the what?"

"The Hurt Patrol."

"What's that?" I stare at him quizzically.

"It was the name of my scout patrol, when I lived with my dad."

"Wait—you were a Boy Scout? How could you be? I didn't think they used to let gay guys be Boy Scouts. How did you get in?"

"I know, right? For starters: That's so idiotic! I didn't even know I was gay when I started scouting. I was in first grade.

But besides that, there were so many gay scouts it's not even funny!"

"Wow. So, did you like it?"

"Not really."

"Because why?"

"The attitude, I guess. The 'us against them' thing. Somebody always had to lose and then be the loser. It was stressful. And I was the new kid. It was like they were all against *me*."

"How long were you a scout?"

"First to eighth grade. It seemed like for hundreds of years, till I was fourteen. Then I quit."

"Was *anything* awesome? Or was it all just bad?"

"Yeah, there was some stuff. There was this giant camping thing they did called Camporee, which was like a series of competitions. I was still all keen to sign up, to please my dad, so I went, and since we'd just moved again, I was late joining, so they put me in this one patrol."

"Like what kind of competitions?"

"Oh, knots, swimming, first aid, keeping a clean campsite."

"What was it called, again?"

"Camporee."

"Yeah, Camporee."

"It was kind of like a competition for who were the best scouts. The scout leaders got all agitated, because it showed who the best leaders were too. Tons of different Boy Scout troops, from the entire US. All these different patrols. We were the Hurt Patrol."

"The *Hurt Patrol* . . ."

"Yep. It was particularly awesome when we were at Camporee because it drove all the scout leaders crazy . . . especially ours."

"Okay. So what's a patrol do?"

"I guess they're like a squad of guys. They hang out and accomplish things, like make a trail or whatever. At our Camporees, it was basically a bunch of guys getting judged on tying knots and keeping their own campsite clean. That was mostly all it boiled down to."

"Okay. So you were in the Hurt Patrol because—"

"Because by the time we moved there, all the other patrols were filled up. So they put me in the only patrol that still had room, like always, and when I got there, I was the youngest, and all bright-eyed and bushy-tailed and started sweeping with a pine branch like I'd seen the others doing, and they took one look at me and were like, 'Calm down, kid, ain't never gonna happen.' "

"Why?"

" 'Cuz they knew we would fail, no matter how perfect we were."

"Why?"

"Because we were the misfit patrol. They didn't care about us. Seriously. That's why there was room for me. They were the guys nobody else wanted in their patrol. They were the freaks. Guys who were gay, or would be soon. There was a guy who had nightmares, like totally screamed in his sleep, and a dude who wet the bed, and two brothers who *hated* scouting, but their dad made them go, to build character."

"I don't get it. The leaders just ignored your patrol?"

"More or less. We were the goofballs. Everyone had grown up together, except me, and had been rejected or kicked out, so they formed their own patrol. The other patrols were like, 'You suck,' and these guys're all, 'Oh, wah, you don't want us. We're so *hurt!*' Everyone knew the other guys hated us, and there was no way we would ever be okay. If I tried to get our campsite ready for an inspection, my patrol was all, 'Don't bother. It won't help.' And it didn't. But at first I did."

"So what happened?"

"Like you said, we were just pretty much ignored. I think

they were hoping the bears would eat us if they left us alone for long enough, but no."

I sit and ponder this information.

"What were the other patrols' names?"

"Oh, you know: Wolf Clan, Eagle's Den, the Bear Nest. The usual randomness."

"And then you guys were—"

"*The Hurt Patrol!*"

"Omg." I laugh softly. "The Hurt Patrol."

"Yep"—Beau smiles—"we had a flag. It was a red cross with a Band-Aid over it. We even wrote a song. Wanna hear it?"

"You guys wrote a song?"

"Yep."

"Okay," I say, "I do." And he sings softly:

> *"They say that we are hurt,*
> *Because we hit the dirt.*
> *But that's not really true,*
> *'Cuz we're not really hurt!"*

He beams at me proudly.

I snuffle-laugh with my face scrinched up in delight, trying not to wake Leo.

"Sing it again," I whisper.

So he does.

I nod approvingly. "That's awesome, Beau! Two thumbs-up."

"Thank you." He nods modestly. "You're supposed to kind of scream the last line—*defiantly*." He laughs under his breath. I glance at him while I drive. Even though I'm joking I hesitate. But then I ask:

"Can I be in the Hurt Patrol, too?"

Beau looks over and grins at me. Joy shines right in my eyes like sunshine.

"Absolutely! You and Lee and me, so far: We are the new

Hurt Patrol, West Coast chapter. Congratulations! 'Cuz we're not really hurt! Now sing our team song with me."

So I do. Both of us sing:

> *"They say that we are hurt!*
> *Because we hit the dirt!*
> *But that's not really true!*
> *'Cuz WE'RE NOT REALLY HURT!"*

We try to scream it quietly, but we get loud enough that Leonie starts to wake up behind us. Beau turns.

"Good morning, sleepyhead." Though it's still dark.

Leonie stretches so her feet hang off the seat.

"I'm hungry."

I laugh out loud. It's like four in the morning. She eats like a mountain gorilla.

"Go back to sleep and we'll wake you up when we find a restaurant."

She does.

We drive on. I'm going very slowly because I'm a little freaked out, as usual, by the density of the trees. I am always a little unhinged about the idea of getting stranded out here so I'm careful. I see shapes in the shadows that I imagine are black bears and cougars fixin' to lunge at the van. I freak myself out.

After a while we see a little spot that looks good called Granny's Café and I pull off. It's still dark, and it's not quite six so we sit in the parking lot. We fade out after I turn off the engine.

The next thing I'm aware of is someone new tapping on the window.

It's some lanky old guy who is telling us the café is open now if we are hungry. Which we are.

We smell frying bacon and traces of gas from the recently lit pilot light when we come in. We're the first customers of the day and the only ones here besides the old guy who runs it with his wife, our waitress. We sit down, and she comes to take our order.

She's a little person. And I gotta say, we act weird at first, even if we don't stare. See, why do we behave like that? We have *all* seen a little person. How silly is it when people wig out over someone because they're different? *So* immature!

Anyway, she's really old too, and both of their faces look a little like these dried apple head dolls my brother used to make for my mom. We order. She smiles at us, which makes her cheeks *super* wrinkly, and takes the menus. We remember our manners and say thanks.

We look around. It's pretty much what you'd think, from the name. Lots of blue gingham ruffles and doodads. I end up having to take the country goose salt and pepper shakers away from Leo because she won't stop messing with them, making them kiss and dance on the table.

Breakfast comes quickly. Killer food, tons of it, and cheap. We grub like wild jackals. The waitress is pretty funny. We ask her if there is anything we should look out for, and she pretends to think for a sec and says we'd probably do better if we stay *on* the road and keep the yellow stripes to our left. Then she nods, all straight-faced like that was helpful.

We laugh, and she brings us another fountain of coffee, which I drain. It's about eight or so in the morning, and I am in *overdrive!* I don't think I'll need to sleep before we leave for Cali!

The sun is behind us as we get back on the road. It's not raining for five seconds. Yay.

We pass Lake Sutherland, which we can't see, on the left and head toward Lake Crescent. It's on our right, and we can see it sparkling as we pass. It's off-the-hook gorgeous. As well as enormous. We get out at a turnout and admire the view. The road is empty, and the morning sun backlights the lake.

Glittering, crystalline and pristine. I hope it stays that way.

We pass on detouring down the road leading to the hot springs after a brief, exasperated (on my part) discussion—because we're *already* on a side trip from our real mission, and all we *don't* need is to go to some clothing-optional hot springs in b.f. Egypt with Leonie the man-eater. We'll never get to Beau's uncle, and we'll never get our various acts together till we do, etc., which is what I start sputtering and whining (really only the part about Beau's uncle, I never actually say the thing about Leonie the man-eater) and to which they finally agree.

We drive once again into the deep dark forest. I'm steadier in the daylight. The trees just look like trees again. It starts to cloud, but it's okay. It's kind of cool, actually—all brooding and foggy and mysterious. Atmospheric.

Leonie's been texting for the last few minutes and has gotten quiet. Beau and I exchange glances. We see a sign for Forks and show her, and she starts to get all excited and stops texting to take pictures. I can see that Beau is also looking around and smiling.

That's good. This is so insane. We're going to Forks.

It's a small town about as far over on the West Coast as you can get before you leave dry land. A sign says it's one of the rainiest places in the world, which is easy to believe. There are gray clouds, and the wind is up a little. No sign of vampires, though.

We drive slowly down the main street of town. We are looking for the greasy spoon that must be here somewhere. They always are. We don't have too far to search.

When we pull in the small parking lot, it's almost full. It's nearing lunchtime and the waitress is busy. The clientele is about what you'd expect: flannel-covered guts and baseball caps for the gents; jogging suits for the ladies. I'd fit right in if my sweats were made of velour and I was, like, fifty. I also spot a few matching bowling jackets, official uniform of the RV crowd.

We are seated, and the place is warm and steamy and smells greasy and good. We are still pretty full from breakfast, but we can figure out where we are going. We order coffee and are about to start tracking the undead when we hear the waitress over the bustling noise of lunch:

"Mel! Mel, damn it! That lil' ole husky dog of yours is out again and running all over the parking lot! Go put her back before she gets hit too! And make sure she stays! 'Cuz that is the level last thing I need again—another dead damn dog making kids cry and driving off business! Hear me? Go get her!"

The guy she's talking to is sitting in the booth across from us with two other guys. They all look out the window and laugh, and the one called Mel cusses and gets up and waddles out the door. We look out our window and see him chase her (a her because she's obviously nursing pups) around the parking lot. She's freaking terrified of him and cowers when he corners her. We see him kick her and grab her by the scruff of her neck and sling her in the back of a pickup. He ties a rope around her neck and comes back in. He is greeted with laughter from the two men he is sitting with, and they return to their coffee. As I return to mine.

I look at Beau and Leonie. They are staring at the dog in the truck bed and then back at the guy, then back to the dog. Beau is pale again, and Leo is getting glassy-eyed.

"What." It's not a question. I'm not thinking about the life that dog has. I won't.

They both look at me. At least Leonie does. Her lower lip is trembling.

"You *know* what . . ." Beau is staring at the dog.

"Call the Humane Society. We gotta go."

"That'll take days." He's starting to get up.

"Beau, you just got your lights punched out a week ago. Just let it go." I try to grab him before he gets all the way up. Man, I thought gay guys were supposed to be all wussy and such. I didn't expect him to be rocking his Jet Li every five minutes.

He stands up and turns to the guys. I can tell he doesn't want to. There's something reluctant about the way he moves that informs me that he'd let it go if he *could*.

But he's not that guy.

"Nice job with the dog." He sounds breathless. His hands shake with outrage and adrenaline, and he clenches them.

The old dudes turn and look at him. He's standing at their table. They are struck dumb.

He breathes shallow and rapidly. "Ever stop and think what a horrible life that dog has? Which you could change any time you want. She feels pain just like you do." Beau hasn't raised his voice, but the old guy Mel sure does.

"What thee hell?! What have we here? Well, la-di-*da!* Mr. Fancy Shews! Why don't you sit the hell down and shut thee hell up and mind yer own gatdank bizness?!" he squalls.

Then he bangs the table. "Who the hell're you, anyway? Just go back to Seattle, ya gatdank vampire turist!" (Which, if he wasn't such a douche bag, would be hilarious.) "You know what, you snotty little 206er?" (Seattle's area code) "I'm-a kick yer ass!"

He struggles to squeeze out from the booth to come kick Beau's ass. His friends restrain him with guffaws. The waitress comes over. The rest of the restaurant is watching. Leonie and I get up. The waitress is red. Her face looks shiny. She's mad.

"What did I just say?! Didn't I just say I have enough to deal with already?" She turns to us. "Listen, you kids just go—now—no, just shut up and get! No, don't worry about the check. Just leave. As for you three: It's something *every day* with you! Mel, I don't know why you drive all the way into town every morning to make as much trouble as you do! Someday I would like just one morning of my life to go smoothly! 'Cuz one of these days I *will* eighty-six you." She's looking right at the old dudes when she says that. I get the distinct feeling they cause more trouble than you think they would.

"I'm-a shoot that bitch, soon as I sell her last puppy," Mel says as we pass them.

Lee stops.

"No, he won't! Keep going and never mind!" orders the waitress. "You, Mel—shut up!"

The door is closed behind us. We walk to our car.

"I'm calling the cops."

"No, don't, Beau. You forget—we're on the lam."

He looks at me with something like pity.

"Rusty, don't be heartless. How can you not stop cruelty when you see it?"

He's right, but all I feel is a boundless irritation.

"Oh, all right! But call from that old phone booth and use a fake name."

Which he does. He picks up the tiny phone book on the cord and reads a name and then an address when asked for one. Pretty slick, I must say. We get in the van to wait for him.

All this time Leonie has been silent. She looks sick to her stomach. I glance at her in the rearview, and she's staring out the window, all gray-faced and stony.

"You okay?"

"Yeah," she says vaguely. She's lost in a fog.

Beau gets back in. He's quiet too.

"So are they going to come?" I ask brightly.

"Yeah." He sounds dispirited. "They didn't sound too impressed."

"Dude, you did what you could," I say as we pull out. I'm

glad to get out of here. "Let's go find whatever *Twilight* thing you guys are wanting and get back on the road. I want to show you the ocean."

There actually is a *Twilight* store in Forks. A bunch of them. And all the restaurants offer stuff like Bella Melts and Edward Rings. I start riffing that the Bella Melt is *way* too cheesy and is it just me or are the Edward Rings always *cold?* They roll their eyes at my hee-larity. We pass a sign for smoked salmon taped to a bumper sticker that says "Werewolves <3 La Push."

I tell you what: These guys ain't dumb. Some of the young people of the Quileute tribe also made T-shirts, which, rumor has it, the elders find hilarious. They're all, "Yep, absolutely. We're totally werewolves. Now gimme thirty bucks for that T-shirt."

And lo, the faithful come on pilgrimage, some wearing street clothes, others in character.

And they come to the store and are taken on a tour (still very popular), and it is cool and it is so amazing and it is hella tight, as well as freaking awesome. For it is the *Twilight* tour.

Or so I was made to understand by the faithful fans that'd already been on it while I waited for *Twi*-dledum and *Twi*-dledee to get back. Heh.

I was going to go too, but at the last minute I just couldn't deal. Beau and Lee were cool, though, and there wasn't time for them to trip about it much, so they went and I stayed. It worked out just fine. I listened to the radio. (And watched this Swedish dude totally lose it because he missed the tour and then angrily try to convince the woman he was with that he was only mad 'cuz he wanted to go on the tour for his *niece*—back in Sweden—of *course* not for him! Har!) And, like I said, shared in the tale of the Holy Tour of *Twilight* with the devotees. So I scored.

As I wait for them I sit and read. I walk or run the engine when I get cold.

Pretty soon back they come. Beau is so cute when he's happy. Like a little kid. He looks relaxed. I didn't realize the trouble in his face till it left. Plus, he's healing.

They both now have a bunch of Edward fan-aphanalia, as opposed to a more even distribution of all three throbs. I am forced to appreciate the awesomeness. So I do.

I also worry about their cash. Like, how much do they have, anyway? I've bought all the gas so far. Not to be douchey or anything. We haven't talked about money. However, I'm pretty sure they are almost flat. I can't bring myself to ask . . . so I haven't said much.

Leonie is happy to have her cool Edward shirt, but I can tell she has a dark cloud over her. I repeat myself several times and finally confront her.

"Dude, what's with you?"

"Nothing."

"Unacceptable."

"I'm okay. But I'm sad about that dog."

Beau looks up like he was poked.

"I *know*. I've been thinking about her all day."

"And her puppy . . ."

"I know." Beau's face is somber.

I try to stop them before they get sad.

"No! Listen, guys, you did *good!* They've probably been taken away from the puppy mill by now, and the puppy will have a good home because it must be cute, and the mom will be too, and soon she'll belong to a nice couple who will love her, and it's all going to be unicorns and kibbles over the rainbow!" I'm trying to get them to smile, but I can see they are thinking I'm just cold. They stare at me in silence.

"Rusty, do you or do you not care about what happens to that poor little dog?" Leo's big turquoise eyes are again all wet and tragic.

"Oh, of course I do. I just don't know what you want us to

do! Should we go steal it and take it to the dog pound or something? Is that what you guys think? I'm not trying to be a butt, but is nobody going to be practical except me?"

They look at each other. Then Leonie looks down and sighs deeply.

"I guess not. They would probably just put her to sleep, anyway. There are a lot of dogs out there." The corners of her mouth quiver and turn down as her voice breaks. I try again.

"Listen. Look at me. We are going to do something really cool now. We are going to see the ocean! I know you haven't seen it, Beau, but have you, Lee?"

"No."

"Well, it's awesome in winter! It's wild and huge and stormy and off the hook!"

They look at each other. Then shrug.

But that's all the encouragement I need and we're off.

I try to think how we can best do this as we leave the town of *Twilight* by twilight. It will not be the same to get there in the dark and then try to show Beau the ocean at night. It will not be Amazing.

Though if you've already seen the ocean and can imagine it when you hear the roar of the waves, nighttime is as cool as anytime. Just not for a first meeting.

I start driving slower as I try to figure this out. I guess we can just pull over and sleep and I can take them the rest of the way in the morning, but it's only like dinnertime and we aren't even tired.

Then I remember the cabins. Dad always said they were a pretty good deal. We'll stay in the cabins.

When my dad used to live with us, he would take me and Paul to the ocean every summer and some winters. Mom didn't go because they were already not that fond of each other, but we liked it. The cabins smelled like propane, and there was a bed in a loft I always got because I was the only girl. Paul and Dad slept in the bigger bed downstairs. There was light and a hot plate, running water, a shower, and a toilet. And that's about all. It was a fun time when we were kids.

I haven't thought about the cabins in years, but now I wanted to go there.

The guy is different than when I was here last, but he's really cool, and when he finds out I used to come here as a kid, he takes some money off the price of the cabin.

It's still more than I hoped to spend. But at this point I almost don't care. I want a shower. Immediately if not sooner.

It's exactly the same since the last time I was here, the last summer before my dad left, except for the cabins, which have been fixed up. I turn on the faucet and do a test flush in the new bathroom, and it works *way* better than I remember. I go back outside and look around. The air is the same. The air is salty. I can hear the roar beckoning just over the beach bluff.

You can smell salt sea air in Seattle because we are on the Puget Sound, but it's different on the actual coast. You can hear seagulls in Seattle, but they too are different on the actual coast.

It's all more intense somehow. Bigger. It's easy to feel epic at the ocean. To feel infinite.

We throw our stuff on the bed, and Beau climbs the ladder to the loft. We hear him exclaiming about the coolness. Leo climbs up, and they are sitting and reading the names that have been scratched into the wood walls. I climb up far enough to stick my head above the floor and see what they are doing, but I don't stay. I know what's up there. They're the same walls. So cool.

I realize as I climb back down that I'm not as out of breath as usual. Running away is good cardio, apparently.

After we shop and eat mac and cheese on the hot plate and settle in for the night, I turn on my phone.

And when I turn on my phone, my friends, I expire from guilt.

My mom has called thirty-nine times. She has also texted me about ten times and she never texts. It takes her like an hour to hit reply, type "okay," and then send it. These must have taken her all day.

I listen to the first part of her first message, which is angry. I go to the next one and the next. She gets more and more angry, like *screaming,* then she gets scared, which is worse, and by the end, she is cajoling and crying, and then in the last message there is only her quiet sobbing and some whispered Hail Marys for my safety under her breath.

I hang up and immediately text her: *Im gud. Beaus gud 2. B hom soon. Lees here 2. LOV u. Sorry. Sorry. Xoxoxoxoxo.*

Then I turn the phone back off.

Beau takes the loft, and Leonie and I have the bigger downstairs bed. During the night, I wake up and hear her thrashing and crying in her sleep. I shake her gently, and she mutters and stops. I float back to sleep.

The next morning I wake up when the light is still gray to the song of seagull screams. I look out the window, and it's blowing and wet and a light rain is sleeting almost horizontally. Don't care, don't care!

Lee is still sound asleep, and I sneak out of bed. I climb the ladder to the loft and stick my head up to see if Beau's awake.

He is.

"Let's go see the ocean."

He agrees, and we quietly leave the cabin after writing a note to Leo saying we were just over the little bluff along the path in front of the cottage and to come find us when she got up if we weren't back yet.

I follow the sound of the surf. The ocean is just out of view, but the salt air is so thick you taste it on your lips. The crash of the invisible water just ahead is like the rhythmic breathing of some immortal animal—never stopping, always stirring—and it is calling me, and I answer, scrambling faster and faster till I hear Beau, some distance behind me, telling me to wait up.

I do. I stop, panting, just behind the rise of the bluff and wait for him. Then together we walk over the crest of the sandy hill.

Even if you have seen the Pacific Ocean a million times before, it takes your breath away. Especially in winter when it's only die-hard wetsuit surfers and seagulls and nobody else. It's violent and endless, and the waves rock in a surging, muddy rage and roll till they deplete, till they are nothing but the laciest white foam to ever tickle a girl's toes.

I take off my shoes. Beau stands staring, amazed at the sight.

"Wow," breathes Beau. "It's so"—he searches for the word—"*real.*"

And it is. Water rules the horizon to eternity.

I pull off my socks. Let the games begin.

"Aaahhhhhhhh!" I scream and run down the path. Onto the beach, landing flat-footed for maximum splat, I race across the smooth surface, leaving fleeting footprints in the surf.

Arms outstretched, embracing the eternal wind. Here I am forever. I am falling. I am free.

I am forever free-falling.

I look back, and Beau has approached the edge of the water. The salty wind whips his hair. He's just standing and looking, mesmerized.

I understand. I was also awestruck the first time. Now it's a reunion.

But first things first; I walk over to him.

"Beau, the Pacific Ocean. Your majesty, this is Beau." Bowing, I make the introductions.

Then I splash him.

"You are now an official West Coaster. Welcome to the Pacific Rim! Welcome home, Lucky of the Left Coast!"

The ocean has a very energizing effect on me. I jump and splash. Very bracing.

I do a cartwheel, but when I do, my hoodie rides up over my gut and I feel my huge flub hanging out in the cold wind. Mortified, I jump upright and shove my shirt down, but I know Beau saw. When I glance over, I see him turning his face so I won't think he saw, but he did. He's just being cool. Then he sees *me* seeing *him* pretending, and shrugs, like "So what?" He beams at me, then holds his face and arms up to the wind.

I feel a sudden stab of love for him. He is kind beyond his years.

We climb on beached driftwood logs far bigger than the trees we saw in the trucks on the road. We walk along their horizontal spines like trails and jump from one fallen giant to another. We sit within them, where the rain can't rot, nor doth rust corrupt, and rest.

"Have we gone far?"

"No. We left my shoes back there by the trail head. See?"

"Oh. Yeah. It seems like we ran a lot farther."

"Because we were running on sand. It's super tiring. Plus, you're still getting better."

We continue resting. The sky is gray, and it's as light as it's going to be at the beach in December. It's cold.

"Let's go get Leonie and get started," I say.

He doesn't respond, and I see in his eyes that he's a thousand miles away. Or two hundred, anyway.

"Beau?"

He looks at me. I see him thinking.

"What's today?" he asks.

"Today is . . . the seventeenth?"

"Winter break hasn't started yet."

"Nope. It starts the twenty-sumpin' this year."

"Are you sorry?"

"What, that I came with? Do I look sorry?" I screw my face into a truly hideous grimace. Then I try for a pensive yet snotty look, like Bella.

He laughs, and we pull each other up and brush the sand off and walk back to the cabin.

To the empty cabin.

We look at each other.

"What the . . . ?" Beau's face is disbelieving. "She's not in the loft. What happened?"

I look. The comforter and pillow are here.

"Let's go see if she's in the van."

But she's not there. Neither is the van.

Beau heads off my meltdown.

"Rusty, I've been thinking. I think maybe she's left."

"What? No way! Why?! Where?!" I start venting. But Beau redirects me.

"Rust! Listen, how many calls were on your phone when you turned it on?"

"Oh, I don't know. Like a thousand!"

"I know. I got twenty-three from my mom. Rust, Leo never turned her phone off."

We look at each other as his meaning dawns in my mind.

She didn't get one call from her mom. Not one . . . all night.

I am shut down. That would be the one number worse than thirty-nine.

Zero.

Poor Leonie! But where would she go? Back to deal with her terrible mom?

Or something else . . . oh *no.* Would she go back to Ratskin? The only one to text her. Thinking he was the only one who cared. Or wait—had that tool called her? Or had the other ones, the creeps who call her T? We'd missed it! We'd been at the ocean for over an hour.

After another hour of discussion, we walk over to a little diner close by. We order eggs and toast and wait and watch the ocean and ponder our predicament. We call and text her.

Nothing.

Finally, after drinking so much coffee that we are completely wired, we get up and sprint back to the cabin. It's noon and it's checkout time. We gather our stuff up and set it outside of the cabin door.

We sit down and wonder what to do next—without a van and with a lot of junk to carry. We're stuck.

We are discussing how sad/mad we feel when we think of Leo's life and whether or not Leonie has lost her mind when she pulls up. Fast.

And, I must say, it is the most *wonderful* sight in the world.

She jumps out of the van and comes around to us. We are standing up and shaking the sand off us and the stuff we've been sitting on.

"I'm sorry! I'm sorry! I didn't think it would take so long! I missed the turnoff! Don't be mad, 'kay?" Her hair looks like she's seen a ghost. She has sunglasses on the top of her head and is wearing Beau's black hoodie.

"Where did you go? Why did you leave? We were so worried!" We are babbling in relief when Leonie shushes us.

"I got something to show you," she says mysteriously. Sort of defiantly.

And then she opens the van side door to reveal the dog.

I stand frozen in place, jaw unhinged.

I just knew it.

And a crappier, more dejected, *miserable* specimen of a dog you are unlikely to ever see. Scrawny, shaking, flattened ears, flattened-down body—just a terrified little animal. Barely more than a puppy herself.

She looks up at us and averts her eyes, then licks her chops over and over nervously.

I got nothing. I just stand there, staring.

You know what we don't need right now? What we don't need right now is a *dog*. Any dog but especially *this* dog. Yes, she's pitiful, so let's get her away from the monsters and drop her off at the nearest PAWS right now before it gets any worse. They won't put her down. Then we can go. We're *busy*.

Beau stands there openmouthed for a sec and then goes slowly down on his knees far enough away so that she isn't freaked out. Speaks to her kindly. Doesn't move fast. Just waits.

She pees. Right on the black rubber floor of the van, all flattened down on her stomach; she just cuts loose. Pees everywhere.

I yell, and she looks away, shaking harder than ever, but can't stop herself.

"Rusty, chill! Stop! I'll clean it up! It's just pee! Shhhh, it's okay." Leonie is sitting down beside her, practically in the pee; she's petting her and holding her around her neck. The dog just crouches there. Like it's too scared to move. Shaking and peeing. I jump out of the van.

Beau comes after me.

"Hey."

I turn around.

"I know this sounds wrong, but Lee did the right thing. The only thing."

"*Not* the only thing! She could have just stuck to the plan, and we would be on the road by now!" I'm boiling. Now, on top of everything else, we have to think up what to do with Rando, the Pissing Wonder Dog! Freaking *great!*

"No, Rust! You know we couldn't! I know you don't mean that. You're just a little riled up right now . . . Rylee. It's good what she did. It's an act of kindness. Of greatness, really. It's okay, Ry. Listen to me: Leo fed the right wolf!"

"What?!"

"Leo fed the right wolf! It's like that saying or whatever!"

"What are you even talking about?! You mean like a *hybrid?!* I thought it was a husky or like a Mal—'cuz it better not be a *wolf!*"

"No, Rust—you know—that saying or fable or whatever, about the two wolves—"

"What are you *talking* about?!" I practically screech.

"Okay, calm down and let me tell you! Are you listening?"

I stop yelling. Instead, I try to stare him down. "Yes. Shoot."

"So this Indian, I mean Native American, kid goes to his dad and—"

"Oh, good that he's Native American. That makes it more profound!" I interject snarkily.

"Will you just *listen?!* So the kid says I'm having this dream all the time where these two wolves are fighting, and they fight constantly and one is mean and vicious and a bully and the other is awesome and kind and brave! But they fight and fight all night! So when the kid wakes up, he freaks out and says, 'What's going on, Dad?' And the dad says: 'Okay, if you've seen them, then you're growing up. There're these two wolves. They're inside everyone—one is good and one is evil. It takes us a while to become aware of them, but they're fighting constantly, inside everyone you know—' " Beau pauses to see if I'm listening.

In spite of myself, I am. Actually riveted. I have never heard this.

"The dad says, 'The wolves are fighting for your soul,' " Beau continues. "So the kid is, like, horrified and says, 'But, Dad, which one will win?' "

Beau pauses again, and I try to look at him indifferently. But I'm caught, and he can see that. He really does have my attention. So he draws it out. He smiles at me and puts his hand on my shoulder.

"And the dad looks at him and says, 'Son . . .' "

I scowl at Beau impatiently. He gazes at me and says distinctly, " 'The one that wins is the one you *feed*.' "

I remember *gasping* like I'd been dunked in cold water and standing stock-still as that washed over me. . . .

Amazement.

(Okay, I know by now everyone has heard it ten billion times, but remember that shivery feeling? That was how I felt when I heard it for the first time, and for me, hearing it was a paradigm shift, like when you learn something that changes your opinion forever. I thought it was so cool it gave me chills. I remember just standing frozen, freezing . . . gob-smacked, *realizing*.)

Till Beau continues:

"Also, this dog is awesome."

At which time I sharply regain focus.

"This dog's been *abused!* It's messed up! How do we know it's not going to go sketch on us and tear our arms off?" I'm coming a little unthreaded. The dog's barely more than a puppy. "Besides, where is her puppy? What, aren't we going to go steal that too?"

"No, because I saw the puppy get sold this morning, with my own eyes, and it's going to be fine," Leonie says as she jumps out of the van and comes over to where we are.

"Seriously, Leo?" Beau looks at her intently.

"Yeah. It's gonna be okay. He sold it to a little kid, a girl, who carried it like it was a baby. I think it's probably going to be wearing a lot of doll clothes for a while. I don't think it will mind though." Leonie considers the puppy's prospects thoughtfully.

I stand in the sand and bellow belligerently.

"So then, if he can sell her puppies for money, he's never gonna shoot her! He was just messing with your minds!" I'm trying to keep them tracking our plan.

Enraged, I throw sand at the cabin. The wind catches it.

"Rusty! Let's listen to her! What happened, Leo?" Beau's voice is soothing. I stop them.

"No! You two listen! Lee, go clean up the pee and we'll get in the van and you can tell us then. Beau, help me put the stuff in there. It's cold and I want to bounce!"

They've stalled; I'm in gear.

So we do.

As we are pulling out, all de-peed and de-sanded, I simmer down enough to remember the tradition. I run back to the trail and find a small round rock on the edge of the path. I put it in my pocket. I will add it to the collection. I bring a pebble from the ocean every time I visit.

This will be the first one without my dad . . . both pebble and ocean trip.

"So, Leo, what happened?" I look at her in the rearview. She's sitting wrapped in the comforter with the pillow and the dog. She's rubbing the dog's ears softly.

"Yeah, Lee, tell us the story," Beau adds.

She slowly comes back to the van from wherever her thoughts were.

"That guy is mean." Her face is somber.

"Dude, tell us something we don't know." Beau is half turned around to her seat. "He should never have a dog."

"Yeah, well, he was a huge poser also, acting really nice to the kid and her dad. Acted like he was all into dogs and patted her on the head . . . the kid, not the dog." Leonie's voice is contemptuous. "Then the second they were gone he was all 'gat-dank dogs' and spitting chew."

"Where were you?"

"At that place where we ate. 'Member? The waitress said they came in every morning for breakfast."

"No, I figured that. Where were you that you could see all this without him seeing you?"

"I was sitting at our same table. I was wearing this hoodie with the hood up and these dark glasses. Like this. Nobody ever recognizes me without my hair. See?" She demonstrates.

"Dude, you look like the Unabomber," I say. Which she did. Beau yelps. He thinks I'm funny.

"Who's that?" Leonie wants to know.

"He's a guy who goes around stealing dogs," I tell her. Beau snorts again.

"Oh." Lee doesn't even know I'm bagging on her.

"Leo," Beau says, still grinning, "Rusty is bagging on you." He eyeballs me in reprimand, even though he's laughing too.

"Oh." Leo so doesn't care. She smooches the dog's head absentmindedly.

"Then what?" I ask nicely, to make up for teasing her.

"So the little girl gets the puppy and then he comes back inside, and I see him talking to his friends and then he goes to the bathroom, so that's when I make my move. I had seen the mom dog in the back of the truck, and when nobody was looking, I just walked out like no big deal and untied her and put her in the van and drove away. Fast. My heart was *pounding!*"

We drive in silence for a minute.

"No one saw you?" Beau asks.

"I don't think so. No one yelled or followed me. My hands were trembling! I drove!"

"Jeez." I finally sigh heavily. "This is awesome!"

"It's fine! It's good! This dog is the *bomb!*" Leonie glares at me defensively.

I frown at her in the rearview.

"Oh, it's the bomb, all right! It just came in and blew our plans to smithereens!"

"Rusty! She's a 'her,' not an 'it'!" Leonie scowls from the mirror. "It's not her fault!"

"Whatever," I say. "Actually, you're right. It's yours."

"Rust." Beau touches my arm. "It's cool. The poor little thing, right? This dog *is* the bomb."

I look at Beau and then back straight ahead. Two against one. Fine; I'm just driving.

We leave the beach like we left the woods, heading down 101. The broken yellow line curves out of sight like the road less traveled. We'll stay on the scenic route and keep the ocean to our right.

We're finally en route to the city!

I drive in silence for a while. Lee and the dog are on the seat behind me, and then the dog gets down and fidgets on the floor, and of course the next thing I smell is *stank*.

I cannot believe this. I start to take a really deep breath for calmness—then change my mind *quickly* and unroll the window.

I look back in the rearview. Begin to go ballistic but again change my mind.

"Leonie, uh, I think *The Bomb* just went off," I say with cheese grating hilarity.

Beau looks over at me. His eyes are amused.

"Um, yeah, so could you start cleaning up the, uh, shrapnel?" Ow, I am just hurting myself! I'm a killer! Rusty on a roll!

Beau stifles a laugh 'cuz I'm a hoot. Then he turns around to Leo.

"We'll pull over and I'll help you," he says sweetly.

As do I. I sing out.

"Oh *yes!* Let's do! I shall pull over *now* because The Bomb shat! This is all part of the plan! Oh, great day in the morning, *yes!*" I'm in my own little groove now. "Yup, yup, awesome pup!"

I elaborately signal to pull over, even though there are no other cars on the road. Leonie jumps out of the car, calls The Bomb, and walks her over to the side of the road, leading her gently by her neck fur flap. Bomb follows her and then pees and dookies everywhere again. Then looks up in wonder when she hears Leo encourage her. Wags her tail once, doubtfully.

Okay. I guess she really had to go.

I calm down after they clean the van out again. We smell like a dirty, dank, doggy day care. On wheels.

I open my door and unroll my window when we are halfway tolerable again and get in. This trip is starting to go completely sideways. We should be past Portlandia by now. Instead, we have left the left coast and are heading inland down 101; we're halfway through the Quileute reservation, which takes up a lot of the far west of Washington state. It's not all timber—a huge stretch of the land is scrub, with little pines and sagebrush. We are going toward Aberdeen. It'll be getting dark by the time we get there because we live in the land of midday night during winter.

We pass the turnoff for Olympia, our state capital. I feel better. We're on the move.

Maybe on the way back we'll explore Olympia, I tell our crew. There's a tree there that was a seed on the *moon*, I think—or orbited it or something . . . Or we'll come back later, when the rhodies are in bloom. Our state flower is the rhododendron, I explain, which is actually a member of the evergreen family, so that makes it perfect for the Evergreen State. I read somewhere that there's a huge garden of them at the capitol. All colors. I like the thought of massive, raucous blossoms, waving crazy in the wind, some growing taller than my head.

They both look about as freaking interested in this as The Bomb does. Fine. Whatever. Knuckleheads.

We continue driving. The terrain has changed from scrub to greenbelt back to tall trees again as we roll south along 101, then back to scrub, as we head west again toward the ocean.

I drive in the dark. When I see a rest stop I pull over and we walk The Bomb and then curl up in the van to sleep. It's only about eight thirty, but we are wiped. I can hear The Bomb snoring as I fade.

I wake to Leonie singing in the dark.

"Mommy's little Bommy loves shortening, shortening, Mommy's little Bommy loves short-nin bread . . ." It's a whisper.

I can see them in the rearview without moving. The Bomb is completely relaxed and blissed out. They are under the comforter, and The Bomb's paws are flopped over comfortably like fins. I laugh under my breath. So crazed.

Then I go back to sleep.

The next day we drive over the Astoria Bridge without hitting any seagulls, which from the looks of it must be a rare feat of skill and luck. The bird bodies are all over the bridge in various states of decay. It's a huge bridge, over the wide Columbia River, and about halfway through the sign overhead changes from "Washington" to "Oregon."

We have crossed state lines! Woo-hoo! Better later than never! We continue down the coast, far from Portland and its zillion bridges. I remember my dad got lost here once, when he went to look at a fishing boat and brought along Paul and me. My dad was in the navy, and I have learned some epic swears from him.

That was a day I learned quite a few.

We'll stay on the coast and ride 101 down. Let the fast guys take I-5; we'll be fine with our scenic route.

I look in the rearview, and Leonie has The Bomb upside down and is holding her like a baby.

"Lee, you guys look silly. You know that, right?" I smile when I say it. I can't help it. They also look cute.

She ignores me and addresses The Bomb.

"Aunty Wusty is just jealous she doesn't have the pwettiest doggy in the whirld. She wuvs The Bommy, too! She thinks The Bommy is the sweetest, pwettiest, goodest wittle doggy-woggy-woggy." The Bomb licks her face. The rest of the information about what I think is lost in The Bomb's neck fur. The Bomb closes her eyes dreamily.

"Yup. That is exactly what I was thinking," I say. "If only there were some *more* dogs to steal!"

Beau looks over, laughing.

"We'll never go home! We'll just drive up and down the West Coast, stealing all the sad little dogs and cats, and we'll keep them in the van and feed them and go for walks on the beach."

"And take them to Disneyland!" I add with snarkasm.

"Yes, we will take them to Disneyland on a Groupon and buy them all mouse hats! It will be the most fun they ever have and we will take their pictures on Splash Mountain so they will remember it forever!" Beau is telling The Bomb this as she is licking his hand.

"And never make them have puppies! At least not until they are old enough! That sucks—asking a puppy to do a woman's job!" Leonie suddenly snarls, outraged and ferocious.

"Dude!" I yell.

"What? It's *true!*" Leo glares at me in the mirror. "She's not a *factory!*"

"Omg! Okay, very true, but don't say *woman!* She's not a woman! She's a dog, for gawd's sake! Don't say *woman* if you mean *female*. It's female. She's a female. Jeez! Also, technically—she's a bitch."

In the rearview, I see Leonie snicker and lean down to stage-whisper loudly near The Bomb's ear: "Well, if anyone's an expert about that, for sure it's Auntie Wusty!" And The Bomb's tail thumps. Her tongue flaps out one side of her mouth.

They are laughing at me.

I do too, a little.

The Pacific Ocean has more than just one mode. From high up in the upper left hand corner of the country at Neah Bay all the way down to the mouth of the Columbia, it is cold and wild and inhospitable, even in the summer. But that's just us. You get to love it.

It's an acquired taste; it doesn't get that much warmer in the summer or that much worse in the winter because it's generally just freezing and blowing and hard to be with. Occasional surfers in black bodysuits ride the bleak waves, flanked by screaming gulls, but you probably aren't going to see many bathing suits on the beach up north, even in August.

We head for the warmer Pacific we have seen on TV.

As we near the salt water again, farther south, I can begin to feel the rhythm and the song. When we travel inland, I grow aware of this great silence—this *lack*—and it's almost unnatural. Too still.

Returning to the ocean renews a subterranean rumble I can hear through the soles of my feet and it just keeps getting louder, drawing me like a magnet till we can actually see water. It feels great when I can see waves again. They are rising and singing in a gigantic chorus. They are calling. We stay near and follow 101.

We discover that occasionally we can drive on the beach so

we do. Minivans are not known for their handling. We push the van onto firmer ground twice and give up trying to do doughnuts.

But we can just drive down the hard sand beach for miles. It's beautiful, though the ocean always looks a little disheveled and muddy right through here. This is as far south as I've ever seen. The waves come in fast. We eventually leave the beach for the asphalt and return to 101. I pull over frequently to let cars go around. There are a lot of turnouts for this. I'm driving slowly because it's so winding and narrow.

Next stop Florence. The white sand capital of the Oregon coast.

You feel the land changing as you drive into the dunes.

It's crazy beautiful when you glimpse the distant hills of sparkling white sand for the first time. I'd heard about the dunes and seen pictures of them when a UK friend posted his vacation shots: "Trev from the Oregon dunes!" He went sandboarding in Jessie M. Honeyman Memorial State Park last summer, but I think the weather this time of year is going to keep us from doing that. I don't think the sand will cooperate. It's wet and makes the board stick and we can already go stand on the sand. For free.

We park the van and walk through the trees up over the crests of the mounds. It is blowing and cold but not too bad. The Bomb is running around and chasing sticks and having a great time. We can see for miles in all directions, mostly dunes, beige and blowing. There is a small blue man-made lake according to the sign I read, and we walk down to it and throw The Bomb's stick in there, and she fetches it time and again, her mouth wide open and laughing.

Beau has a good arm. He makes her swim far out for the stick. Then we get the idea to drop a rock into this three-feet-deep creek and The Bomb dives for it. She is so crazy! We can see her looking underwater for it and then plunging down and grabbing the same rock, over and over! It's bananas!

I feel myself warming to her *very* slightly.

After getting way too wet and having to go buy some towels at a thrift store we discovered in Florence, we search out the library so we can go online and find a youth hostel to spend the night.

We need to keep this trip cheap. There is a youth hostel in Bandon, just a few miles south that has rooms available. That would be about the right amount of driving and then we will make the push into San Francisco tomorrow.

I need to get a map. San Francisco looks way more complicated than Portland to drive into.

We get into Bandon later that afternoon. The marina is everywhere in this small town, and the sun is still setting on the ocean. It was cloudy, but the sky is clear near the horizon and the sun casts surreal colors on the water, just for a minute in its setting.

We find the hostel. We park and go in.

There is room in the hostel, and the shower is the best, most remarkable experience I've ever had! Even better than at La Push, because now we've become embedded with sand. It's weird. When you're at home, a shower or a bed just feels normal, but on the road it becomes a treasure. It is amazing, beyond imagination luxury.

Strange . . . when and what we take for granted.

We each get a bunk, and we are the only three out of four bunks in the room so unless someone else checks in tonight that makes it private. The guy who runs the place, whose name tag says Guy (and whose mustache is gigantic and waxed pointy!) listens to Leonie's sad tearful plea for The Bomb to come inside too, or she'll be lonely. At first he's all no way, no how. Then when Lee really turns on the waterworks he says that The

Bomb could come in for a ten-dollar deposit, as long as she didn't make a mess. *Maybe* refundable.

I look at both of them, and they look back, all pleading and broke, and I reluctantly fish a ten-spot out of *my* pocket.

And yeah, it better be refundable.

I don't think The Bomb has ever been inside a room before. She comes in and I think, *If she pees, I swear I'm gonna . . .* But she doesn't. Leonie sits on the bottom bunk and pats it and calls her, and she jumps up and slides alongside Leo's leg with her ears all flattened back and her tail thumping. Then she proceeds to go mental and jump from one bottom bunk to the other, back and forth, making this weird under-her-breath yipping song. Then she runs around in a circle, jumping on and off the beds like a wing nut till Leo pats one of the top bunks and The Bomb jumps up on it too—then proceeds to tear around *all* the bunks, top and bottom. She goes so fast she becomes a blur—up, down, over, around, *underbesidealongyondernearbyadjacentupon*—faster and faster, till we make her stop and she lies on her tummy, panting and snuggling in the bunk beside Leonie.

"I guess The Bomb approves," I note.

Beau throws his stuff on the top bunk without being asked. He knows I don't want to haul my big butt up there and also that Leo and The Bomb would be better on the ground floor. He does it before I have to make some stupid joke about my size that I don't think is funny but is expected by society. I see he is intentionally doing it before the subject comes up so I won't be embarrassed. Again, he is saving me pain.

Beau is quite a guy. He forged kindness from the torment he's faced.

Not everybody does.

I think there are two kinds of people, or maybe two ways of handling abuse from others. You get really mean and beat the others at their own game, or you evolve and swear never to treat others like that.

Or you just withdraw from the human race and become en-meshed in a lumpy chain-mail shield against mean people. Which is what I did. So more ways than two, I guess.

The problem with withdrawing from the mean people is you never know who the mean people are going to be, so you shut down everyone. Which is also what I did. And from which, my friends, I suffered even more, upon recollection. I do not miss my depression. I do not miss being broken. I do *not* miss the void.

I never knew how much I wanted to be part of a gang till I had one. Even a gang of misfits.

Especially a gang of misfits.

I wake up in the dawn of the next morning, which isn't all that early in the winter, though it is lighter here in south-central Oregon than it is in Seattle. I get up and I see The Bomb's head pick up. I take the leash Leonie made for her out of some plas-tic grocery bags (it's kind of cool; she tore one into strips and braided it, and she made her a collar that way too) and show it to her. The Bomb jumps down like she needs to go out.

I'm a little surprised she would even want to go with me, but I open the door quietly and we head out and down the stairs. It's early and there is no one at the desk, so we make our way out the front door unobserved.

Outside is gray and a steady wind is blowing, but it's not raining and it's not that cold. Seagulls cluster around me in midair because this is apparently a tourist town where they get fed just for being seagulls.

"Get lost! Bug off!! I'm from Seattle!" I wave my arms. "So unimpressed!"

Our freaking seagulls do tricks for fries. At least on the water-front and on the ferries.

If you have the nerve—their beaks are huge close-up—they

will swoop down and take a french fry from your fingers, slick as a whistle. We found as kids that if you don't look, it's much easier. We all have *that* picture (though we never took it till not-from-town friends or cousins came to visit)—one of us with the seagull in mid-snatch, fries and feet and fingers and beak all a big yellow blur.

When we get to the sand, I throw a stick for The Bomb and she runs madly and catches it. I throw it higher, and she catches it like a pop fly. I fake her out, and she goes left when I throw right. The second time she doesn't get fooled by the same trick and gets the stick.

The Bomb might be a real smart lil' doggy.

And isn't that just what we need, a real smart doggy. . . . I remind myself to roll my eyes when she brings the stick over and drops it at my feet and waits.

On the way back, I stop and get a small coffee and a two-dollar map of California at the gas station. I walk The Bomb off the leash back to the hostel and then put her in the van with the window open a little.

Inside the room the two sleeping beauties are still sound asleep. I pull up the blackout shade and open the window a crack. It's breezy. They stir.

"Get up! Time to be off with you!! Up and at 'em! Hip hip *hooray!*" I clang gleefully.

They groan and fire pillows in my direction, but that alone cannot reverse the clock and it's time we should be going. I go find out about my tenner. I mean to get it back.

The rest of the day is driving. We leave Oregon and enter Cali in heavy fog.

Leo takes a picture of the "Welcome to California" sign in the drifting mist. The background is completely composed of shades of gray. It's weirdly beautiful. For some reason it makes my nose sting; that's my version of getting verklempt. I turn my lights on low and drive slowly as shapes shift.

We arrive in Crescent City around one thirty in the afternoon. It's a pretty town. There's a huge beach, and we walk and throw sticks for The Bomb and get something to eat.

We are developing a routine: eat first, and then find a library. If you are patient (or if you go to a smaller town), there is always a computer waiting at the library.

Which happens to be the case in Crescent City.

So we find out that San Francisco is still like six hours away. For some reason I thought we would get there at around sunset and we would just drive up to his uncle's house and go get some food and have a bath, you know, be welcomed with open arms by Uncle Frankie.

Instead it's getting on toward two in the afternoon, it'll be dark again in about three hours, and his uncle hasn't even called Beau back. We have his address from a card he sent for Beau's birthday; I googled the directions when we were online. Beau says that his uncle and he never really talk; he just gets a birthday card every year.

Whatever. It's more than I've been getting the last couple years from my dad, never mind some uncle. He has decided he has forgotten Paul's and my birthdays or something. The last card I got was for my fourteenth birthday and had a picture of a unicorn and was covered with glitter and fuzzy velvet card fur. It made me wonder how old I am in my dad's mind. It was exactly right for a five-year-old.

And that was more than Paul got. Nothing came later that year for his birthday.

The weird thing is my dad signed that card "All my love, dad." Well, two weird things:

1. He never capitalizes *Dad* when he uses it as his name.

2. He neglects us, bailing emotionally while claiming we have *all* his love.

What am I supposed to make of that?

But I meander . . .

I sit at the computer in the library with Beau. Lee and The Bomb are outside. I can see them through the window. They were dancing but got bored.

They now sit, huddled and waiting.

"What part of San Francisco does he live in?" Beau is no more familiar with "the city" than I am. He squints at the map on the screen as I type.

"Well, the address is right here at the balloon." I show him. "It looks like he is kind of near Amoeba Music, which I've always wanted to go to, so that's the Haight-Ashbury district." I look at Beau. "But I really don't know if we should just show up on his porch and be all, 'Hi, Unc!' "

"Yeah, I know." Beau looks worried. "I've thought about that too. I've called him twice."

"What do you think the deal is?"

"I dunno. I know he talks to my mom on occasion, even though she isn't his sister—my dad is . . ."

I snicker. He glances at me reproachfully.

"Dude," I say, "I know what you meant."

"It's crazy how well he and my mom like each other because my dad hates him."

"Did your dad ever say why?"

"No, but my mom said that because Uncle Frankie was older and gay everyone in their school thought that my dad was going to be gay too, so they were ready for him. It messed him up, all the crap he had to deal with."

"So they bullied him before he even had a chance in high school."

"Yeah."

"So that sucked, but—I mean, no offense, how old is your dad?"

"Yeah, I know, maybe he should be over it, but I'm not sure some people ever *can* get over things they experience early in life."

"I so don't believe that! I think if you turn your fine mind onto a problem you can change it."

"Yeah, but what if you don't have a fine mind? Or if you don't perceive it as a problem? Or you just won't? He is not a guy who analyzes things. He thinks I am making a choice. The one time I tried to explain, after the cops left, he was freaking out so bad he punched me in the mouth. Then every word I tried to say, he punched me again. So I shut up. Then I left. And to this day, I don't really care if I ever see him again."

Beau goes quiet. His handsome, healing face is hard. Not great memories for him and his dad.

So what we decide finally is that we will drive down till dusk and then will spend even *more* money by spending *another* night at a hostel or motel and then we will call his uncle again in the morning and tell him we will see him that afternoon. Then he will invite us to come over and let us stay with him and then he will say this and that and solve all our problems forever.

So that's the plan.

We get back on the road.

Almost immediately we are faced with a choice. Stay on 101 or turn down the "Avenue of the Giants," which is where the last of the huge redwoods are. I say stay on the road.

So of course you know what Thing One and Thing Two want to do, don'tcha?

Yup. So we go down the avenue (which isn't really all that out of the way and totally worth it). It runs parallel to the highway, and the weather's dry enough that we get out and take pictures of Paul Bunyan and Babe the Blue Ox, and Beau takes one of me and Leo in the van inside that tree you can drive a car through, and I take one of them inside the single huge log that was hollowed out and made into an entire cabin. Windows with curtains even.

I gotta admit, it was fun.

When we pull back onto the highway, we are soon faced with yet another choice. Stay on 101 and go inland, or head over to Highway 1, probably much more slow and winding, and follow the coast.

Unanimously, we choose Highway 1. It's about the ocean till we get to our destination. On this we all agree.

Highway 1 in Northern California is one of the most beautiful places on earth. It has to be. As it clears farther to the south, it gets ever more amazing. It's ridiculously, excessively beautiful. At one point I pull over, and we just stand spellbound for half an hour. The hills to the water. Again: Sky to sea = eternity.

We shout out the names of the towns as we drive by them. Westport, Fort Bragg, Casper, Mendocino. We pass a sign for Albion and I start to explain that was the old name for England, and their eyes glaze *immediately* so I stop. I concentrate on the concrete.

I was right though. The roads are slow and winding. There are more and crookeder switchbacks than I've ever seen. At some points there is only one lane. I focus hard and drive.

We study the map I got at the gas station. It's like impossible to figure out at first. We are so totally out of our depth. I *know* I need a smartphone but, like I said, I'm waiting; Beau's is at the bottom of Lake Washington; and Leo, well, you know. But I show everyone how. Paper maps are a lot more work than computer maps. There are no little balloons showing where you want to go, plus they take up a ton of room. It's just harder.

But we work it. We study up and decide we will spend the night at the hostel in a town called Point Reyes Station. It's about the right distance.

Beau navigates and I captain. Leonie sings. The Bomb's tongue flaps out the window.

We stop and eat at a roadhouse café, appropriately called Queenie's Roadhouse Café.

Food fit for a queen.

Leonie is out of money. We have still never discussed who all is paying for what, but I knew it would happen when all she had to start was less than forty bucks. I start to blow a gasket, but then I remember how Beau took the top bunk, etc., without saying anything to embarrass me, and so I do the same now and just pay for her. We can use my college money bank account for now. I'll figure it out some other time.

Afterward we go for a walk and The Bomb detonates. Lol.

We continue down the Shoreline Highway, as they call Highway 1 through here. It's straight but narrow like a country lane. We make good time. We own the road and the quiet and thoughtful ocean over on our right.

There a couple of hostels to choose from at Point Reyes. The one we pick looks super busy and fun. We drive up and sit still in surprise.

It's totally a youth hostel and about a second from the beach, and there are millions of young people milling around even now at this time of year. People coming and going and it's a festive-looking place.

The only problem is we are all under seventeen, which hasn't been an issue so far, but I read in the info it's a lot cheaper to stay if you say you're a minor. What worries me is if we all admit to being underage, will they even let us stay? Or get weird and call the cops? I'm still pretty sure we're on the lam. And if we don't get the discount rate, it's twice as expensive. Plus, there are *so* many people here. The joint is jumping! And I noticed Leonie eyeballing these two cute guys. So that's freaking wonderful.

We sit outside in the van and consider before we go in. I don't recognize the music that's playing. I know of the three of us I look the oldest so if anyone is going to play the sensible elder statesman it should be me.

We get out of the van, leave the window open a crack for The Bomb, and lock it. We stand there and look uncertain for a sec, which is about the worst thing you can do if you are trying to pull a fast one.

"I'll go in and say we need accommodations for three UM," I say, practicing my older, deeper, sensible voice.

They both look at me blankly.

"What does that even mean?"

"Unaccompanied minors. My brother Paul and I traveled that way."

"No, that sounds too weird." Beau frowns. "Why are you suddenly tripping? We have stayed a bunch of places, no big deal." I agree. I don't even know why I'm suddenly tripping.

Then I do. I realize it's because there are so many people around our own age and I'm used to that always becoming an unpleasant situation. Also Leo, who is a piece of work to keep out of trouble around guys.

Also, money. We're just chugging through it.

I go inside and am just about to go up to the front desk when Beau comes up to me.

"Listen, Leonie asked this guy to be our big brother or whatever if we need him to. We can totally get the cheap price now!" He looks pleased.

I do not. Of that I am sure.

"Beau! No! Yeah, I *bet* she did! Omg! For what in return?

She does *mental* things, y'know, Beau!" I look out the front door as best I can. I don't see her.

It's my turn at the front desk.

They totally do not care how we got there, and when we say we are students, they don't even card us and we get the rate. I don't know why I get myself so cranked.

We hurry out to find Lee, and she is talking to this guy with a beard that looks like Jesus. Assuming that you think Jesus looked like a hot white guy with a beard.

They are deep in conversation, and she is twiddling her hair. Beau and I exchange looks, and we go see what she has blabbed so far.

"So, yeah, we're from Seattle."

"Cool . . . the Emerald City, right?"

"Um, yeah. I think so."

"Nice. How old are you?"

"Si—uh . . . eighteen."

"Great." Jesus looks really happy. I pipe right in.

"Such a lie! Omg! She is *sixteen!*"

He looks at me and then back at her. A few times. You can see he's hoping she's the one telling the truth but that he's pretty sure it's me. He gets a little flustered.

"What?! Seriously?! *Omg!* Listen, um—Leonie, you shouldn't tell people that you're of age when you aren't. Omg, you said your friends were the ones who were underage."

"So what does it matter how old I am? I'm old enough." Leonie glances at me savagely. Whatever.

"So what?! So it's a *huge* deal! You're underage! Honey! Do you not get that? I was going to ask if you wanted to go get something to eat maybe and then who knows. But sixteen?! That's jailbait! Are you crazy?! *No way!*"

Leo looks at him angrily. "Don't worry about it! I can take care of myself! I won't tell anyone! I don't even *care!*"

Jesus looks at her sorrowfully. "But you should care! I wouldn't do that, 'cuz if I did, I would be using you. I'd be taking advantage of you. Can you see? *I* wouldn't do that, Leonie."

Jesus leaves us. Fast.

Leonie stink-eyes me. Hard. Starts to say something snotty, but I short-circuit her.

"Oh, Leonie, don't you even dare be mad at me! What were you even thinking—if you ever *do* think—trying to get us busted much?" I am boiling with anger. I'm keeping my voice down with difficulty and hissing like some giant teapot. "You don't even get it! That was the appropriate response when a grown man finds out some random chick is sixteen years old! Not like despicable Ratskin, the child molester!"

She glares at me, then turns without a word and lunges off. I turn to Beau.

"Beau, we are in the first room on the right. Go find her before she goes off looking for trouble just to show me, 'kay? Which I'm sure she will find." He nods and disappears after her.

I take our stuff back to the van so I don't have to rent a locker, then get The Bomb and her leash and head out to the beach.

The Bomb is like a people magnet. Especially for kids. She is getting much more confident and friendly and not so startled by every little thing. It's only been a couple days and already she is adapting to her new reality. Plus, her milk is drying up fast and she's not so skinny.

We wander around, and I throw sticks we find on the beach but neither of us has any heart for it. We sit on a log. I do, anyway; she stands on it, and we watch people get firewood for a bonfire on the beach. We stay far back from the circle. I look to see if Itchy and Scratchy are at the fire but no luck.

We wander and wait, and I finally put The Bomb back in the van, get her all snuggled in with the pillows (and her thick fur),

and grab the sleeping bags to go to the room and read. I get
something to eat from the vending machines and wait and look
around and still no crew. They've been gone a while.

When I go back to the room, I suddenly feel very alone,
even though there are two other people sleeping in nearby
bunks. I am reminded sickeningly of how awful my life was before. How blank. I hear the old oppressive desperate static of
solitude and silence.

I crawl in my bunk and wait, my internal emptiness eerily
echoing, frozen in place.

When I finally hear them come into the room, I get a little
unhinged with relief. But when I hear them whispering, I feel
my temperature start to rise.

They are high . . . like really, *really* high.

It's late, and there are other people besides me in the room.
Beau and Leonie are both laughing and trying not to, and this
results in them laughing like hyenas and not being quiet at all.

The other people in the room start to complain and so I grab
them both and pull them out of the room and into the van. The
Bomb is seriously glad to see them, and they are deliriously happy
to see her.

After a little while, it starts to dawn on me that they are not
just high on weed; it's something different and stronger. They are
weaving and laughing in hysterics. And saying weird things . . .
like weirder than usual.

I get them in the van and start the engine because it's cold
and we don't have our sleeping bags since they're back in the
room.

The Bomb is sniffing them and wagging her tail uncertainly.

"Yeah, check it. She can tell you guys are messed up." I indi-
cate her hesitation.

"We're fine. She knows *shwe* love her!" Leo is defensive and
slurring. Her hair is wild and snarled.

Beau just tee-hees helplessly. Then Lee does too. Then they start to shush each other so that they start laughing harder and harder till eventually they are just clicking.

"*Ack, ack ack ack ack yackackackyackyack.*"

Flopping over and flailing their little fins and making that little *tick* in their throats that is only one step away from crying and two from peeing your pants. I roll my eyes as I watch them in the rearview.

I roll with *epic* numbskulls.

They stop quacking and quaking finally and lie still, propping each other up, holding their collective tummies, wiping their eyes, getting their breath, and snorting in relapse till they sit quietly in some new phase of highness. I watch them in the mirror. Then I turn and face them. We all look at each other.

"Rusty, you are so beautiful!" Leonie bursts out. "Your face looks like chrome in the moonlight! For reals!"

This sets Beau off again, and he has to repeat "for reals!" several thousand times like some extra chunky nut bar. Then Leonie tells him to shut up. Then he tells her to shut up. Then she says, "No, you shut up," then he says, "No, you shut up," and thus they continue, gasping and writhing with glee for several hundred thousand more repetitions. I shake my head.

"You guys are freaking hilarious. Seriously. I wish Conan O'Brien could see you; you'd be totally famous." They grow palsied with laughter. Their eyes bug out. "*Yak! Yak! Yak! Yak yak yakity yak yak!!*" they inform me. They shake when they laugh like a bowl full of jelly.

I wait them out, my eyes skyward.

Then I continue cautiously. Their eyes look weird. Like pure black.

"So what did you *do*, exactly? What did you take? Did you have something to drink?"

"No! We know better than that! No roofies! We just bought

a joint off some dude. It tasted weird, though. Beau, did you think it tasted funny?"

I look at Beau. He nods and slides down the backrest onto the seat.

I freak.

"And you smoked it anyway?! Idiots! What is wrong with you?! Somebody probably messed with it! I *knew* it!"

"Dude, seriously, we only smoked some weed," Leo insists. She pauses and looks at me intently. "Omg, Rus, listen. I see the flesh on your face, Rusty . . . and it's *glittering!* Omg, Rusty, you are totally like Edward! Beau! *Rusty is like Edward!*"

"That is so tight, Russss . . ." Beau sounds like a spider from Mars. He reaches up and traces his finger down the inside of the van window. Draws rainbows in the condensation.

But Leo isn't done. Not even.

"Omg, Rusty, seriously—wait—oh no, your face is *falling off!* It's totally dropping off in clumps, like—glitter glue! On your lap! *Ahh!* It keeps doing it! Yuck! Dude! You're freaking me out! Make it stop!" Grossed out, she flaps jazz hands at me.

Beau turns slowly and looks at me owlishly, then turns back to Leonie. Shakes his head.

"Leo. Leo. Rust *has* no control over her face. . . . You must stop it, Leonie." Beau is very solemn. He's all profound: a faded Yoda. "Rusty cannot control what her face does. *You* must control her face. You made her face fall off with your mind . . . so only *you* have the power to put it back. So put it back on her, dude. Put her face back on! Wait . . . first . . . can you see what's underneath?" He looks at me, squinting.

"Underneath are . . . eye sockets . . . made of diamonds," Leonie whispers. She's awed. "And . . . wait—there are tears on your cheekbones . . . made of pearls! Oh, poor Rusty . . ."

They both squint at me.

"Yeah, I figured. . . ." Beau closes his eyes and conducts music only he can hear.

Leo looks at me. Then she frowns. She knows the look on my face, whether or not there is flesh on it. "Just don't lecture us and harsh our buzz, 'kay? Don't."

I look away from both of them. I don't want to lecture. I'm not gonna . . . but I have to.

"Sorry, I am *so* going to lecture you! You were so lucky! Whatever you smoked wasn't just some pot; it was mixed with who even knows what by some sketcho! I'm surprised at you both! You should know better than to take stuff from strangers! I've seen how you are when you're high—I've seen you a lot, Leo—but you are acting much weirder this time."

They look at me like, "Oh boy, here we go."

"But, Rusty, you said you thought weed should be legal," Leo begins feebly.

I start lecturing them like a librarian. An insanely bad-tempered librarian.

"See, and this is exactly why! 'Cuz it'll be a little more rational—not to mention harder for you two to get your lil' koala paws on!"

"Nuh-uh, Rust, it would be exactly the same." Leo is stonily certain.

"How?! This way you could get popped and maybe go spend some quality time with a bunch of *seriously* bad kids whose best day was just smoking some weed!"

They stare at me and nod, bemused. "That's true, Rus," Beau agrees.

"Oh, well, whatcha gonna do?" Leo asks. Then she gets distracted and looks alarmed. She checks the skin on her face to make sure it's still there.

I practically screech I'm so vexed.

"*Re*-legalize it nationally! It's too stupid. Beau, you said your mom and Matt smoke; I know my mom has too, 'cuz I smelled it when her friend got chemo! And it's not like she's some *Scarface* drug mom—she's an RN, for gawd's sake!

What—are we gonna hafta go spring our old-ass parents from jail for blazin'? Or: '*Hi, honey, it's Grandma. I got busted for torchin' a blunt—again. Would you come spring me?*' Seriously?! Plus: *so* counterproductive. It doesn't make sense, and kids *know* that. Then they don't respect other laws that do!"

My fond and captive audience looks at me. Leonie nods to Beau sagely. She explains.

"She gets like this. . . . She has 'theories' and she can keep going for hours. She's like the Energizer Bunny."

Beau nods. "I've noticed."

"Not to mention the money you'll get from taxing it!" I add. "Good-bye, Great Broke Ass Recession—Hello, National Health Care! *Hello, College!!*"

"It's cool, Rust. We totally agree with you." Beau's voice is soothing. So I chill out.

Literally. It's cold. I had shut off the engine, but now I run it again.

I change the topic to what's been on my mind.

"Turn your phone on and see if your uncle has called, Beau."

"I did. He didn't," Beau answers slowly.

We sit and think. I do, anyway. They just coast.

Leonie stirs from her reverie. She turns to look at Beau, reassures herself that his face is still totally covered in skin, then settles back, thinking out loud.

"I don't even know what you think he's going to do that will help. I mean, *I* know what will help. It's actually easy, hon: Just don't *be* gay, Beau. Find some hot chick and get over it! Wait, I know. . . . We should totally go out! I can fix this! I won't *let* you be gay, Beau! I can totally hook you up. You should choose me. I got this." She pats his face as they sit slumped together in the backseat.

"Omg, Leonie, sometimes you are such an epic spaz," he

tells her lovingly. "Listen, I am *so* gay. I am sooo hella gay you wouldn't even believe it. You are totally hot . . . but it just doesn't thrill me, you know? No offense, honey." He pats the hand patting his face.

"How do you know? Have you even tried? Have you ever even kissed a girl?"

"Yuh! When I was fourteen. I kissed her, and we made out, and it was okay, but mostly it was just *weird*, you know? She wanted to be my girlfriend too, and I tried to be all, 'Yeah— absolutely!' But it didn't take me long to figure out that I was way more into hanging out with her older brother. They never knew that, though." He laughs in remembrance.

"Well, I think you should at least try!"

"Leo, you shouldn't do that with other people's feelings. I found that out . . . very bad."

"Well, fine then, suit yourself. How about we just move to some big old gay town and you can be like the gay mayor! That would work too." Leonie looks modestly proud of her brilliant suggestion.

"Yeah, see, no way." Beau shifts and gets a little crabby. "It's crazy for me to have to do that. Why? How is it even that big a deal? Why should *I* have to go away and leave my friends and family to live in some gay concentration camp? How 'bout everybody who's not gay doesn't worry about it, and then maybe I could be the mayor of Anydamnplace, USA, who also happens to be gay, but so what, nobody cares? And the world would go on spinning along just the same as before I was the mayor of Anydamnplace, and everything is just as good or bad as it had always been. Why is that so impossible?" He has his irritated face on again.

"It's not, Beau," I tell him. "It's the future. We just have to go get it."

"Fine. So that is what I am going to find out how to do."

Leo's suddenly cross, probably because it dawned on her that Beau turned her down.

"Or whatever! What's Uncle Frankie going to say to us, anyway, that's so hella off the hook? 'Come on down to San Francisco and get your gay on happily ever after'? *Please.* He doesn't know you. He doesn't know sh—"

Beau interrupts her.

"Maybe he does and maybe he doesn't, but he's the only gay guy I know, or even know of, and I want to at least meet him."

"Well, I certainly hope it helps!" Leo sniffs. "But *I* think you're deluded!"

I feel it's time to remind Leonie of a thing or two.

"Oh, what about you, missy? Like *you* have it all together?" I catch her like a mousetrap.

"What? You do?"

"No, but let's just talk about you for now: You let anyone put their dirty, freezing hands all up on your body and let them call you crappy put-down names, which you then respond to! Omg, Leonie, you need to step up! Tell those sorry butt-wipes to step *off!* And to *shut up!* You are worth *so* much more than that trashy behavior! And you're beautiful. Like ridiculously, unbelievably beautiful! You don't even have to be a freak like us; you just are here because of your own crap behavior!"

I'd been wanting to say that! But I also knew she wouldn't want to hear it. And I was right. She yowls like an angry cat.

"*Whatever!* Then we are all here because of our own behavior! You're a freak 'cuz you eat too much and got all big, and Beau's here because he chooses boys!"

We both just stare at her. I face palm. Some of the more priceless things that come out of her mouth are almost beyond belief. Honestly, I occasionally wonder how she can feed herself.

Patiently, Beau tries again.

"Leo, remember? So *not* a choice. I just am gay. Otherwise I would choose you! Think about it. How could I be all leaned up against your hot self and still be able to concentrate, right?" He tickles her under the chin playfully.

I also chime in, in my own defense.

"And I totally admit that I eat way too much, but, Leonie, come on. You also have to acknowledge the fact that different bodies process food at different rates. Some people have a more efficient metabolism. They just burn it off faster. You eat *tons* more than I do, and nobody would ever guess that! Just sayin'."

All of which is true.

Our rejoinders to Leo's little outburst being over, we simmer down again. Silence reigns unbroken for a few minutes.

Then she adds indifferently as an afterthought, "In that case, it's not my choice either. My stepdad started molesting me when I was a little kid."

Beau and I are not sure what we just heard. We just sit, blinking. Finally Beau speaks softly.

"Did you just say that your stepdad molested you?"

"Yeah . . . when I was, like, *little*."

"Omg, Lee, how little?"

"I don't know exactly." She shrugs. "I can't remember a time before he did."

We do not know what to say. It's hard to breathe. Finally I venture a question.

"Didn't you tell your mom?"

"Yeah! Are you kidding?! I told her at least three times I can remember!"

That is so unbelievably messed up I cannot imagine it. My mother would have killed anyone if they'd even *looked* at me. . . .

"What did she do?"

"Nothing. She acted like it wasn't true. She didn't believe

me. Then when I told her again when I was older, she said I had encouraged him . . . which was *so* not true."

Beau and I try to wrap our heads around this.

"Where is he now?"

"Dunno. I think he took off when she chased him around with a knife and threatened to kill him for cheating on her . . . with someone besides me."

"Oh, Leonie, why didn't you tell me this before?" I can't believe there is so much I don't know about her. Or how much crap I've given her.

"Yeah, well, there's more if you want to hear it."

"Do you want to tell it?"

She shrugs. "Sure. Why not? I'm wasted. So they took me away from her after that, 'cuz the neighbors called the cops, and I went to this foster home. . . ." Her words drift off.

"But that was good, though, right?" Beau's face is intense.

Lee snorts bitterly.

"Hardly. It was exactly the same, only where I was placed there were two guys now instead of one."

"*Two* guys molested you?"

"Yeah."

"Who were they?"

"Other random foster kids."

"How old were they?"

"I dunno. Older than me."

"How old were you?"

"Ten."

I am completely shut down. Everything makes perfect sense now: Ratskin, Turbo, all the jerk asses getting over on her—her absent mom and silent phone and empty fridge. . . .

"So then what happened, Leo?" I ask, my tone uncustomarily kind.

"Um . . ." She looks up, thinking, and then stares accusingly at me. "Wait—you're not going to start being all nice to me, are you? Because that would be weird."

I swear I'm about to bust out crying. The thought of poor little Leonie, with her big eyes and sweet nature all alone and bad people doing whatever they felt like to her.

"No," I manage to rasp. "Same as it ever was."

"Good. 'Cuz I'm fine. I hardly even remember it anymore."

Which I seriously doubt.

"Why didn't you tell us?"

"I dunno. It doesn't really come up in conversation. Whatevs. Why think about it? Haters gonna hate. Just have fun now is what I say." She looks out the window, then leans her head on Beau's shoulder tiredly. "It's all good. Who cares? I can't even remember that little kid . . . the little girl I was."

Beau puts his arm around her shoulders protectively.

"I wish I'd been there. I would have kicked that guy's ass. I wish I was your brother."

"I wish you were too." They snuggle a little. I can see whatever stuff they're on is wearing off and that they are wiped. The Bomb has been very quiet during this last hour or so, keeping her worried eyes on Leonie and Beau and then turning to me like, "What's their deal?" When she sees them calming down, she gets on the seat with them and snuggles up in the mix.

I don't blame her. They look like a litter of puppies.

After a little while, I hear them snoring gently. All three of them. Then I doze too.

In the gray dawn I wake up and go back into the hostel room that we paid for but none of us slept in. I take a shower, grab our stuff, and load it carefully around my sleeping beauties. They slumber on, completely unaware of how well they're being looked after.

And off we bounce.

* * *

We still have a fair ways to go. I'm pumped to see the city even though I have so many new thoughts in my mind. The pile of flesh in the back mutters and moans in its collective dream, but I'm wide awake and hitting on all cylinders. We drive on.

And omg, coming into the city by way of Highway 1 is the tightest route! The iconic Golden Gate Bridge is our road, but it's not just because of Golden Gate; you can see other bridges and buildings and skyscrapers glinting in the sun, which is even partially shining at the time we get there. I wake the guys up when we're on the bridge to show them this vision.

I know I will always remember this:

The fog and clouds part over the mauve water; the sunshine sparkles white-gold, illuminating the city on the hill; everything becomes shimmery and ethereal; luminous and otherworldly in its perfect, transient beauty, and suddenly we realize we are weirdly *happy*.

I know because we all look at each other, smiling. I can see it in their eyes and faces too.

We made it!

They immediately fall back asleep. I keep on truckin'.

So now we're in San Francisco. I'm on Market Street and I need to find Nob Hill.

These are the words I have read. I have no idea what they mean.

And apparently my navigator is Rip Van Winkle, who is going to sleep for a hundred years, like in the fairy tales.

I find a place to pull over. Get out the stupid paper map and start to figure it out.

After fifteen minutes, from the backseat I hear Leo start to groan.

"Oh, ow, ow, omg . . . I'm gonna barf! Oh *no* . . . move!" She pile drives through the door of the van and spews vigorously all over the streets of San Francisco, then leans against a streetlight, retching.

The Bomb is whining nervously. I hear more gagging from the backseat, and then Beau projectiles through the van door. They stagger around the sidewalk ralphing and heaving and generally giving the streets of the city one more shellacking. I get out and head over to them.

They are greenish and shaky. Their skin looks slick and wet. I get some ice from a bodega behind us and hold it to their faces. Then they suck it. And barf again. I make them try to drink some water and that doesn't work either.

After ralphing about twenty times, they are both exhausted and clammy, sitting on the curb beside the van in a three-minute loading zone. It's cloudy again and they are shivering. I give them the towels from Florence to wipe themselves off. Luckily there is no spew or crap in the van for a change and I can put them back inside and under their covers. Shaking with chills, they immediately fall back asleep.

I sit and have a little chat with myself about what we should do at this point. I seriously doubt that if I show up at Uncle Frankie's house with Pinky and the Brain here, covered with barf and in need of a bed, and say, "Hi! We tried to call, but oh well! Could you help me hose them off?" that we will get the reception we were hoping for. I have to get them someplace we can have some time for them to recover from this fun, fun hungover part of their little misadventure before we go find Beau's uncle.

And where that someplace could be I have no idea.

I decide at last to go up to the Haight-Ashbury neighborhood. I want to explore the Haight, and also Amoeba Music is there and I seriously need to see it. I figure I can get a parking place and something to eat and maybe by that time they will feel like finding out where in the world is Uncle Frankie. I navigate with as much trouble as you think I would and go up an enormous hill and then take a wrong turn and go down another one and then I'm suddenly far from the street I seek . . . I think. I go down a one-way and think I'm circling around, but no. I have no idea where I am or what neighborhood this is. One-way streets have surged me far from where I meant to go. Exasperated, I park the van and pay for a couple hours at the meter. I'm getting hungry.

They slumber on, except for The Bomb, who is riding shotgun while Beau sleeps. I smooch her forehead and her tail thumps. I leave all the windows open a crack and lock the doors and go find something to eat.

I wander around looking at the shops and people for almost two hours. Then I go back to check on the sleeping beauties. Nothing. Still sound asleep. I wonder if they will wake up hungry or sick. I *know* they will wake up stinky. In fact, the entire van is reeling in reek—like wet dog and armpits and puke and feet. I open all the windows another inch and try not to heave as I leave. I find a deli I'd passed earlier. I order a sandwich and sit and eat and read the *San Francisco Bay Guardian,* which is like the *Stranger* in Seattle: bands and club dates and wild personal ads. I'm worried so I can't concentrate. Also I'm not as ravenous as usual, which has happened a few times on this trip. I decide to take the other half of my sandwich to go and check on The Bomb to see if she needs a walk. As I roll along I hear this voice.

"Hey, girl! Hey, girl with the box! You gonna eat that?"

I see these two hippie chicks sitting on the sidewalk. It's not raining but also not very warm, and they are just sitting on the nasty, gum-pocked sidewalk. Eyeballing my half a sandwich box. Intently.

Without a word I hand it to them. They are about a block from the van. I walk over and get The Bomb and put some money in the meter, all of which takes two seconds, and when I get back to where they are, the sandwich is gone, as well as the pickle, and they are licking their grimy fingers to get every last potato chip crumb and sesame seed.

"Thanks, girl! You rock. Hi, cute doggy. Got any spare change?"

I smile at them and shake my head as I walk The Bomb. I will try never to judge anyone again. Who knows how or why they are here or from what hell they escaped.

I will do what I can to help; I just wish them the best and leave it at that.

What to do . . .

After our little jaunt, I take The Bomb back to the van and put her away. The hippie chicks are gone, and I'm bummed because I was going to ask them if they knew a place where we could hang out for a couple of hours or days that wasn't too sketchy. I guess we'll find a hostel if we have to.

I drive us around. I accidentally go down to Chinatown and see Alcatraz in the distance from the wharf. Some lady tells me how to get to Lombard Street, and so I head down Lombard. Beau and Leo really don't appreciate the long and winding Lombard as much as I do. They groan and yell and tell me to knock it off. So far they are not enjoying San Francisco.

I play music and try to learn the city as I drive around. I listen to the Art of Noise.

"Where are we?" Beau gets into the front seat beside me. Slowly.

"Well, um . . . we're not in Kansas anymore, Toto!" I bellow. "Aahhahahahahaaaaa!"

He winces and grunts at me, pained and reproving. Like he might barf again.

"No, Rust! Do not say that awful thing! Omg, *so* played!"

I cackle with glee, caused by trotting out that dusty Kansas line yet again.

"Omg, I know! *Sorry!* I was a'feared I'd be a sayin' that—sooner or later!"

"Rusty, never again. It's just . . . *too* . . . horrible. . . ."

"You're right! *Never* appropriate! And *not* funny! I promise: Never say it again! Never ever! Wait—say what?"

It's a relief to see Beau smile. He's feeling better.

The Bomb is also glad. She gets on his lap and smooches him, so now there are two passengers in the seat. They rubberneck while we roll.

San Fran is a lot like Seattle in that it's beautiful and salty and full of seagulls. Also hilly.

I have heard about this flock of parrots on Telegraph Hill. There is a documentary about it. I look for someone to ask for directions.

But Beau has other ideas. He's feeling well enough to be sarcastic.

"Let's get to my uncle's so we can rejoice that he's moved away or whatever!"

"Okay. I Google-earthed his address at the library. It's an apartment in Nob Hill. I'm pretty sure we aren't far."

Nob Hill is an old part of San Fran, and the buildings are all brick and cobblestone and cool.

We finally find the street that has been our North Star and troll the block looking for parking. We see some eventually and get out, just intending to scope out the place.

We are almost there (with The Bomb on her leash) when we see this other guy with his dog. You can tell it's a pretty old dog, and so we hold The Bomb back from getting too close.

They are just standing there, waiting for the old dog to dookie. They look bored, both the dude and his dog. The dog squats finally. We politely look the other way, and the dude cleans it up with a bag.

"Good job, Sylvester! Good boy!" the guy tells him placidly.

He throws the bag in a garbage can and uses some hand sanitizer from his pocket. Mission accomplished.

Sylvester wags briefly and lifts his leg on a phone pole. Then he sees The Bomb and loses it.

He starts barking and runs up to us on his expando-leash thing, then starts sniffing The Bomb.

He's a Bomb-sniffing dog. Har.

We just stand there. The Bomb cringes submissively.

Then the old dog starts humping The Bomb. And she totally *lets* him.

Leonie screams and pulls The Bomb away in disgust. The other dog starts barking at her in a threatening way. Beau looks over to the guy.

"Hey, could you maybe get your dog?"

"Sylvester! No, no! Come here!" He pulls the leash so it starts to retract. "Right now, mister!"

He looks at us like it was somehow our fault. Instead of his nasty dog's.

"Excuse me. Do you live in this building?" Beau asks him politely.

"Why?"

"Do you know anyone named Frankie Gales?"

He looks at us again. Hard.

I start to think, *Oh no, please don't you be Beau's uncle.*

"Why do you want to know?"

"I think he's my uncle."

The guy just coughs like he's been punched lightly in the gut. Stands there, looking up.

"Okay," he says after a minute. "Come inside."

We follow him and Sylvester up the stairs to the third floor. We look at each other and shrug.

"Frank? I have a surprise for you," the dude says as he opens the door to the apartment.

And standing there, we see a short, buff guy in a T-shirt and jeans, unpacking books onto a bookshelf. His T-shirt is black. His arms are *ripped*. He stops putting books away.

"Frank? Yes, well, these kids just blew in. Apparently, they're looking for *you*." The guy has kind of a snotty smile on his face when he says that, like he's enjoying himself at the other dude's expense. "You should probably check your messages soon."

The short, ripped guy looks at us blankly. Beau speaks first.

"Hey . . . I'm Beau Gales. Are you my uncle Frankie?"

The short guy just stares at us all jaw-dropped. Gobsmacked.

The other dude snorts. "Ho-kay! I'll just be in the kitchen washing my hands, *Frankie.*"

His tone makes us look at each other in a confused manner. What?

The ripped dude is still staring at us in amazement.

"Wh-where did you all come from?"

"Um, we started in Seattle."

"Yes . . . I'm sure. . . . And you drove down here *why?*"

Now it seems kind of idiotic. We eyeball each other again. I speak up.

"Because Beau wanted to meet you. We all do, but you're his only uncle."

He looks over at me.

"And you are?"

"Rusty."

He looks me up and down.

"Of course you are." His tone is amused.

Gee, really? I've been served! (Oh, I'm so *hurt.*)

He turns back to Beau.

"So you drove what, eight hundred something miles, without even calling me first?"

"No, we did call! You didn't pick up. We called like twenty times."

"I was at a weeklong retreat because this world is driving me crazy, and now here you all come the second I get back, to drive me back to crazy town! Great! Just great! Really! Exquisite timing!"

We hear laughing from the kitchen.

"That somewhat expensive peace didn't last too long, did it, *Frankie?*"

Beau's uncle turns to the disembodied voice in the kitchen.

"Knock it off." He turns back to us. "Just call me Frank, okay?"

"Okay. Whatever." We shrug. We glance at each other. Whatever.

"Why?" Leonie asks.

"One: Because I said so! Two: Because it's my name. 'Frankie' has bad associations for me."

"Wait . . . my mom calls you Frankie." Beau's expression is confused.

Uncle Frank's face softened.

"Gina? Yeah, well, that's different. *She* can."

We just look at him. He looks back at us. You can tell he's deciding. Then he does.

"Listen, do you guys want some tea or something? You may as well come in and sit down, since you're here."

We have all been standing in the doorway. We go into the room where he was putting away the books. The little old dog is a lot less awful now that he's inside and comes up and wags his tail and is friendly, but we are not. We only give him a courtesy pat till he has redeemed himself. The Bomb is quietly tense.

The other guy comes in with four green bottles and hands us each one and cracks one for himself. I look at the bottle and it's something called "gingerade." I try a sip. It's pretty good.

Dude's still grinning wickedly. He sits down in an easy chair. He looks at us, all disgusting and hungover and trashed, then stares at Beau's face and giggles a little. Sylvester comes over and flops down at his feet.

"Maybe you could do some sightseeing with Uncle Frank while you're here," he suggests. I hear attitude in his voice. He smiles über sweetly, but he's pissed.

"Hope so. What's your name?" Beau asks, smiling in a neutral, if somewhat hesitant way.

"You may call me Captain Marvel." Dude sits up very tall. Waggles his eyebrows and eyeballs us, unsmiling.

This guy is like a crazy person. We look at each other like *what?*

"Why would we do that?" Beau asks carefully, like this guy might go off.

"Because I am!" He cackles maniacally. We gather ourselves to run if we have to.

"Stop scaring the kinder, Oscar, right *now*." Uncle Frank rolls his eyes at us as he re-enters the room. "He's been designing his pride costume all day—months in advance; he's decided he's going to be Captain Marvel on skates this year. That's the only reason . . . so don't worry—he's just a *little* nutty." He smiles down at him.

"Wait—you march in the Gay Pride Parade?" Beau asks Oscar, like it's too cool.

"Indeed. Are you surprised? You've seen the one in Seattle, surely?"

"I haven't lived there that long. There isn't one where my dad lives. That's for sure."

Frank laughs out loud. "I imagine not. . . . How is that big jerk, by the way?"

"Jerkier than ever." Then Beau and Frank both laugh. They look at each other like, "Hey! Maybe you're okay."

Captain Marvel pipes up.

"Oh, good times! Maybe he can come visit, too! That would be wonderful!"

I glance at Leonie, and we shrug. What's the dude's problem, anyway?

Beau also shrugs. "Yeah. Not probable," he says.

"Honestly, Oscar, could you be just a little snarkier?" Frank looks over at him. "I know this is crazy, but let's just roll with it, okay? This is *exactly* what the message of the retreat was: Letting go. Discovering peace. Let's not argue with the path."

"I see. And this is peace how?"

"By accepting that the kids are here and maybe with a new outlook for us too. A good wind . . . if we go along and see where it leads."

"I'm not babysitting!"

"Honey, no one is asking you to. But if I had gotten the calls, I would have said to come down, so let's pretend it's all been planned from the start and our nephew is here to visit now. He's brought a couple friends. Isn't that great?"

We glance at each other. He called him "honey." Leonie's eyes grow wide. Her mouth opens to say something. I try to signal her to please not be random.

Okay, I was pretty sure they were more than "just friends" already, but now I'm certain that Oscar the Grouch here, aka Capt'n Marvel, lives here. He is Uncle Frank's *partner*. His *boyfriend*—maybe his husband! It's *their* apartment.

They live together; we invaded and he's mad.

So . . . here is that which *so* freaks folks out. Two dudes live *together* and share a *bedroom!* Okay? Everyone survive? Did we spaz and soil our britches? No? Double check. Okay? Let's roll.

We've shown up with no notice and that's why he's being such a wanker. It's Oscar's apartment, too, that we have invited ourselves into. We should have guessed!

I turn to him.

"Dude, sorry! We didn't think there would be anyone else when we came to visit."

He looks at me with a fraction of a pause. But then:

"Well, for your information, *dude,* I too live here, so indeed, *hella true dat, dude.*"

Leonie squawks, but squelches it when he stink-eyes her.

"It just sounds so preposterous. When *you* say it," she explains apologetically.

Which is tragically true.

Adults should never, ever, ever, ever, everevereverevereverever try to talk like teenagers. Ever.

He gets up and gets another gingerade. I'm not even half through mine yet. Apparently, he can just shoot them. Maybe that's his superpower. He does give me kind of a smile as he passes.

I feel special.

Oscar picks up the leash and puts on his coat. He and Uncle Frank look at each other hard. Then he leaves. He takes Sylvester and his green bottle.

Uncle Frank stares at the door after he goes.

"How long do you guys think you will be visiting?" he asks us. He sounds kind of fearful. We look at each other and shrug. He looks from one to the other of us. "Have you at least called your mom, Beau?"

"No."

"Oh, boy," Uncle Frankie mutters. He walks over and stares out the window. They have a pretty good view. "Well . . . wow!" He looks at Oscar. "Okay . . . I guess this is good practice for 'letting go.' "

He turns and gives us a rueful smile. We smile back, but with worried eyes.

We shouldn't be surprised. We are a pretty big interruption. I don't know what else we expected when we arrived unexpectedly.

Frank goes into another room. Their bedroom.

"Should we just leave?" whispers Leo.

"To where?" I hiss. "This is our *destination!*"

Uncle Frankie comes out with a big old photo album. Stuffed with pictures with a giant rubber band to keep it shut. We look at him in surprise. I thought he might be calling Gina or something. He smiles, and we can tell he's made up his mind about us.

"Whatever, let's go with it. Let's enjoy the time we have together. I have baby pictures of you, Beau," he says. Leonie and I crack up. Awesome! Plus—the *relief!*

"Yay! Yes! Tiny baby Beau! Woo-hoo! Let's see 'em!"

Beau looks at us reprovingly, but we can see he's intrigued.

Frank sits on the sofa in the middle of their cluttered living room. He beckons us over.

(I must say right here, my friends, I'm a little disappointed in their apartment. I thought gay guys were supposed to know how to decorate and all, but their apartment is really *not* fabulous. The coolest thing they have is a poster for this show or band or something, *Zoroaster,* with this weird, like mermaid-squid. Also, their bookshelf is so full of books it looks like it might topple over any second. Remember that show *Queer Eye for the Straight Guy*? Well, these dudes need queer eye for the gay guys. Just sayin'.)

"Beau, sit here and look at these . . . all of you. I haven't looked at these in so long!" He opens the yellowed book. "Oh, look—first page, here you are! The whole front page. All you! You're about ten months old here, as I recall. . . . Yeah, it says so, right there."

Beau concentrates on the fading photos. They lean together, over the album, as they grow more absorbed in the pictures. Beau's uncle turns a page slowly and then another and then stops. He points to another one of baby Beau right here in San Francisco, down in Chinatown, but this one with his mom.

"Look, here's Beau again . . . little chickadee . . . And look at your mom . . . look. How 'bout it? Was she not a babe? Like a movie star!"

In the picture Beau is blond and chubby and adorable, and Gina looks a lot like Leonie, only with long dark hair. She has crescent moon earrings. She looks really young and beautiful. Like a Madonna and child.

They look. Frank grows quiet after a minute and almost reverent. He whispers to the image in the photo from long ago.

"Gina, look at you, so beautiful. Wow, it seems like last week. . . ." Uncle Frank pauses and frowns. "Dear God, look at us . . . so different then. Where did our little time go?"

Something sad catches in his voice and makes me look at him. It's almost like a prayer.

Beau and his uncle sit spellbound by the breathtaking picture.

"I've never seen that photo." Beau is mesmerized.

"Your mom's a goddess." Frank looks at Beau and smiles. They smile at each other.

"I'll make you a copy," he tells Beau. "We'll make that a project while you're visiting."

"Cool." Beau nods in pleasant surprise.

We look at other pictures of Beau, which stop abruptly when he's about three. There are several of him in San Francisco with Gina and a handsome man who must be his dad and a much younger Uncle Frank. The handsome man is not smiling in one single picture. He is noticeably glowering.

Pictures of him stop abruptly too. Uncle Frank doesn't comment. Neither does Beau.

After a while we decide to go walk the dogs and then find something to eat. Oscar returned a while back, but declines another walk when we ask him to go with us. He tells Frank maybe he'll come to dinner and to just give him a call when we're ready.

Sylvester has also amended his evil ways during our visit. While we were in the apartment, he and I had a stare down till he caved and now he is being very apologetic. Which is fine. He's being very friendly (though fortunately not *too* friendly) to The Bomb, and that is also good.

She is ignoring him.

We walk a couple steep uphill blocks to the Fairmont Hotel, where Uncle Frank says Beau stayed when he was a baby. We leave the dogs outside with him and go into the lobby for a sec. It's amazing: ornate, like *gigantic* high ceilings, and gilded, sparkling golden everything. We rotate, staring, our mouths dangle open briefly and then we go back outside to the dogs. Uncle Frank laughs when he sees our faces.

"Dazzling, isn't it? Just one more reason to make San Francisco your next vacation destination!" he tells us delightedly as we walk on. He is kind of making me laugh with the random way he phrases stuff.

"Is there anything you want to see while you're here? This city is made for tourists."

I pipe up.

"Amoeba! I totally want to visit Amoeba Music!"

Frank smiles and nods. "Okay!"

We go back to drop off the dogs at the apartment and see if Oscar wants to come with us. It's dark by the time we return. We went for a long walk.

He's sitting by the window, with a book open and the lights off. He has a different photo album, older than the one we were looking at. I don't think from the look on his face he even realizes he's sitting in the dark. He's holding the open book in his lap. He closes his eyes when we come in, but other than that he doesn't move.

Frank stands still and then sees what he has.

"Oh, dear . . . Oscar de la Renter, why do you have that picture book?" Frank's voice is so tender and sad. He slowly comes into the room and gently pulls the book away from Oscar and whisks it into the bedroom. He comes back out and signals us to come into the other room, which is where we will be staying.

"Hey, kids, why don't you go get your stuff and give us a minute, okay?" he says.

So we do. We take The Bomb so she won't be a hassle.

We dawdle. We lollygag. We try to take a long time.

Both of them look like they've been crying when we get back. Their eyes are red, and their noses are plugged up.

We pretend not to notice, and Frank says we'll go without Oscar because Oscar doesn't feel too social right now, but maybe we'll bring him back a little something to eat later.

Frank hails a cab on the streets of San Francisco, just like in the movies. We pile in.

"Haight and Ashbury, Amoeba Music, please, and make it snappy, jack!" He's clowning. The driver grins and says, "Okay, my friend!" And we *scoot!*

Amoeba Music is awesome! Just amazing! I stand staring. It's freaking ginormous!

We fan out. I walk and gape.

There is so much music and so many old-timey ways to play it that I am a little overwhelmed. I look over at Frank. He smiles. Beau is over by the counter, and Leo is somewhere out of sight.

"You know about this stuff, right?" he asks as he gestures to the stacks. "Before CDs and cassette tapes, up to about the late '80s, there were primarily record albums."

Duh. But I nod as we wander over to enormous racks of records. I start flipping through. Frank searches the *R*s. He grins as he finds one and hoists the album out of the stack: *Rocket to Russia* by the Ramones.

"I loved this album! Hee-hee! Check out these giant things we listened to in the day! I played mine to death . . . scratched up both sides. It sounded just gawd-awful after a couple of years."

I find an album that I'd heard in Mr. J's class—Kate Bush, *The Dreaming*—and I hold it up and smell the oldness of it as Uncle Frankie continues.

"That was the problem. You had a needle you set down—gently—on the record, which was made of super hard vinyl and really easy to scratch—way easier than CDs—which if you did would skip over entire lyrics, or endlessly repeat them, 'like a broken record,' which meant the record was ruined and you had to replace it . . . a lot. Also, you couldn't really take your music with you in the day; it was too heavy and awkward."

We walk it over to the counter dude and ask to listen to the Ramones album. He takes it out of the cover and holds it by its edges. Checks its face in the light for scratches. Holds it out for Frank to examine. He does.

Pristine.

Dude sets it up, expertly drops the needle, and gives me the headset. I put it on and am enveloped in super-fast-driving-eighth notes: "We're a Happy Family," which is a really funny song you should google if you don't know. I take the headphones off and laugh.

Frank puts them on and starts bopping. We grin at each other. He kind of yells.

"Regardless, the sound is so great some people still prefer albums. Plus, there was artwork on the covers and that was cool. The covers meant something. We all had the same music . . . the same experience. I heard someone say that we used to have a few deep collective taproots in our culture, that have now become shallow ground cover. There's just so *much* stuff!"

He takes off the headphones. I've found the Beatles stack

nearby. He walks over to where I'm standing and nods. Watches as I flip through the stack.

"Look—*Sgt. Pepper's Lonely Hearts Club Band*! See, that's a perfect example. We all knew it as the first 'concept' album. It had a theme instead of just being a bunch of songs."

He picks it up lovingly.

"*Everyone* had this album. We all grew up with these faces and costumes every day in our consciousness. And it's hard to explain what it meant to the era. . . . I can still sing every word on this album. Want me to?"

I shake my head emphatically no. We laugh.

We go deeper inside the store. It's so much bigger than I expected that I am still kind of blown away. There are so many things I have read about right here in front of me. I feel like I'm in a museum. The Amazing Amoeba Music Museum!

We stroll over to Beau and Leonie. They are at the counter looking at lighters shaped like guns and unicorns. I walk right by a Beatles "butcher" album cover hanging on the wall behind the counter. I can't believe my eyes and turn around. I've read all about it and there it *is*—right there!

Frank sees me looking.

"Ah, yes, the infamous butcher cover. Are you going to be okay?" He's teasing.

It's like five feet away from me! The sixties Beatles, all wearing doctor coats and doll parts and splashed with red paint. I just stare at it, intrigued. *This* was what was so shocking?

Leo and Beau wander over.

"Omg! They want two thousand dollars for *that?!*" Leonie is scandalized.

Frank laughs.

"Look it up, you guys. It was a *huge* deal when it came out in the sixties. They had to stop the presses . . . literally. Everyone thought it was so horrifying they changed the cover."

We stare at it again. We try to see it like they did. . . .
Whatevs . . . they thought it was so bad at the time but now
that we are used to so much worse it just looks kind of cute.

After Amoeba we amble into this candlelit café around the
corner and are treated to a delicious dinner. I haven't been to
many fine dining establishments during my life yet, what with
the single parenting budget and all, so I don't have a lot for reference, but I must say this was the best dinner ever. There are
more forks and weird spoons than I've ever seen on a table per
place setting, but I carefully watch what Uncle Frank uses. Little dish on *left* for bread: Check. Use fork on the outside left
first: Check. Give up fork with salad plate, switch to inner fork
for meat: Check. Knife in the right hand, fork in the left to cut:
Check. Eat with the fork in the left hand for some random reason: Check.

Beau watches me and copies what Uncle Frank does too.
Lee is oblivious. She's just chowing down, gobbling like a wild
animal, as usual.

Don't care. She's getting a free pass from me for quite a
while. I give her my dinner roll when she finishes hers. Uncle
Frankie takes note with his eyes. He doesn't say anything, just
looks at me for a sec.

We talk about easy things: getting the print of his mom made
and framed for Beau, stuff we want to see while we are here,
bands that came from San Francisco, things like that. Frank
gets really excited when I know so many songs of the retro
bands he listened to in the day. He seriously cannot believe I
know of the band Romeo Void, but when I quote a song lyric
and mention the saxophones, he's all impressed. Never say
never!

"That's great! We loved that band! And now I'm friends
with her, on Facebook."

I am quietly felled by how *cool* it would be to be able to just say stuff like that so casually: "Yeah, I'm chill with a bunch of rock stars . . . no big . . . you know." I wanna be like this!

Beau and I exchange glances. Omg; *so* glad we came!

We finish a *sick* dinner, the kind where Leo's meat is called medallions and my salmon is on a cedar plank and everything comes on gigantic plates drizzled with a bunch of arty sauces, complete with dessert and coffee and then, exactly as we are finishing, they bring the to-go order for Oscar.

When the bill comes, I slowly reach for my money like a gunslinger, mentally doing the math since he really hadn't offered, exactly, to take us out, but Frank shakes his head at me.

Uncle Frank picks up the check.

"Put your wallet away, Rusty! Tonight is an extra special 'Welcome to The City Celebration,' and it's on me."

Yay!

"So what do you do, Frank?" I ask him, while we wait for the bill to come back.

"Well, I used to be a sous chef for a couple of swanky joints around here, but then I got hired as a personal chef."

"Cool. Who for? What all do you do?"

"Oh, you know—one of these richy-rich Silicon Valley guys you've never heard of. He lives here in the city, except he's in Nice right now, since I'm taking some vacation time. Mostly I create meals designed to keep him healthy. I'm studying to be a nutritionist."

"Cool." We gaze at him. He smiles at us and takes a pen from his pocket. He clicks it against the tablecloth dreamily and adds an afterthought, "So I'm in school, too, or at least I will be when the quarter starts again."

"How long till you graduate?" asks Leonie.

"I will be a nutritionist this time next year!" he answers, as the receipt comes back to be signed. "And I can hardly wait! I think we can prevent so much illness—in fact, I think we can turn the clock back on some diseases, just by eating right." He smiles at the waiter and scribbles away, then sets down the pen and closes the little bill thingy.

We leave.

When we get back, it's almost eleven and Oscar and Sylvester and The Bomb are all on the sofa watching TV. The Bomb is cool; she has forgiven Sylvester, and he is being a nice respectful doggy so it's all good. Oscar has his arm around each of them, and they are all watching a movie about some punk rocker who likes to take *everything*. He's a wreck, of course. All three viewers are very concerned.

"What are you three up to?" Uncle Frank asks when we get inside.

"We're just watching poor Sid and Nancy, who have lost their way, as always . . . *spectacularly*."

We watch too, but it's too depressing; in the scene he's bellowing because he's messed up on heroin and has to go do a concert, but can't sing. So he just staggers around, bleeding and grunt-screeching, and it sucks so very bad.

We are seriously freaked out after about one minute, and Oscar looks up. Then he giggles abruptly at the horrified looks on our faces.

"I *know!* Never do drugs, um-kay? 'Cause drugs are bad, um-kay?" Which makes us feel better, 'cuz it's true, um-kay?

Seriously. Watch *Sid and Nancy* sometime—*so* wasted.

Uncle Frank shows us how to make the sofa into a bed. He also has a chair that turns into a bed so it's like a dormitory in their spare room/library/office. We get all settled then go out and watch Jon Stewart and Stephen Colbert with them in their living room. Stewart and Colbert are, as always, hilarious. Stephen Colbert kills it on *Late Show*. We miss them; we haven't watched TV in a while. Or been online. At all.

We've been off the grid.

The guys go to bed and leave us up alone after *Late Show* is over. We turn down the volume and just start flipping through random channels. We are tired too and go to bed pretty soon after they do.

I have the nightmare again for the first time in a long while.

My mom is outside, and she can't find me and she's calling, "Rylee! Ryyyleeeeeeeeee!" And I am trying to go to her, but I'm frozen in place. Dad is gone and Paul is really little and I have to find him and get to Mom and I can't move. And there's something else. I don't know what, I've *never* known what, but it's coming—fast—and I've got to do something about it. Hurry! They are counting on me! *I* have to save them! It's coming—maybe from everywhere—I don't know. And I can't budge and I try to call out to warn them . . . tell them to run . . . to save themselves . . . because I'm failing . . . I'm *failing them!* But I can't make a sound, and I try to open my mouth in a silent scream, and then I can't breathe and I'm suddenly falling *up*, rising rapidly, flailing, tumbling, then *plummeting*—

I yell and jerk out of sleep and sit up, panting. I have tears on my face. I swipe them off.

Dream crying—only for the advanced multitasker.

I check to see if I'm broken by the fall.

Nope.

The Bomb lifts her head, and Leo opens her eyes for a second, and they both look at me, before Lee plunges back into sleep. The Bomb touches my hand with her nose and lays her head back down.

I lie back down, trying to be chill, but I do have to pee so I get up. As I am going past the living room, I notice that the TV is on mute and that Oscar is sitting in front of it on the couch with the photo album Frank magicked away earlier that afternoon. I head to the bathroom, and on my way back, he looks up at me and gestures with his head to come into the living room. He puts his finger to his lips like "keep it down" and pats the couch beside him. I go over and sit down on the couch too.

The TV is on some station with some lady blabbing away silently and a bunch of tickers all over the screen telling you crappy things about the economy and terrorists and such. The screen flickers on us like a fireplace. We sit and watch the mute people argue in their little boxes from their different distant cities. Everyone has the whitest high-def teeth you've ever seen. Freaking neon. I can see the beard stubble on Oscar's flickering face in profile. He looks down at the open book on his lap, then over at me. His smile is remote. I look at the book too. Photos of young folks.

"Dear . . . dead . . . friends." I see a glass of red wine beside him on the coffee table. He's been drinking and is a little emotional. I look at the book. It's an old book, the kind with photos that slip into sleeves. We look at the pictures. All young people, men and women, wearing the clothes of the late seventies—the dudes with these giant handlebar mustaches and mullets and really short shorts, which just look too hilarious to me because they are *so* not in style now. And the girls! They totally have armpit hair and unibrows! Seriously! The hot ones—*all* of them.

It's kind of horrifying, but fashion always is once it changes, right? The pictures from the eighties (even if I do like the music from back then) look ridiculous too, with their big old psycho shoulder pads, crazy clown-face Nagel makeup, and upright wall o' bangs. And I *know* pics of our generation's sad saggin' britches are going to be material for mirth and blackmail forever.

Hee-hee . . . I can hardly wait.

There are photos of a young Oscar, and he has his arms

around everyone and he's smoking cigs in a lot of the photos, which he sees me notice and whispers, "Everybody smoked then," and turns the page. There is a gang of friends all dancing on a huge boat in the summer. Everyone is tan and young, and there are some huge crazy-looking women there, and when I look closer at these amazons, he snorts. He points to one with a giant beehive hairdo.

"Oh! I can't stand it! God save the queens! Ahh! See, honey, those are drag queens. Men that dress up like women and then lip-synch, at least in this case." He laughs nostalgically. "So funny! This was long ago and far away.... It was a magical time, in a magical land called Fire Island, and all the beautiful men in the world were there . . . and a lot of the beautiful women too. And a lot of beautiful men dressed as, um, maybe *not* so beautiful women. Oh! And here's me! Here I am at a party I threw. I'm Oscar de la Renter. See my foil hat? And look at my costume! I went to the Goodwill and got this *tacky* bathrobe and hot-glued a bunch of stuffed cats to it. I was managing an apartment building, and that's what all my renters were like."

We both snort. But quietly. He turns another page.

"Oh, my, now this child was a *dear* friend!" Oscar laughs. "His name was Mark, but we called him Jojo. Look at that hair! It's just grown out natural for about two years at this point, and it's a 'fro the size you just don't see nowadays. Oh dear . . . that child was so *not* on the down low! We were so young then! Look at us—*such* babies!"

Oscar is just blabbing away to himself. I'm not even sure what he's saying, just that he hasn't seen these pics in a long time and they are evoking a bunch of emotions in him. He smoothes the picture of the young Jimi Hendrix–looking man with a nostalgic touch, smiling, tracing his freaking *huge* 'fro. The sun is shining through it in the picture so it looks like a halo.

I gather up my courage, along with my big mouth.

"Was he your boyfriend?"

He stares at me and kind of gives me a look like, "Okay, you asked."

And I did. So he tells.

"Yes. For a little while. But he was my friend forever."

"Did he die?"

Oscar answers slowly.

"Yes . . . yes, he did. When he was twenty-six years old."

I don't know what to say. He was less than ten years older than me, since I'm almost seventeen. I just sit and then Oscar turns the page. There is another picture of Jojo, obviously a professional shot, like for an actor or a model. He is *so* handsome. It's in black and white, in front of some body of water, and there are leaves and trees behind his face and it's an amazing shot. Oscar touches it with an air of satisfaction.

"He got a lot of work from this shot. I took it. It was his head shot for years."

"Are you a professional photographer?"

"Nope. Just occasionally lucky."

He looks at me and winks. He's actually pretty nice.

"Was Jojo your only boyfriend, till now?"

He looks at me and laughs out loud, and then claps his hand over his mouth.

"Oh, sweetheart! Hardly." He is smiling at me like I'm adorable.

"But it seems you were like *deeply* in love. . . ."

"Yes. I was. We were."

I once again sit there with nothing whatsoever. We both sit and think about what to say next.

Oscar goes first. He sounds tentative, choosing his way carefully.

"Listen, I don't know what your parents have told you about homosexuality—"

I jump in.

"Not much, but that's not the point! I'm old enough to think for myself. And I think it's just fine!"

He looks at me and chuckles. But not in a making fun of me sort of way.

(Believe me—because *that* I can recognize.)

"Well, *good!* That makes it easier to talk to you. Lots of kids have grown up being taught to hate gay people without ever having even known one single person who was gay by parents who didn't know anyone gay either. It's ludicrous. But sadly, there are a lot of people sleepwalking out there."

"Sleepwalking how?"

"Not thinking for themselves. Y'know? Just lurching through life without examining anything."

"Yeah," I say. I do know.

"Yeah. Well, back in the day we did have a lot of relationships. There are a million things I could say here, but suffice to say, it was a different mind-set. Gay *and* straight people both had a different priority after the pointless bloody Vietnam War ended. Make love, not war! Oh dear, and a lot of one-night stands. Bad, bad idea! But it was the seventies.

"People thought sex was safe, and a lot of young people were very promiscuous; they slept around a *lot*, sometimes with strangers. Men and women . . . though gay men the most, I must admit. And it was a bad idea, it turns out, like how everyone smoked cigarettes back then too. We were responsible for a lot of self-destructive behavior. And, child, did we ever pay for it!

"It was a strange time. A sea change . . . everything was being examined. Gay people were finally beginning to not only admit being gay but to rally for equal rights. Women wanted control of their own bodies, and they were marching right along beside us. Public opinion was starting to become more open, less hateful . . . till religious zealots got ahold of politics. They spread the hate. They said the whole AIDS thing was a punishment from God . . . a judgment."

I look at him carefully. I'd heard that. Never from my mom, but I had heard that before.

"Never mind that it's afflicted the gay community in America and the West, but that in Africa and other places in the third world, it is very much a heterosexual disease. Inflicted on women and girls who have no power over their lives. Nobody mentions *that* fact too often." Oscar stretches and puts his stocking heels on the edge of the coffee table. He continues.

"So here's a confusing message from the God of Love: 'Okay, I unconditionally love you, because I made you, but I also hate gays, and, uh, African women, and oh yeah, when I'm angry, I kill! Like a *lot*. Okay, figure *that* out and have a good day! See you this weekend! Praise me!' "

I snicker, and he looks at me. To see how I'm taking it. I'm fine; I agree. He goes on.

"*Right?* I pity those who demean the notion of 'love' like that . . . and as for God, it's amazing how 'he'—always he— agrees with their ideas so completely!"

Oscar glances at me, and I nod. I've often thought so. Especially the "he" part.

"I know! How'd they get so certain? Dang, must be nice!" He sighs.

"Certainty can be very addictive. It's a relief to stop asking questions, turn off your mind, and close the books. . . . And some people have. Others never asked a single question in the first place. They're the same luminaries who declare Harry Potter—who, by the way, is not real—to be an enemy of God who should be put to death. They claim things like the earth is six thousand years old, when there have been *toilets* found that are older than that! I mean, for cryin' out loud! You hear that and you're like *seriously?* How can you even function in this world, running on that much stupid? It's hard to respect other viewpoints when they are so unfair and unbalanced. Kind of takes your breath away, y'know?"

He takes a sip of wine and continues.

"The second you start to consider the possibility—what's so wrong with two grown-ups who love each other and who want to get married?—is the moment you take that first step forward toward empathy." Oscar smiles at me and checks again how I'm taking this. I nod.

"I agree! Especially when everyone makes such a joke of it like getting married five or six times, or married and divorced the same day. I mean, like: *What??*"

Oscar nods. "That behavior is legal? They *can?* But *I* don't get that right, at all?" His brow furrows. "I can't marry the person I honor and make sure that the things everyone wants for their loved ones are there for us. Things like the certainty that if I am hurt and hospitalized in *any* state in the union, he can be right there beside me. Oh, Rylee, do you have any idea how important that is? It has happened a lot, that the family of one of the members of a gay couple won't let the partner into the room because they are prejudiced against gay people."

I stare in disbelief, and he looks at me and nods. "People have *died* without ever seeing their loved one, and they were right there! How could anyone be so cruel? And why would they be? Because they disapprove? They don't like it? For real? How is that allowed?"

"People are bullies when they get to call all the shots." I say what I have noticed.

"Boy, that's for sure! 'Absolute power corrupts absolutely,' as they say. You know, I'd like to call the shots for a day! That would be a horse of a different color, let me tell you, because I have a lot of opinions!" Oscar pauses for air.

I smile. I'd like to see a world with Oscar in charge. That *would* be a horse of a different color! He's not quite done.

"But you know what? I tell myself, 'So what?' Big deal whether or not I approve, right? This world will keep right on turning. Maybe it's none of *my* business!"

His eyes are blazing in the TV light. But he keeps his voice down. "And you know what else, Rusty? I'm not religious anymore but Frank is, and he told me once the one thing he's found that is the same in all the religions he's studied is the Golden Rule. Y'know? Do unto others? Treat other people like you want to be treated. He says there's a version of it in all modern and ancient religions: Christianity, Judaism, Buddhism, Islam, Taoism, Hinduism, Jainism, Wicca, Zoroastrianism—I mean, you name it! Shouldn't that alone mean something? If it is that historically universal to empathize—to feel for each other—chances are that the concept has proved beneficial. Why don't we just lose the ideology and keep the psychology?

" 'Do unto others,' by the way, doesn't equate with just letting others run over you like a doormat either. Not if you believe everyone was born with the potential to be a decent human being. You can't allow others to treat you badly. You have to stand tall and remind them. For their sake as well as yours . . . you see? It's subtle. You have to think, and that is hard."

Oscar stops talking and takes another sip.

We sit in flickering silence. I think about what he said.

I think Oscar is pretty cool. I think he might be right.

The next morning I wake up to the sound of voices. Beau and Frank are planning.

"I know the best place to get a reprint, maybe framed by the next day! We'll see if that can happen. Consider this your Christmas present, to make up for all the others you never got, okay?"

Beau laughs. "Awesome."

Which reminds me that it's Christmastime. We haven't been really feeling the Christmas spirit yet, since every day is Christmas at the ocean. For me, anyway.

It makes me think about Mom and Paul. I can actually see them in my mind's eye.

Usually I make their Christmas presents. I make Paul blue-gray shirts to match his eyes and sew clothes for Mom that fit her exactly. I wonder if Paul has gotten his growth spurt that Mom has been predicting all year and how her seven millionth diet is going, and suddenly I miss them so bad my nose swells shut. I roll over, avoid squashing The Bomb, and reach for my phone on the end table beside me. I don't even listen to the messages I know are there. I text: *Were here. Were gud. LUV u!!!!!!* and send it. Then I turn my phone off because I would cry if she calls and I hear her voice, and I can't yet. I'll rust shut if I start.

So I get up. Leonie is still sleeping, as is Oscar. The Bomb jumps off the bed and yawns and wags and bows to me in a big stretch. I bow to her too. Do a couple of toe touches. Not as hard as it was! I do a few more. Like I said, I think running away is making me springy.

I wander out to where I smell coffee. Beau and Frankie are sitting at the cluttered table in the cluttered kitchen with the picture of baby Beau and Gina Madonna, which they have taken out of the book and put in a big old ziplock bag.

They are going on an errand, just the two of them, which I think is a great idea.

"Good morning, sleepyhead." Uncle Frank pours me some coffee and hands me cream.

Yummy. Their coffee is as good as Seattle's. I feel my batteries charging.

"So whatcha doing today?" I stand at the window, which has a small but amazing view.

"Well! I think after the picture extravaganza, we will go get some lunch and then maybe walk up the Coit Tower and look at the city. Then we will come home and I will soak in an Epsom salt bath for three or four days and try to recover."

I crack up.

"Cool! Then in that case I think I will ask Leonie and The Bomb out for a walk. I want to walk the Embarcadero and maybe check out Chinatown if there is time."

"Sounds like you have a plan. If you need a map, ask Oscar. He can set you up on the computer or just draw you one on a piece of paper, how to get wherever from the apartment. *If* you can wait that long. I don't know when he'll be up. Poor thing couldn't sleep last night."

Which I know. We sat up till past three a.m.

"Just be careful if you are out after it gets dark, which is like four thirty in the afternoon, because some neighborhoods get pretty scary at night, okay?"

"We won't be out that late," I tell him. I figure we'll walk and eat and then come see if Oscar is awake. I don't want him to feel like he is babysitting, but I do want to hang out if he's up for it. I want to hear him talk some more.

They leave. It gets quiet. It's nice in the apartment with everybody else asleep and just me and The Bomb looking out the window. It's not rainy, just sort of foggy and cool.

Eventually Leonie gets up. She wanders in barefoot, blinded by sleep.

"I smell coffee."

"Here, I saved you the rest. I figured you'd be up soon and want some."

"Thanks." She takes the oversized mug and breathes it in, then looks around foggily.

"Where is everybody?"

"Beau and Uncle Frank are getting that picture made. Oscar is asleep, and here is your ever-lovin' Bommy, right here." The

Bomb thumps her tail and gets up at the sound of her name, then kisses Leo's hand. Her devoted subject.

"What should we do today?" Leonie is amusing me. She is mostly still asleep. She sets down her coffee cup, scoops up The Bomb, and holds her in the rocking chair, which The Bomb is too big for. One of Bommy's hind legs sticks out in an undignified right angle.

"I'm going to post a picture of you two like that," I threaten, laughing.

"You have to take it first." She smushes The Bomb back onto her lap, as her hind end is sort of sliding off. The Bomb tries to go along with it, but then gives up and hops off to lie down at her feet.

"Well, I did take it. I have it here, in my mind's eye," I say.

We sit and drink coffee as we prepare to seize the day.

I read that the Embarcadero is this long, cool place to walk dogs, etc., so we head down California to Market to go look for it. It's not half bad outside, at least by Seattle standards, though I see long drawn-out expressions of freezing misery on the San Franciscans' faces as we pass. There are Christmas decorations blinking on all the streets. There's a waving Santa with a sandwich board advertising half-price vitamins. He waves at us. We wave back. The Bomb doesn't bark; she's not much of a barker, but she frowns at him hard.

It's a fair walk, but The Bomb is pulling Leo and I'm keeping up with them so we move fairly rapidly. I'm out of breath by the time we stop.

The Embarcadero is perfect for a walk. We meander along and pass under the Bay Bridge. The sun comes out briefly and then darts back under the cloud comforter. We examine the view from under the bridge. Everything has been tagged by graffiti.

BEAU, LEE, THE BOMB, & ME / 151

After some more brisk double-time, we find an awesome place called the Hi Dive. It looks like an old shack, which we like, so we decide to give it a try. The food is great. We get an extra side of scrambled eggs for The Bomb, and Leo gives it to her while we are still eating and she is waiting outside on the sidewalk. We all eat breakfast for lunch after which we unhitch The Bomb from the Hi Dive sign and continue our quest for knowledge.

We end up walking all the way down to Pier 48, which is like two or three miles. The Embarcadero is real flat, and they offer to rent bikes periodically along the way.

The bikes would be fun, but I'm still in my thrifty mode. I pretend not to see Leo's "hey—I got an idea" face as we pass the rental kiosks.

We continue our walk.

After pausing on a nearby bridge, we decide to keep going for a little longer. We walk along and find a cute little park called China Basin where we sit and let The Bomb run around dragging her plastic-bag leash, chasing invisible squirrels and sticks.

We flop down on a park bench and look around at the beauty of it all.

"This is cool," Leo observes. "I like San Francisco."

"Me too." I close my eyes, and immediately my hand is brushed by something slobbery and rough. Bommy is sticking me with a stick. She wants to play fetch.

So we play a slightly different game. This one is called "I sit and you fetch." That is where I sit and she fetches. It works well with my present energy levels. After a while, I stop and lean back against the bench.

"I've been thinking . . ." Leonie says. I groan and slide down the backrest in a heap.

"What? You don't even know what I'm going to say!" She elbows me a little.

"You're right. I just figured you were going to drone on about Ratskin."

"Oh. Well . . . I was. But not like you think. What I was going to say is I'm kind of thinking I'm not getting a very good deal out of this . . . thing . . . with him." She looks at me like she's discovered something terrible. And is being really disloyal by admitting it.

Now, I can hear you thinking that I probably jumped up and down and yelled, "Duh! Duh! Duh!" at her, but I did not.

She's already feeling guilty. I don't need to yell anything. I need to remember to breathe very calmly. I close my eyes like a priest at confession and lean my head back against the bench rest.

"Go on," I say like Jon Stewart.

"I don't know. I was just thinking how The Bomb goes along with whatever some other dog wants to do, and it's so disgusting. It's like that with him and me. He calls me, and I go to wherever he says, night time or pouring rain or whatever, but I can't call him or ask him to meet me, ever. And it would be easy for him! He's the one with a car! How is that fair? It's not! *It's not fair!* It sucks!" She is indignant.

What?! I open my eyes and smile at her. Big. This is new.

It's a beginning.

"Atta girl!" I mean it. "It sucks for real!" I sit up and hug her shoulders. "Yeah, baby!"

By the time we head back, it's starting to get dark, even though it's barely past four in the afternoon. It's around the winter solstice, so the days are their shortest. I'm embarrassed to admit I'm not exactly sure what day it is.

Not Christmas—all I'm sure of is that.

On the way back, I start to limp a little. My feet hurt. It didn't seem like we walked very far at the time, but now it does. Eventually we turn off the Embarcadero and onto Market, then California—same route we came.

When we buzz to get in, Oscar's voice comes over the intercom.

"Where did you go?"

"For a walk."

"I figured that. Where?"

"To, um, China Basin Park?"

"Oh my lord, child! That's about thirty miles!"

I laugh.

"So not! Can we come in—I mean, may we?"

"Oh. Yeah. Sorry." He buzzes us in.

When we get upstairs, Oscar actually looks pleased to see us.

"Oh, dears, I'm so glad you're back! I didn't know where you'd gone, and neither did Frank when I called him, and then neither of you answered when Beau gave me your numbers and, well, there are some pretty dodgy places around here and . . . So! I'm glad you're back!"

I look at Leonie. Why didn't her phone ring?

"I got mad and turned mine off, just in case you-know-who *did* call." She shrugs. "Else I'd just talk to him. I know I would."

I'm so proud of her I'm speechless. Oscar continues.

"Anyway, they should be back any minute, and I said I'd take us out tonight! How fun does that sound? San Francisco is known all over the world for its great food!"

I'm stoked. Sign me up. Last night was awesome. I look at Leonie, who is smiling.

We nod.

"Yay!" She looks out the window. The dark is upon us. Just as Beau and Uncle Frank arrive.

I'm totally looking forward to seeing Beau's happy face after a long day with his favorite uncle, but when he comes in, neither of them look very thrilled. Beau's face is red with temper or exercise; I can't tell. Frank just looks aggrieved. Like he'd really like to figure out how to do something he's been failing to accomplish all day.

When we ask about the picture, they say it wouldn't be ready before tomorrow, which is still really quick for this time of year. When we ask about the Coit Tower, they look away from each other before answering.

"It was awesome!" Beau is trying to be enthusiastic.

Leonie and I, and even Oscar, all look at each other. It's totally obvious Beau and Frank had a disagreement or something during their day together. Maybe not a fight exactly, but a disturbance in the force for sure.

"Did you see the view?" Oscar asks.

"Yes, Oscar, we were up there. How could we not?" Frank can only be described as snippy.

"Well, *okay*. I'm glad you had such a great time. Maybe you should go again tomorrow," Oscar answers sarcastically.

Frank just glares at him and stomps off into the bedroom. We hear the bath running.

Oscar looks at Beau.

"Well, that seemed to go well." He arches his eyebrows at Beau over his reading glasses.

"Omg! Whatever!" Beau flops down on the sofa.

"Beau, what happened?" Leo and I say it almost in unison.

"I asked him what he thought I should do about our stupid school and this gayness thing. It was useless! *He* was useless! All day he was like: 'I don't have the answers. How can I tell you what to do?' And I'm just looking at him. I'm all, 'Seriously? I come all the way here and you got nothing?' " Beau runs his hands through his hair so it looks like he's been battling a strong wind.

We are subdued. We thought Uncle Frank would know.

Leo is first to speak.

"Well, why not? Hasn't he been gay a long time by now? He should know how it works."

Okay, so Beau and I are used to Leo saying randomness, but Oscar slowly turns his head and does a "take" on her. Then he looks at me. I just shake my head like, "It's all good." He turns back and nods at her.

"I guess the problem with the 'gayness thing' is there isn't just one way to be gay. There's no figuring it out. There's only coming out, and in that case, you can only be true to yourself. Remember—" He points to the long thin sign over the massive messy bookcase:

This above all: to thine own self be true.

He turns back to us, gesturing to it.

"Do you have any idea how long it took me to understand how profound that is?"

I don't think I've ever thought much about it.

"It is so important! To use your time here well! To learn who you are . . . and not squander it! Our time here is the only thing that limits us, when we've had such a lucky start!"

We just look at him. *Us?* Lucky? He continues enthusiastically.

"Yes! Think about it: We are healthy, well fed, wanted, *surviving*, first world, intelligent, and compassionate human beings! We are the stuff that stars are made of! We have the ability right now in this new millennium, to do almost anything we want, if we can focus and not just spin out bickering. Right?! That's where we fail! If we can't grow beyond our old-fashioned worn-out bigotries and get along, how do we expect to negotiate this brave new world?"

We look at him thoughtfully. Then Beau shrugs in annoyance.

"I still need advice! Look, I'm a kid! Someone needs to tell me something I don't know!"

"Fine then, here's some advice: Figure it out! Harken to your better angels. You're a big boy! What does your gut tell you?"

"I don't know! Nothing!"

"Try harder. Reach down and feel your heart."

"Okay! My heart says find some place I can feel at home! Which I don't have a clue how to do! I'm lost, okay? I can't find my way home! That's what my heart is *screaming* at me!" Beau looks like he feels like crying. He's getting red again.

"Good! That is a great start! Once you can identify the problem, you can begin to create the solution."

"Great! How? I'm trying! I need magic!"

Oscar laughs a little snarkily.

"Oh right, I forgot the magic! Lemme just grab you some of my fairy dust here."

"Fine! Get me some! I need it! If someone had an answer, I would be *so* glad."

"Well, lil' snapper, let's try then: Where do you like best, of the places you have lived so far?"

"Nowhere."

"Very helpful. Where did you dislike the least?"

Beau looks at us.

"I guess Seattle. Before all the crap."

Leo goes, "Yay!" quietly. I smile too.

Oscar looks at him, shrugs, and nods.

"There you are. Go home."

Beau looks at him incredulously.

"Are you kidding? *Seattle sucks!*"

Oscar snorts.

"Hee-hee! Sorry. I saw the punk band Fear open a show there once with that line." He cackles again.

" 'Cuz it *does*."

"Yes, well, it certainly impressed the milling audience! Mr. Lee Ving immediately had their attention. They began throwing things at the band and spitting beer at him onstage . . . but I digress."

"So you're saying go back there?"

"I'm saying follow your heart! Stop thinking about being stuck in high school, which is going to be over in a nanosecond, and start to think about who you are going to be in your early adulthood, which will be upon you in another nanosecond, and then it too, will be gone one more nanosecond after that! Start to plan now to make a difference, because you are going to be at your peak very soon, but someday you will become tired."

We know that this is true, but we shrug. Too far away. Don't care.

Oscar looks at us in exasperation.

"Do you know the worst thing about getting old, or at least older? I'll tell you my opinion: It's getting tired! I'm not there yet, but I've heard that this world, so interesting and sparkly, grows dull and the joke ceases to amuse. Then you are worn out and don't care. Which is fine, as long as you have something to show and point to when you need it . . . that you can announce you have accomplished: a mission, a passion you have nurtured—be it children, books, music, science, whatever. Because then you can settle down and remember to enjoy yourself, y'know? I did a play back in the day, *Auntie Mame*, with exactly the line: '*Life is a banquet and most poor suckers are starving to death!*' "

We look at each other. Beau rolls his eyes at us. Very bad mood.

Oscar stops his diatribe briefly to choose a bottle of wine from their wine rack.

I've noticed he drinks a fair amount. I hope not too much.

He seems just fine, though he does like to talk *a lot*. At least what he says is mostly interesting.

I also like how Oscar throws in quotes from other people with his conversation. I don't know who said what mostly, except the Shakespeare one, which I'm pretty sure is *Hamlet,* but I'm going to look them up. I can tell they are quotes because he strikes a pose when he says them. Holds up one ironic finger, like proclaiming "the beauty of it all." He stops to go check on Frank.

Uncle Frank is still in the tub. We hear a startled splash and muffled conversation.

As it turns out, tonight we will go out to dinner with Uncle Oscar but not Uncle Frank.

"Kids, you know what? I think let's just us go. Uncle Frank was just snoring—sound asleep in the tub! I had to wake him up. Let's get ready while I make sure he gets to bed, then out we'll go, and we can talk about him all night!" He disappears.

He cracks me up. We listen to the indistinct voices from the master bath and getting-out splashes. We can see Sylvester jump on their bed through the open bedroom door, then Oscar comes back out and closes it behind him. We put our coats on and prepare to leave.

"He's awake now, but he'll be out like a light again in a second. Where all did you guys go today, that he's so exhausted?" he asks Beau as we start down the stairs.

"Shopping. Then all the way to the top of the Coit Tower. It was awesome up there! It was a little cloudy. Frank said it's an even better view in the summer when it's clear."

"Then you need to come back to see it in summertime!"

Beau glares at us as we start down the hilly sidewalk.

"Uh, yeah . . . doubtful." He sounds pretty chilly.

"What? You can't have a disagreement and still be friends?

Goodness, that's terribly fragile of you! Both! That's what families do, I thought." Oscar tsk-tsks all the way to the restaurant.

Beau has nothing to say the entire walk.

Which isn't too long. We enter this amazing restaurant, a different amazing restaurant: vegetarian cuisine. Which I have *no* experience with and am delighted by. We all are.

Oscar orders for us, and there are these giant mushrooms for the entrée. Like giant.

"These are portobello mushrooms, which I think are more delicious than any other. Aren't they? I've been trying to eat lower on the food chain. I think they taste like steak." I totally agree. I think I'm going to research vegetarianism.

We are awarded our salads because that's what it feels like; the salads are *so* good.

We dig in. Too good to talk. We look at each other and nod with our mouths full.

As they are clearing for the next course, Oscar pats his mouth with a linen napkin and addresses Beau.

"Would you like to hear a few things about your uncle Frank?"

We sit up. We all would. Even if Beau's still ticked.

"Let me start with the story of why Frank loves your mom like he does. To infinity and beyond. I told him I was going to tell you, if you didn't know, and he said fine.

"Okay, you know you lived in L.A. once when you were a baby, right? You do? You don't? What does shruggy-shrug-shoulder mean? Well, whatever, you *did*. You moved there when you were the age you first appear in our photo albums, not even a year old yet. You all used to come up and visit us a lot, hence the pictures. Your mom and dad. They'd moved from the Midwest out here, because of this thing I'm going to tell you.

"Your dad and mom and Uncle Frank, then Frankie, grew

up and went to school in the Midwest, the name of which town escapes me, but it wasn't very big and there weren't many people who were different there.

"Now, even though you might have noticed Frank is not as fabulous as *some* of us, he was different enough to get himself noticed by the gentle townsfolk around the time he was a teenager in . . . oh, let's call it Hooterville till I remember the name."

We snort. Oscar is so snarky. He enjoys our enjoyment and continues.

"Well, they formulated the enlightened opinion that their town didn't need no stinkin' fags; at least that's what the more charitable townspeople determined, and thus the fireworks began!

"According to Frank it started with just a *little* harassment. Just words and spit wads and 'bumping'—oops, sorry, accident!—when they were in junior high, which is what we called it. I don't know what you call it now . . . middle school?"

We nod. That crap all sounds totally familiar. Oscar's brow furrows as he describes what happened next.

"Yeah, so okay, it started small, but when no one stopped it, it escalated, quickly but surely, till kids were doing things like putting syrup in Frank's car, which completely destroyed the engine one year. He said it took him three months to save up enough to repair it. It wrecked his whole summer. He had to walk everywhere he wanted to go, and *that* can make a child nervous! And why, again? Oh right! Because someone disagrees! I forgot! Well, *boo-hoo!* Silly mean people and their attitudes! It's hard sometimes to remember to let it just float away."

He's being all campy to stay light and not get too angry. He tosses back the last sip of wine and continues.

"Any-hoo, when your mom gets to high school, this has already been going on for a couple years and everyone is pretty used to him being treated like crap. Including him. But not your mom! She immediately starts to patrol the halls with Frankie. They become inseparable. She didn't just let things pass; she spoke up and yelled at the jerks. She returned the name they'd poisoned—carloads of buffalo screaming out in falsetto 'Frankieeeeeee!'—to the proud name that your grandma gave him, given with love in honor of her dad.

"So, of course, this confuses the cretins. They wonder if she's his girlfriend. I'm sure they had never heard of a fag hag, as they're so flatteringly called, or they would have called her that too, though in this case she was just behaving decently. You haven't heard of it either? Whoops, I did it again! Well, it's a girl—or woman—who likes to hang out with gay guys."

"*Fag hag?*" We exchange glances. What?!

"I don't know where it came from. I imagine some dreadful place where they hated gay allies as much as gays. Hopefully that will change forever. That's what I work to accomplish."

"What's your job?" asks Leo.

"I'm at GLAAD."

"About what?" She looks puzzled.

"No, I didn't say I *was* glad. I said I'm *at* GLAAD."

"Oh. What's that mean?"

"It stands for Gay and Lesbian Alliance Against Defamation."

We nod, though I've never heard of it. Beau has, when he was going to the websites, and sits up, in spite of himself. I see him start to listen. So I ask Oscar more.

"What all do you do?"

"We are changing the image of the LGBT community, going after what is now hate speech and showing that it's just *not* okay to dump on us anymore. We have been considered fair game for a long time, but those days are finally drawing to a close. You would be amazed at what is still allowed *before* it's considered hate speech! Right now I'm after a school that has a horrible reputation; they have a bunch of bullies that apparently everyone knows about, called the Fruit Juicers." He shakes his head and rolls his eyes. "Which isn't even particularly clever."

"What? Why *Fruit* Juicers?" asks Leonie.

"Because that's something else homophobes call gay people: 'fruits.' "

"*Why?*" We look at him in bewilderment. He shrugs and smiles, wide-eyed.

"Who knows … because we're crisp and refreshing? I know, right? What does that even *mean?*" Oscar makes a face and laughs. "But hang on, let me finish the story about Frank.

"So they start going everywhere together. Because Frankie had been disrespected for so long, it takes a long time for the good people of Hooterville to adjust their thinking, but they did.

"Now they were mean to Gina, too, for hanging out with the town weirdo! Who says people can't change, huh? They easily can, and they did—for the worse! After a while, wherever she went, the catcalls and insults started up. According to Frankie, they were at least as awful, verbally, to Gina, because the girls got involved too. And why? Because they were jealous! Just look at her, for cryin' out loud! She should have gone to L.A. to be in the movies!

"Soon they make plans to leave their crappy town after Gina graduates and go somewhere where people are more open-minded and -hearted. Then Frankie sees an ad for sunny California, to 'come for a day or a lifetime' and 'live out your dreams' and all these hot people on the beach, in bathing suits, having a good old time! So he goes to L.A. and sees the sun set on the ocean and the way things can be, out in the orange groves, and he falls in love with the place."

Oscar orders another glass of wine. We're almost done with

the entrée, slowing down, still picking at the food, but comfortably full. We are busy listening. We wait as he nibbles.

Oscar thanks the waiter when the wine comes. He sips and swirls the red in the glass so its shadow-light makes a ruby jewel tone on the textured plaster wall. He sighs.

"Where were we? Oh, right, L.A.

"Okay, so Frankie comes out and falls in love with the place. That's where we met, in L.A. I had come from the East Coast and was searching for someplace. Did I mention I lived in Seattle, too, for a second? Yeah . . . I did. I like Seattle; it's just too cold. Anyway, I come down from the north to see the scene I'd heard was in L.A. and lo: It's just as much fun as they said. Lots of beautiful people, all trying to get a break, make their mark, and become a star. Lots of beautiful men, and so many of them gay! Out in the open gay! I remember being thrilled, and I was from the East Coast. So imagine when Frankie came from the Great Plains! It was life-changing to him. He'd never seen the like.

"I remember the first time I saw him. I was not looking for a relationship. Jojo had been gone for a while; I could finally get my head around that, but I did not want to care about anyone anymore. I'd lost so many friends by that point I was sick of it! I was sick of loss and death. No more loss for me.

"Imagine, you guys, if everyone you know started getting sick . . . if your friends started *dying*, at almost your age, just dropping like flies—like a sniper attack! Seriously, try to imagine all your friends leaving you.

"It's weird. You become disoriented after a while. Then you think, *Oh no, I'm not going to lose you too!* every time you meet someone you think is great. You refuse to engage. You start running scared. Running on empty . . . it's awful. Emptiness is awful. Being alone is awful." Oscar sighs and sips and fiddles with the garnish on his plate. The waiter comes to clear the course.

I stare at him, riveted. Everything he is saying is echoing through my mind like truth. The *worst* thing is solitude when you are not in the mood for it. Worst. Oscar resumes.

"Loneliness can *eat* you. It destroys. It's a wasting sickness. Loneliness leaves no memories. Your time passes, and there is nothing to consider. A life lived in loneliness is like an exile, like if a tree falls in the forest and no one hears, did it make a noise? If you live and leave no mark, no trace . . . there was nothing you loved, well, that's not a life well-lived. That's a near miss and a waste . . . a life lived in fear. That's how Scrooge lived, and he wasn't exactly a role model for a happy life, until the end, when he finally understood.

"So I meet Frankie and he meets me, and though I'm older (and I'm feeling *a lot* older than he does, at the time), we hit it off, much to my chagrin! I wasn't going to fall for anyone again! But there he was, looking so cute and bright and shiny! I couldn't resist! No one could! He was the life of the party wherever we went. It was so much fun that summer!" Oscar looks into the past, and his eyes twinkle in remembrance. I wish I could see what he is seeing. Abruptly, his thoughts return to us.

"And then we got serious and I felt like I couldn't live without him. It was just terrifying." I see Leo start to listen very closely when he says that. He goes on.

"Do you guys know what 'a point of reference' is? It's sort of like a yardstick to measure other things by. Before LA, Frankie had no point of reference for how awful it really was back in Hooterville, but when he saw how people *can* just get along, the thought of going back became intolerable. He got really glum when it was autumn and he was supposed to return. Even though you can't really tell when it's fall in L.A. 'cause it's still sunny and seventy degrees."

"Did he stay?" asks Leo hopefully. She wants love to conquer all immediately.

"Sort of. He kept putting off his return. School started for Gina again back home and he was still here. I remember him feeling bad, but then the thought of returning to those, um—"

"Monkey people?" I interject helpfully.

"Hah! Precisely! The thought of returning to those monkey people became more than he could handle. Fall turned into winter, still sunny, but now a hazy sixty-five degrees, and winter turned into spring. Spring is beautiful in L.A.!" As he speaks, our waiter comes up to us with a look like, "More yummy treats in store for you!" Oscar doesn't see him for a sec.

"And here is Frankie. He's not in Hooterville. He's deserted your—oh, hey, wait, do we want some dessert? I do, and coffee. Yes, thanks, dessert all around. Get the chocolate bomb, kids. If you like chocolate, it's a masterpiece!"

We do, because of our "Bomb," and when it comes, we toast her with gooey spoonfuls of triply decadent fudge.

"So what happened to my mom?" Beau redirects Oscar.

"Well, she wasn't too happy about it, as you can imagine. He was gone to the coast, but she was stuck back in Hooterville and the cattle were lowing whenever she went outside. By which I mean the townspeople were still being mean. She and Frank used to talk on the phone every day, which used to be *expensive!* She stopped begging him to come back for her, but he still called because he felt so bad. She said she'd be okay, and she'd come out as soon as she could. He said there was something in her voice that really worried him. So he finally went back to see her.

"It was so bad! Apparently she was now not only considered 'the crazy chick who loves gay weirdos' but now they were whispering that she was 'easy,' as we said back in the day, that she'd sleep with any and every guy who asked! That used to be an even worse insult than it is now! Everyone was calling her a slut and all kinds of rotten things. The fact that it was all lies didn't stop anyone. The rumor mill was spraying sludge full blast.

"During her last year in high school, your mom got a job at a nursing home—because she is *awesome*—and by now she has become an aide and has started saving money to leave the hellhole, which makes Frankie feel so much better that he returns to L.A.

"So he's left her again.

"That was the year your dad started high school. You know your mom is older than your dad, right? *Whew,* finally something I didn't give away! So when your dad starts school, the whole thing starts over again, only your poor dumb—sorry— dad isn't even gay! They are just being horrible to him because of his brother whom they cannot torment anymore! Which gives your daddy just an *awful* attitude. . . .

"Of course, Gina isn't going to let that be the case, either! She's known him for most of their lives. She starts to walk the halls with *him* too, which makes it worse for her, but that doesn't stop her. She put his safety before her own; she saved him from getting beat up more than once just by refusing to leave! She used to carry a PE whistle, Frankie said, and she'd blow it if anyone started to mess in any way, shape, or form with your dad. She didn't care if that made it worse for her. She was so done with that town!

"She was getting ready to get out of there when the bad news came about her mom, your grandma. She was sick. *Very* sick. I guess your grandma almost died, Beau. Thank God she got better, but it took years. She had something called Guillain-Barré. It's a terrible disease that goes on and *on.* . . . I don't really know what that is, but she was in a wheelchair for a couple years, I think, and at one point, I remember Frank saying she was on a breathing tube. But your mom stayed right beside her. It was a good thing she was a nurse's aide because it made it a little easier on them both, her and her mom.

"So anyway, she didn't go to L.A. I think she probably started going out with your dad when she couldn't get away. He was the closest thing to a friend she had in that town after Frankie left. And you can see why he fell in love with her—she's amazing! I'm not saying your mom never loved your dad because I don't know . . . I mean, Gina's *so* loving. . . . And there was no one else in town that was decent to her."

Beau just frowns and looks down.

Oscar looks at me when he continues, though he's still addressing Beau.

"Maybe that can help you see your dad with just a little compassion, if he was in love with someone who didn't feel the same way about him? There is nothing worse than unrequited love," he adds. Beau grunts and inhales to say something rotten—but too slow.

Oscar cuts him off. "No, I *do* know—he's been a jerk. You are very entitled to that opinion. . . . So eventually they got married and then there you were a year after that. By the time your grandma felt better, your mom had already made some life choices that she couldn't just walk away from; she couldn't just pick up and leave for L.A. Though eventually she did manage to get out here. She got your dad to agree to move out.

"By that time we had gotten over West Hollywood and had moved up here to San Francisco. That visit was the first time either of them had seen San Francisco. Predictably, your mom loved it and your dad hated it. Notice his happy face in the pics? Yeah, exactly! *Way* too gay for his comfort zone. So they continued to live in L.A. for a couple of years, and he hated it so much they left and then I'm not sure where you all went after that. I know Frank was *so* sad that your mom had moved away.

"What I always thought made sense was how your dad could find somewhere else *exactly* like Hooterville to live, someplace small and suspicious. Someplace like his hometown, but where no one knew he had a gay brother. That became his quest. And your mom went along with it till she couldn't stand it anymore."

"She went along with it until he turned on *me*," Beau says stonily. "That was when she left him. She lived this crazy life just for me, and I didn't even realize it at the time! I was such a jerk to her! I said I wanted to go live with my dad when she wanted to get married to Matt! That's the only reason I was even back with my dad! I was mad because I wanted it to always be just her and me! She put off marrying Matt for *years*. They didn't get married till, like, last year, just 'cuz *I* didn't want her to! Even though I liked him fine! I remember back when she first said she wanted to. She goes, 'Why do you get to do what you want, and hang out with your friends, but I don't get the same right?' And I was such a douche I yelled, 'Fine, I want to live with my dad!' So eventually I did . . . and *that* went well, didn't it?" Beau looks miserable. "I actually thought if I lived there and tried to act like my dad thought I should it could all be different, you know? That maybe I could turn into the son he wanted, all tough and badass and whatever it is, but no. He would just stink-eye me with this look, whenever I forgot to be a tough guy and was singing or something, this disgusted look of . . . *disgust*. Whatever, I'm just sorry I yelled at my mom so much."

Oscar wags his finger at Beau gently.

"Not your fault, chimichanga. Kids are always awful to their moms. They are unaware their mother, or either of their parents for that matter, had a life before them. It's when you grow up that you realize she was a person before you were around to take up every last waking second of her day, and that she still is. Don't kick yourself too hard, just be super nice to her when you get the chance." Oscar winks at him kindly, then giggles and polishes off his wine.

"Shall we go?" he asks as we stretch.

We are finished. The chocolate bomb was delish. We lay our

napkins gently on the table as the to-go order is brought with the check. Oscar snatches it up with a flourish.

"Me! I'm getting this!" He announces it like I'm even trying. I see him calculate the tip on his phone. His signature is huge when he signs the bill.

We can hear Uncle Frank on the phone to someone when we climb the stairs to the apartment door. His voice is kind of loud. Oscar puts his finger to his lips for us to be quiet so we can eavesdrop.

So we do.

"Oh, it was worth it, I guess. I don't know if I learned anything. To be honest, it was kind of depressing. I know, I'm getting old. We both are. Oscar's turning *fifty* this year! Oh yes, he *is*—as in the one that starts in a couple weeks. Yeah, *that* next year. Do you know what an oddity that makes us in certain crowds? Outside this town, I don't even know if there are any gay men left around that age. . . . No, it's true. It did seem a little like a holocaust. For years it seemed like I went to funerals every day. And the ones a few years older than us? Yikes! Oscar is seven years older than I am and our friends that age and older were hit even harder. We tell each other, 'Hey, it's a miracle we're even still here,' when the chips are down. So *many* aren't.

"Oh, sweetie, I *know! How* did we get on this tragic topic? I know, right? 'The Big Gay Holocaust.' Oh, what? I can't say that? Jeez, I lived it. 'Cuz why? Would somebody be *mean* to me? Hahaha! I know. I am awful. I try!

"Probably because we were looking at the old photos . . . I just don't want your poor boy to think that this is all we ever do—sit around surrounded by costumes, sketches of superheroes, and pictures of the dead. Yeah, I am, but whadaya gonna do? It's laugh or cry. Oh, honey, he is *so* beautiful! He looks just like you! But he's annoying like Jason!"

We grin at Beau, and he rolls his eyes.

"Oh, I totally saw it! Yes, yes, yes, yes, too, too true. Well, how the hell did I get to be gay Mr. Wizard? Then how come he ends up *here* looking for the answer to life, the universe, and everything? Hmm? I wonder where he could have gotten that idea. Yeah! You did so! Don't lie. You know you never could. Ha! Hahaha!! I have no idea. Not very long. I'd think, any minute. They've been gone for hours. Actually, Oscar is being really amazing. I know, right? But no! He didn't run screaming—almost, but he stayed right here!"

We grin at Oscar—he rolls his eyes like, busted! We hear Frank pause, then continue:

"He's so funny. I think he's really enjoying them. I heard him giving them some long-winded lecture about the price of beans in China or some awful thing, and they were actually responding, speaking in full sentences and making eye contact and everyth—I know, wouldn't he? I often think what a great dad he would have been . . . the *best* dad. Yeah, sometimes I do still wonder. Oh well, maybe next lifetime. Oh, honey, that's so not going to happen. Oh, right, two gay guys in their fifties. Well, I might as well be—yeah, we were always going to be at the top of that list, for sure!"

I sneak a look at Oscar when we hear Frank say that. I understand then that they had tried to adopt. Oscar isn't aware I'm peeking at him, and his face wears a wintery expression, just for a second. Then Frank laughs. "He's fine! He's good, actually, better than ever. Yeah, I do, *crazy* time. Remember? It was like night and day when he first started to take it. Yeah. I could see him coming back to life, y'know—back from the brink? Right? Oh, what, maybe thirty or so. We have a little joke that his superhero name is really Lazarus McPhoenix. Ha, I *know!* Thank the dears who invented the cocktail!"

I sneak another glance at Oscar. He's listening carefully, and his eyes are still distant, but then he sees me and winks. The next thing Frank says regrabs my attention, though.

"So how do you like his two little friends? The big girl, Rusty, what's her real name? Rylee? She's a card! Do you? Okay, that makes me really like her too then."

It's weird to hear yourself discussed. I feel embarrassed he called me "the big girl"—though I *am*—but also very pleased to assume from what I heard that Gina really likes me. Plus, that I'm a card!

"What about the pretty girl? Lee? What a beauty!"

I glance at Lee; she's listening too, liking what's being said.

"I know, I haven't really either, except that I think she looks like you, in the day. Yes, you did! You looked like that one girl in that video! *I* can't remember! The hot one! With the hair! Yes, you did, yes, you did, yes, *youdid, yesyoudidyesyoudidyesyoudid*. Hahaha—*and* you taught him to call me Frankie! Yes, you did! Then who did? Hah! Yes, you did! Yes, you did!"

We all grin at each other, even Beau for a sec. They sound like we do.

"*Yesyoudidyesyoudidyoudidyoudidyoudidyoudidyoudid!* Aahahaha!"

Oscar looks at us and raises his eyebrows. He shakes his head.

"One can intuit when the conversation will disintegrate. Let's go in." He unlocks the door and opens it.

Uncle Frank is staring at the ceiling, holding the phone, and lying on the couch. His swinging leg is sprawled over the back of the sofa like a nine-year-old, but when he sees us, he immediately straightens up.

"Hey, guess who just walked in?" He looks at us and waves at Oscar. He points at the phone and mouths "your mom" to Beau, who glares at him without response. "Should I put him on? I'll give him the phone to say hi." He reaches out the receiver to Beau. "It's your mom!"

Beau just backs up. He grimaces and shakes his head and puts his hands up like "no way." Goes in the bathroom. Frank stares after him and then at me. I shrug. I don't know why Beau is tripping on his mom. Frank tells Gina, "Hang on for a minute." Then he knocks on the bathroom door and waits. No response.

Then Frank comes back out and just hands the phone to *me*.

I stare at it for a second, then I hear Gina's distant voice, like a trapped fairy inside the phone.

"Hello? Beau?"

The way she said his name makes me answer. It's so full of longing it hurts to hear.

"Hey, Gina. He's in the bathroom. It's Rust."

"Oh, God, Rusty. Is he okay? Are you guys okay, honey?" Her voice is a comfort and a stab. It's a little wobbly.

She sounds so sad. I feel so bad.

I swear I'm not sure I even want to have kids. It's starting to look way too hard.

"Yeah. We're great. It's been awesome. The ocean and driving down and they have been *so* chill since we got here. We've gone out to dinner twice! Tonight was vegetarian. Giant mushrooms. Yum."

I don't know what to say. I'm just riffing, feeling a little rattled to be put on the spot like this. I grimace at Leonie, who gnaws around her big old fingernails and shrugs helplessly. Some backup she is. I'm running out of steam here. Gina speaks again. Her voice is even sadder.

"Rusty, listen. Is Beau avoiding me? He is, isn't he? Could you try to get him to talk to me?"

"Yeah, just a minute. I'm going to give you back to Un . . . Frank now, 'kay?" I hand him the phone and head to the bathroom, where I hear the sounds of Beau trying not to cry, which sounds exactly like holding your nose and gagging with your mouth closed.

After several exhaustive snorts from behind the door, I stop hesitating and knock.

"Beau? It's Rust. 'Sup, son? Are you okay? Whatcha doin'?"
He chokes off mid-snort.

"I'b good." His nose is totally plugged.

"Come say hey to your mom. She says hey. Come on." I try to sound enticing. Fun!

It's like trying to get a feral cat in a carrier. I don't even get close.

"Dah . . . just say hi frob be, too, 'kay?"

"No! Just come say one little word and then she will hang up! Dude!"

"Dude! Dough! Go away!"

I try the door, but he's locked it.

"Beau, your poor mom, right? She is *crying*."

"Shut up! *Shut up!* So is yours!" He starts crying again really hard. Still choking.

I am torn. I look into the other room and try to listen again. I hear what sounds like him punch the wall. Great. But—poor Gina. Should I stay or should I go?

Then I hear Leo in the other room. She has the phone. I go.

"They went to the top of the, um, Coit Tower, and then they came home. Like all day. Um, I'm not sure. He was in a hella bad mood, so . . . hey—are you still going to sue the school?"

I steamroll in to grab the phone and glare at her. She has this way of saying *such* the wrong thing at the wrong time! We need to talk about happy things right now or we will never get Beau out of the bathroom! I stand and speak rapidly into the mouth-piece.

"Gina, it's Rusty again. He's good, but . . . he, uh, got in the tub before he knew it was you!"

"Rusty, I'm pretty sure that's not true. He's just sitting there, isn't he?"

"Uh, no . . . he's in the other room."

"Well, just tell him somethin' for me, would you?" She's trying to sound chipper, but no, she sounds choked. "It's why I called: To say if he'll just come home, I'll drop the lawsuit and we'll find a different school or he can graduate early. There's a program I looked into called Running Start. We can work it out, just *please* come home. Would you do that for me? Please?"

Her voice goes completely, and she tries to hold it back, but the last word sobs low in my ear. It travels into my brain and hurts me.

"Yup. I will. I will tell him that and I will get him to call, 'kay?" I grind through my throttled throat, also trying to sound chipper.

Awful to be sorry! I'm wishing I was still detached. It seems like things used to be easier to ignore.

"Okay, honey. Tell him come home and we . . . start over, okay?" She sounds strangled.

"Will do. Will do. I should probably go. . . ."

"Okay, I won't keep you. But if he gets that message, it might make a difference, is what I thought. Tell him I love him . . . *lots* . . . and thank you, Rylee. He's lucky to have such a good friend."

"Yup. 'Kay. Bye." It's all I got. I hang up and lean over, pressing my aching voice box. I wipe off my face, all sweaty with guilt. I feel like I've been sprinting. Underwater. I concentrate on deep breaths. Then I return to upright.

Everyone has shut up and is kind of staring at me. Leo is the first to speak.

"What did she say?"

"To tell Beau to come home and she won't sue the school," I repeat. Everyone looks at each other. Everyone looks at me.

We hear Beau from the bathroom blowing his nose and clearing his throat. When he comes out, we look at but pointedly don't comment on his swollen red face. He stops when he sees all eyes upon him.

"What?" He sounds surly. I answer him.

"Your mom says hi. I'm sure that's what she called for, to hear your voice, and also she says if we come home she'll drop the lawsuit and you can do whatever instead—switch to another school or do Running Start or whatever. Whatever you want, she just says to please come home."

Beau stands and stares at me.

"So not my home." His face is remote and inhospitable. Inexorable. Implacable. Grim.

I stare back at him. He shrugs one shoulder. He speaks like he's accusing her.

"It's *her* home; she just feels bad because she agreed I could live with my dad for that time in Kansas, and it sucked and now she's all sorry and wants me to come back so that she can make it up to me."

Leonie and I look at each other. *Okay, and your problem is?* It sounds pretty good to us. But not to Beau.

"Just forget it! I didn't choose to be there—or anywhere! I feel like I've been blown around without a choice of my own for too many years! What am I, a freaking tumbleweed?" Beau's face is already red, and now it's glowing brighter. "No roots ever, just blowing in the wind? I'm *sick* of being the new kid! As if everything else wasn't enough, I always have to be the new freak, too! Why don't I just paint a big old target on my back? Because I am!" We can see him getting more and more angry again. He turns his back on us violently.

"I thought you guys would be able to help me! But no! Apparently there are no answers! It's always going to be like this! *Omg, I hate* my life! I *hate* those jerks at school, and I hate that no one seems to know how to make it stop!" He pauses and looks directly at Leo and me. "I hate everything about my life except you guys . . . *I feel like killing myself.*"

He's not yelling now; he's speaking through clenched teeth. His fists shake.

The despair in his voice terrifies us all. We stand frozen for a second. Then:

"*No!!*" We all scream in unison. "*God, Beau, no!*" Everyone panics.

He stops when we yell like he's dazed, and holds up his hands. He closes his eyes. Catches his breath and gets a grip.

"*Okay!* I'm sorry I said that! I take it back—*please* don't start worrying about that too! I'm *not* going to. I was just venting! But sometimes I think what difference would it make? What am I here for? When, exactly, *does* it get better?"

He eyeballs the uncles.

"No offense, dudes—but look at you! You guys are old now! Your whole lives have been used up waiting for stupid people to give you your rights! Which they never did!" Beau is regrowing enraged at the outrage. "So now I still don't have any rights, either! If things don't get changed, they never will! I'll wait my whole life for something I should have been born with! How is that progress? Freaking whatever! I'm so pissed off! This is an epic injustice! It's bigotry! It's . . . freaking"—Beau sputters, at a loss for words—"*un-American*—injustice shouldn't be allowed!"

He shuts up and scowls and slams himself down in the chair by the window, then folds his arms up tight.

Oscar and Frank take a few deep breaths. They look at each other before they say anything. That was a lot of stuff.

Frank speaks first.

"Look, Beau, to start with, I'm sorry about today. I didn't mean to get so impatient with you, it's just I felt I was explaining the same thing over and over. You thought I was going to have some magic beans or something and then you'd just climb a beanstalk to a better land? Great! I want to go there too! Sounds awesome! But please, don't think we've just been waiting for our rights."

"Well, where are they, then?" Beau says like a brat.

"Omg, Beau! We have done so much. There's just so much left to do! You know, being 'outed' used to be the worst thing that could happen to someone. There was no movement *until* us! We were zapping homophobic politicians and businesses before you were even born! Do you even know what a 'zap' is?"

"No." Same way.

"Really?" Frankie is sarcastic. "Well, *quelle* surprise! *I* do. You lie down on some filthy city sidewalk and refuse to get up. You and your friends, some of whom are so sick they can barely walk and are only there for you, because it's too late for them, ignore the hate and the spit and the snot raining down and you block the entrance to their vile little endeavors until you are all arrested and hauled off to jail. Violently. There they ensure you are given a record, which, by the way, makes it nearly impossible to travel to other countries. Which is ridiculous!"

Frank's voice rises a little, and Oscar looks at him. He subdues himself and takes time to chill. Beau scowls.

"Don't ever think we just sat around!" Oscar adds, but more gently. "We were an angry bunch of activists with nothing left to lose. We watched our friends and family die in droves, and from the government?" He looks at Beau, who gives him nothing. So he answers himself.

"Not a word or a care or a cure." Oscar shakes his head, still somewhat disbelievingly.

Frankie resumes. They kind of tag team Beau.

"*We're old now?* Good lord, Beau! Like being snarky much? Why don't I get my damn hankie so you can dry yourself behind the ears?! But you're right! We *are* old! You want to know how aggressively old we really are? Oscar's so old he worked on The Quilt! Do any of you even know about that? Really? Not even you, Rusty?"

I shake my head. I don't know about a quilt. Uncle Frank continues.

"Okay, briefly, there were so many deaths in the early years that the survivors decided to make a quilt. It would have a panel dedicated to each life that was made by the loved ones—who they were, where they lived, what they loved, stuff like that. Things the friends and families could design just for the loved one, in this big creation of love. We hoped it would help comfort us and ease our hearts. . . ." He trails off. We wait. So Oscar takes a round.

"But nobody imagined how long things would go on before we stopped ignoring the growing crisis and did something about AIDS! The quilt kept getting bigger and bigger, until its size alone became an accusation, and still nothing! Years passed. The quilt could only be shown on a football field, it had gotten so huge. And even with all those panels, it was just a small percentage of the dead. It was insanity!"

Back to Frank:

"Right?! Apparently, the government didn't feel much sense of urgency, judging by the time it took to notice hundreds of thousands of young Americans dying horribly. They almost ignored the epidemic! And why? Because the young folks were dying from this thing the press was calling 'gay' cancer!" Uncle Frank snorts and shakes his head in derision. "And you know what? We were so used to it, at first we just thought it was a new way of hating on us—call this death sentence a 'gay disease.' "

" 'Cuz it's not, right?" asks Leo.

"For the record—not just gay men—*anyone's* blood can be infected, so being straight was a risk, as well," Frank says wearily. "We started using this strange new term constantly: safe sex. But since we were mainly the ones dying, it wasn't that surprising no one cared."

Back to Oscar:

"Not the only ones, though, Frank; don't forget about the others who didn't get it from sex or drugs. *So* many, like this one little kid, Ryan White, got AIDS from a blood transfusion when he was eleven, I think. Even he was shunned and hated. . . . I try to remind myself everyone was just *so* afraid."

Right now I think Oscar is trying to remind them both. Frank just frowns and jumps in.

"It was such a long horrible mess that there were rumors that the government had *introduced* the sickness into populations they thought no one cared about, to test a new biological weapon of war. Dear God . . . so many good people . . ."

Uncle Frank puts his hand over his mouth and stops speaking abruptly. He shakes his head and looks drained. He looks at us like his charge just ran out.

I think he's cried all the tears he can cry for his friends and has discovered a new way of coping with his ceaseless grief, which is to *rage*, to tell what really happened, for as long as his anger lasts. And through his anger and pain, to preach tolerance, that there is no upside to a hate-filled mentality for anyone.

Like the crazy man said in the one thing he got right: "Can we all just get along?"

I remember Uncle Frank just got back from a Buddhist retreat. Interesting . . . I think I'm also going to research the tenets of Buddhism. I don't know anything much about it. I don't know anything much about a lot of things. I keep finding out how much stuff there is to learn.

Beau, however, is not impressed. He's listening but all folded up in the rocking chair with a snotty look on his face, like he's not convinced. He rocks the chair hard. It thumps rhythmically.

He addresses himself to Oscar because Frank looks like he doesn't have a lot of fight left in him at the moment.

"I didn't know that—about the quilt. That sucks. But there

must be something you can think of that can help me *now*." He looks away, his lips pressed in a thin line. His sigh is impatient and despairing.

I think he is substituting anger for the huge, sad, freaking disappointment he is feeling.

Oscar takes the reins.

"Well, little Tootsie Roll, *I* have an idea: Go back up to your wonderful mom and don't give up the lawsuit! Be the change you want to see! Cowboy up and work the farm! Make it your home, make it safe and welcoming so that your many friends will all feel at home because they can be whoever they were meant to be! A giant, diverse, big, happy family! Why not? Do it! Time is passing, as you so gob-smackingly noted just a moment ago. You pick up the cudgels! You carry the mission forward!"

Beau looks like he wants to explode.

"I don't want to! I don't want to have to be that guy! I just want to live a regular life and be happy. Why do *I* have to make it so?! Get somebody else!"

They just look at him. He thumps the chair faster and looks out the window. Then turns back. Pissed.

"And another thing!" His arm flails like an unbalanced windmill, as he jabs his finger in accusatory annoyance around the room at the haphazard, and admittedly half-assed, decoration of the walls (unframed posters, mostly) then back at the uncles. "This apartment is *not* what I expected, and you guys don't act like I thought you would! It's like you're not even very good at being gay!"

Oscar looks at Frank and cackles. "Here it comes!"

Beau continues without a pause.

"I thought it would be really cool, and you would be really gay and I would say, *Oh, there's my gay uncle! He's so gay! Oh, good! Now I know what to do!* But no! Apparently the first rule is there are no rules! Awesome—that's not confusing at all! Frank, you don't even act gay. And you, Oscar; people can totally tell, but I thought there was like ... a ..."

"A club?" Oscar interrupts wickedly. "Like the Fabulous Big Gay Clubhouse of San Francisco? I *know!* We need one so bad!"

"Don't make fun of me! This is serious! It's my *life* we're talking about, you guys!" Beau gets out of the rocker and paces over to where Leo and I are. He sits on the arm of the couch by me. Frank sighs.

"Beau, look, I'm sorry if I disappointed you by somehow not being gay enough for your expectations," he begins. "I'm sorry if there aren't any sequin rainbows, or life-size cutouts of Liza and Judy for you here—"

"And Babs!" Oscar warbles. "Do not *ever* forget Miss Barbra Streisand!"

"But believe me, I am gay! I didn't, however, mean to ruin some stereotype you have. What was I thinking? *Let me try to be different for you!* I can change! Sorry if I let you down!"

"I haven't let you down!" yells Oscar. "I am so gay I have never even *visualized* a woman's boob!"

I laugh out loud—then quick, make it a cough. (Omg—Oscar! So freaking hilarious!)

That makes Beau even madder.

"Great! I'm glad this is so freaking hilarious! Whatever! This whole trip has been such a waste of time! Stupid! And I'm still lost! Thanks a lot, everybody! My so-called friends and family! Thanks a lot, loved ones!" He suddenly jumps off the arm of the sofa and bolts out the front door of the apartment. We hear him pounding down the stairs.

Then silence.

We sit speechless for a moment. Then Oscar goes to the window.

"Oh, that little idiot!" He moans. "He's heading straight toward the Tenderloin!"

Frank jumps up in horror. We all do, though Leo and I have no idea what that means.

"Oh no! He's *just* like my brother—the hothead! I'll go after him!"

"No, Frankie! Don't—it's not safe! Call the cops!"

But Leo and I don't wait to hear. We are already through the open door and down the stairs. The Bomb lunges after us. We skitter down the several staircases. We can hear Oscar and Frank shouting frantically at us to come back, but it grows quieter as we keep going.

Downstairs, we look around, and I can see tiny running Beau, already blocks ahead of us. Oscar and Frank lean out the window, still yelling, then Frank disappears and I know he's coming down.

We turn and bolt to the van, which, luckily, is parked pretty close. We get in and start driving in the direction of our last glimpse of Beau, who has by this time completely disappeared.

"You keep looking on that side, and I'll look on this one. Look into that park, or whatever that is, over there. He's got on his blue hoodie and his Vans, right? Okay, keep your eyes peeled."

Great. Apparently, on top of everything else, I'm going to start talking like my dad.

We troll up and down the streets. No Beau. No how. No way. Oh, boy.

We also remember we forgot our phones. Mine was charging, and I don't know why, but Leo just left hers on the coffee table. Which I mention.

"I wasn't thinking about it. You left yours too."

"Yeah, but mine was charging, else—"

"Still, you didn't go, 'Oh, lemme just go get my phone and then run out.' Noooo, you didn't, so neither one of us remembered our phones!" She stares at me triumphantly. I look at her. She lifts her chin, in challenge.

She's right. I didn't.

I really like how she is standing up for herself. It makes me smile. I pipe down and drive. We continue our patrol.

The area Beau disappeared in looks like it has green spaces and plenty of parking. I haven't really researched this neck of the woods yet, but I've heard the name of the neighborhood frequently: the Tenderloin.

I don't see anything out of the ordinary; actually, it looks like it was nice, once. The houses around are big and pretty old, which I guess everything in San Fran is by Seattle standards. Some have lead glass windows, and it's a shame if the neighborhood was once good in the olden days, but now it's too sketchy to live here.

We are at a loss as to what to do. I don't want to call the cops, and I don't want to drive around losing precious time that could keep him from getting jacked or mugged in this dark, frightening place, and my nerves are jangling. We troll up and down, back and forth.

I hate to admit it, but I'm scared stiff.

I tell Leonie to get the flashlight out of the back and shine it out her side into the unlit areas, to see if that helps. She does, but it doesn't.

And time is passing. That's not good. I slow down and double back to where it looks like there might be some quiet place for him to think and chill out.

I am really feeling the cold tonight, as is Leo. We ran out without our coats too. And we're in the heated van. I wish Beau had more than that stupid blue hoodie.

All of a sudden, we hear The Bomb go "woof" real quietly, almost like a doggy whisper. I'd never heard her bark before, and when I turn to find what she is looking at, I see Beau walking into the freezing wind, all hunched over with his hands in his pockets, in front of us about a half block away.

"Omg, omg!" Leo squeaks, pointing.

"I know, I know! I see him! But he's almost in that park, and I can't get close enough in this tuna boat. Let me try to park. He'll just run again if he sees us."

I look, and we're on Leavenworth. I reach for my phone to call and tell the uncles, then remember I'm phoneless and re-curse my haste.

I turn the corner so his back is to the van, but keep him in my sight. He's really good at disappearing. He's got his head down against the wind so low that he can't see very well, which is lucky because it's not as hard to shadow him as it might have been if it was warm out.

So we do. We shadow him. We cross Turk. We follow him at a snail's pace, inching along just far enough back that if he turned around we could just be another car on the road.

He's obviously cold. His arms are clenched against his slim body, and he staggers occasionally like he's being bludgeoned by the wind.

He looks lost and miserable. He keeps trudging, apparently deep in thought.

We keep after him. He crosses, a little way farther up, and now he is on the wrong side of the street. I can't just turn after him because then he would see us.

"Keep an eye on him, Leo!" I say as I try to do an end run around him in the van.

"I can't—he's starting to walk into that park or whatever. Over there. See him?"

What is he thinking? I have known not to walk around at night, especially into parks, since I was like a one-year-old. All

I can think is he's not thinking. He starts to fade into the night. He disappears again. I slow to a stop and try to see where he went.

"I can't see him! I'll go get him!" Leonie unbuckles and opens the door and is gone.

I sit in the van as she too runs out of sight. I can't believe it.

I see The Bomb in the rearview looking after her, not yipping or anything, just darting back and forth frantically to try and see her.

Seriously, this has now officially become a disaster. I pull over to the curb. There is a ton of parking—*not* a good sign. I park and open the door. The Bomb looks at me eagerly, whining softly.

"No, Bommy, I didn't bring your leash. You wait, and I'll be right back with Ren and Stimpy," I tell her as I shut the van door in her face. I don't lock it in case they come back.

I am not keen on walking around at night in the hood with no dog or Taser or friends. It's not a smart move. I leave the sidewalk and start into the park. I figure I won't yell for them unless I can't see them right away. I fear yelling would be counterproductive. I fear it would bring weirdos, and they wouldn't be the right weirdos. They wouldn't be *my* weirdos.

But Leo doesn't share the same thought process. I hear her hollering after about ten minutes. I double back in the direction I came.

"Beau! *Beau!* Why did you run out like that? Come here! We've been going crazy!"

I can't see her, but I follow the direction of her voice. I see a copse of trees. And shadows.

I approach. The shadows turn into people and things.

Beau and Leonie are sitting on a park bench. I come up behind them.

"What are you guys thinking?!" I explode. "Like, danger much? Let's get out of here!"

They jump ten feet and turn around. Stare into my wild eyes as I hiss, pissed: "*Yeah!* See! I could have been some random jacker, coming for your wallets and your life! I am seriously amazed at how stupid you two act sometimes! Omg! Come on!" I look around. "This is a dodgy place to be! Are you trying to get us killed?! Hurry up, let's bounce!"

I glare down at them like a parole officer. An insanely cranky parole officer.

They look up at me, all woeful. Leo has her arm around Beau in a futile attempt against the cold.

"Beau doesn't want to go back," she explains. I put my hands on my hips.

"Well, too bad because we are! What are we going to do instead? Drive away tonight? Hardly! Beau, whatever! You have to learn to solve problems, not just run from them. That's all I've seen you do so far! Come on, dude! Cowboy up and ride the pony, or whatever he just said! You can do it! You can figure it out—even without the magic pep talk! Jeez! And as for you, Leo! What were you thinking—just jumping out of a moving car like that? For gawd's sake! No—I know! Why don't you just audition for freaking Cirque du Soleil?! You can put all that talent to work as an acrobat! Leo, the Amazing Bailer! Omg! You know, people would be sad if you got run over by a bus because you jumped into traffic! Jeez!"

They stare up, shivering. Pitiful and shivering. Not even able to speak in their own defense.

I just look at them and shake my head disapprovingly.

I am so glad to see them it hurts. I could hug them both.

They stand up and we start back. I figure we will stop at a bodega and call the uncles, and then I remember that Beau has his phone, and as I start to say that, I hear a noise. We stop.

A guy comes out of the shadows. He's skinny and gangly and has sores on his face. We stare.

"Hey, kids, got any money?" He's sniffling. He wipes his nose on his sleeve.

He's wearing a gnarly fur Santa hat and a grubby sweatshirt that says "Just Do It." He looks like the scrawny dude in that Nirvana video. His pants are extremely saggin' and he has to hold them up when he walks. He's wearing dirty dress shoes without socks or shoelaces.

"No, sorry, we were just leaving," I say as we keep walking. He joins up.

"Yeah, where to? Can I come? Come on. I need a place."

"Nah, sorry, dude. We're just going home. Sorry, we don't have any money."

I notice we keep apologizing to the dude, who is the one panhandling us. Society. Jeez.

But I am sorry. Sucks to be him.

However, he still needs to leave now.

We walk back to the van with our unwelcome visitor. He sees where we are heading, but we don't know what else to do.

"This your car? Hey, great! Let's all just stay there! Yeah, that's a great idea! And I bet you have some kind of money or something I need in there, anyway! Right? All right! Let's go!"

Beau turns on him.

"Listen, dude, just skip it! I've had a seriously crappy night, and I'm not in the mood! So leave us alone and get lost!" He advances in a threatening way.

Dude doesn't say anything, just pulls a gun out of his raggedy saggin' jeans.

"Or not." He gestures, quite calmly.

We just stand staring at the gun. Shocked silent. Petrified in place.

"Now listen, guys, why don't you open the door, and then

we'll figure out what's really mine in this here van. Or maybe I'll just borrow the whole van itself, okay? So open the door."

We don't answer right away. I'm not sure we can speak. Or move. This is so bad.

"Hello?! Am I jacking a bunch of statues? *Habla* English? Open the damn door!"

"It's open already," I grit between clamped teeth.

He partially turns around to the van, which we are now right beside, keeping the pistol on us. I look, but I don't see The Bomb. Part of my mind starts to spin out of balance. Where is she? Where did she go? Did someone steal her, the one time I left the door unlocked? How could she even go with them? What kind of doggy loyalty is that? Just when we could finally use her! My mind is racing.

We are in a mess. But not the tweaker. He's super happy.

"Well, that was real friendly of you! You must have realized you were going to have company!"

He struggles to slide open the side door while not turning his back on us. It's tricky since the beach if you don't know how to shove it. He finally gets it open, trying to watch both the door and us.

"Look out for The Bomb!" Leo squeaks in a panic.

"Oh, really?" He turns around to us sarcastically. "Really?! A bomb?! Nice try!" He wipes his nose on his sleeve again and laughs all phlegmy. "Like you punk-ass little bitches would have a bomb in this beater! But good one, kids! Really quick think—*aaaahhhh!!*"

Then everything happens at once.

The Bomb, who had been crouched down, shaking and silent and pushed beyond her endurance, catapults out of the van and chomps him—right on the ass! *Deep.* Right through his boxers, which were all that was covering it. I heard it—till he started screaming. It was gross. Then he tries to run, but The

Bomb still has ahold of his entirely hanging out boxers butt, and also Leo is right there and sticks her foot out so he trips. He goes over with The Bomb on top of him, and the gun flies out of his hand to the ground. He scrabbles for it, but Beau steps up and soccer kicks it away. I see it scuttle over in my general direction, and I run to it.

Then I do what you are never supposed to do:

I touch it.

I pick it up. I recognize it.

It's the exact same kind of gun my dad gave me, a .38 special. I remember him saying it was the most common handgun in America. And apparently he's right.

I know mine doesn't have a safety so I handle it very carefully. It's extremely dangerous. It's cocked and loaded.

I uncock it quickly and dump the chamber. There are four bullets.

During this time, Leo has pulled the bloody Bomb off the tweaker, who is trying to get away but instead is staggering around, looking for his gun, dazed and unable to run, holding his mangled butt, which is massively bleeding through his pants.

Beau is dialing the cops.

We stand and gather our thoughts and catch our breath and wait.

We can already hear sirens.

Apparently I don't roll with knuckleheads. I roll with superheroes!

And The Bomb, who is! Our dog truly *is* the bomb! She's our super dog.

It's too crazy. We get our picture in the paper, all of us, under the headline:

Dog Foils Attempted Robbery in Tenderloin

It's a good shot. Hopefully none of our parents will see this before we get back and have a chance to downplay the whole thing. That's *all* we need. We haven't told them about anything or even when we would be home. We haven't spoken to them on the phone yet.

Too much explaining.

The article said the tweaker needed forty-five stitches to sew up his butt. *Dang!* I hope he can get into rehab. Sucks to be him. Maybe he can start again.

The uncles were livid, as you can imagine. But they were so relieved that they didn't even yell at us or anything; they just hugged us and cried . . . and so did Beau. It was epic!

And that's not all. After the newspaper article came out, Leonie got a phone call.

Beau and I overheard it.

We were in the uncles' apartment on Christmas Eve, waiting for them to get back from Christmas shopping. We were admiring our finishing touches on the Christmas tree.

Suddenly Beau and I hear a different ring tone than either of ours. It's Leo's. We don't recognize it because we've never heard it before. She picks it up in surprise, and when she sees the caller ID, she dashes into the other room.

Beau and I look at each other in dread. Freaking Ratskin.

We sit down and stew in horror as we hear her begin to speak.

"Hello? What? Well, why are you? I meant what I said in the text. Because I turned my phone off. Don't text me anymore and don't call either! I meant it! When I said I'm breaking up with you . . ."

Beau and I look at each other in disbelief. *What?!*

She goes on.

"Oh, I am serious. Why do you think? No! It's not stupid. This whole thing is stupid, is why. Oh really? What? What exactly do I get out of this? Yeah . . . whatever! Or maybe I realized it by myself, because I'm smarter than you think I am! Maybe because I realized I wouldn't let anyone treat a dog like you treat me . . . literally! Oh, really?! Whatever! Rusty doesn't tell me what to do! She doesn't even mention you anymore! No, she's not going to tell anyone, so just calm down. I just said not . . . omg, is *that* what you think of me?!"

Leo stops talking and listens for a minute. When she speaks again, her speech is rapid and furious: "*No!* You listen! You know why? I did start to think it's true; he *is* way too old for me, but now I think *I've* outgrown *you!* Omg! *Stop!* How old are you, anyway? 'Cuz you're acting like a baby! Because you act like a spoiled little brat is why! You only ever think about yourself, you only consider your *own* comfort, you never come pick me up, no matter how crappy the weather, or how late it is. You will never take me anyplace—well, *why* do we have to be so careful? Yuh-duh, because it's against the *law!* Oh wait, why is it against the law? Sorry, what'd you say? Sorry? I can't hear you! Oh, right, because it's despicable, is that why? Even if you won't say it, you know it is—and if you don't, then you shouldn't be around us young girls!" She listens for a second then *screams* into the phone.

"GET LOST! Leave me alone! I think you're a perv! I think you're a jerk and a jackass and a loser! I think you can't score with women your own age and so you hit on girls who think you're so cool they go along with whatever crap you suggest, and you're really good at picking out the ones that are too messed up to know it . . . like *me*."

We hear her voice begin to break. "Omg, you are unbelievable! You are seriously going to tell me you love me now? Well, finally! Not a moment too soon! You think I'm a tool, don't you? Shut up! Shut *up! Liar!* Don't say it! Don't try that lame crap anymore! I'm sick of being a fool for you! Don't ever call me again! *Ever!* Understand?! *Never! Do you hear me, DOUCHE BAG?!*" BAM! We hear her throw the phone against the wall.

Echoing silence.

Beau and I stare at each other with wide eyes.

Wow. We never thought we'd see the day.

After a minute, when we still don't hear anything, Beau gets up and softly knocks on the door.

"Lee?"

After a pause, she answers.

"C'min."

Leo is sitting on the bed trying to put her phone back together. She looks up at us and shrugs. Her eyes are bright with unshed tears. There is not enough love in her world for her to reject it lightly. Even its ugly counterfeit doppelgänger, which is all it ever was with him.

We feel so bad. But glad. Like if someone you love is sick but finally getting better.

We sit on both sides and hug her while she cries and rock her gently.

When the uncles get back, they see us all red eyed and stuffed up. They are justly concerned.

We tell them everything: all about Lee, her sorry affair with Ratskin, and her crowning triumph. It seems like the only possible thing to do. They are scandalized by the situation and proud of her in equal measure.

Then she reveals her straight-up, true, brave self.

"He was all worried you were going to say something, Rust, and I said calm down 'cuz you aren't. But do you know why you aren't? Because I decided I am. I don't know how yet, but I am. Also I've been thinking about some stuff and I have a few suspicions. Why did I ever think it was just me? He probably does this every year! And even if he doesn't, *I'm* still worth him getting into trouble! He started giving me the eye in ninth grade! I was fourteen! That's so . . . *icky!* It's disgusting. He's such a creep. He said I made him feel so young, but what I am figuring out now is he made me feel so creepy! I didn't even know. I just knew someone thought I was special. Or even knew I was alive. Do you have any idea how much it hurts to be so lonely? It sucks so bad. . . . Omg, I was *such* a tool!" Her eyes fill up again.

One thing I think every person in the room is well aware of is how much it hurts to be lonely. We can all relate to what one would do to not feel that sad.

Oscar sighs.

"Come here, lil' punkin. It's such a big hard world out there some days." He sits on the couch and holds his arms out to her. Leo goes over and sits beside him, drooping. He puts his arms around her and strokes her hair and hugs her. She leans on him and silently begins to cry. He just hums a soothing little tune and pats her back and just lets her mourn.

I think Oscar would have been a great dad *or* mom. Just sayin'. He's so kind.

And in the middle of all this: It's still Christmas Eve.

It's weird, usually I'm Mom's right-hand man, getting presents ready with her and running errands, etc. Since I can't help like always, this year is going to be so different for them.

Suddenly I'm missing her and Paul massively. She must be so worried; she has no idea what I'm doing or when I'm coming back. I wish I was there.

I haven't even heard her voice in what feels like a long, long time. It's starting to make a hole in my life.

So Beau tries to distract me.

We get the idea to leave Leo with the uncles while Beau and I go shopping. We should give them a Christmas present for being so awesome.

It's cold and foggy and the Salvation Army bell ringers are

out in force. We give them some change, and they do a special thank-you ring with their bells. They have nice bells in San Francisco, tiny silver chimes. Plus, here they just wear regular clothes, no tacky Santa hats. Seattle's bells are big and loud and clank like a herd of stampeding cattle. Very annoying.

We ponder what we should get for the uncles. What do you get two gay guys with everything? We wander around, this time keeping our bearings. We smile at the passersby and hear carolers. It's magical.

We look at each other. Are we finally getting the Christmas spirit? We smile with shining eyes.

We still don't know what to get the uncles. We wish we could give them what they want most. We decide not to get stuff for each other because then we can get them something really nice.

But what?

Suddenly, as we are walking by a kiosk, Beau discovers the perfect thing.

When we get home, Leonie is taking a bath and the uncles have run out for a minute. It's getting dark.

We rustle around in the kitchen looking for some snacks. All they have are healthy snacks. We find energy bars and fruit wraps. Lame.

Leo wanders in wearing Uncle Oscar's robe. It's purple silk and floor-length (on her) and looks regal. Her red-gold hair is all washed and shiny and hangs in long ringlets, which it always does when it's damp. She looks splendid.

"Hello, gorgeous!" Beau is enthusiastic. "You look like you feel better."

"Yeah, I do." But her voice is listless. She's still bumming.

"Where are the uncles?"

"They said they forgot one last thing. They didn't think they'd be long. Everything is going to close soon since it's Christmas Eve."

We show her what we got the uncles. She perks up a little.

"I think that's awesome. That's from us? Like, from me too? Yay! They should love it!"

"Yeah, we thought so too! Hee-hee!" We all high-five each other. Snap!

We decide we are going to be the change we'd like to see; we're going to clean their messy apartment. We start by straightening the books that have been left open or stacked on the shelves and surrounding floor. Beau begins dusting the furniture. Just that in itself makes a huge difference. Then we find a mop and broom and sweep the entire apartment and mop it. They do the dishes pretty regularly so the kitchen isn't too bad and the bathroom is strangely spotless; it's just the living room and their office that look like hell in a handbag.

As I'm stacking the papers that are all over the desk and floor, I make an interesting find.

Just sitting on the desk under tons of clutter are two small ring boxes—each holds a thick gold wedding band. I open the boxes gently. They are pure heavy gold, each with an etching of two vines that twine around the ring. I hold the little boxes so the vines catch the light. Already purchased, affirming the uncles' belief in a better world, two silent tokens of faith and trust just waiting for the imminent eminent day when it *is* better, when our uncles can wear them and their commitment be nationally recognized and even celebrated.

I close the boxes and set them in a position of honor on the freshly polished desktop.

After we finish, we sit and look out the window. The apartment looks amazing and smells great. We found some incense, and now we breathe the scent of lilacs and lavender pine.

We can hardly wait for the uncles, who don't keep us waiting for long. I start to crack up as we look out the window and distantly hear Uncle Oscar singing randomly, "Syl-ves-ter-er!

Here-ear we are! We are bring-ing you-u a prez!! Tra-la-la-la! La-de-da-da! Dippity-do-holly-day!" to "We Three Kings."

We snort and look, and they are coming across the street, arm in arm. The lights of jolly old San Fran town are twinkling behind them, extra brightly for Christmas. They wave. They look so happy. We wave back, and the dogs wag their tails, and Sylvester, who has been listening, yips a chipper greeting.

They have mysterious bags and have to go immediately into the bedroom from whence we hear crackling and cackling. We are *so* curious. When they come back out they have this fake innocent look like "nope, no presents for anyone in there" on their faces.

I feel like I'm six again, in an awesome way. Who says there are no jolly old elves?

Later, when we are making cheeseburgers for Christmas Eve, we realize that either tonight or tomorrow we need to call our moms. It will be too mean if we don't.

And besides . . . well, y'know . . . we *do* love them.

We decide to call them tomorrow on Christmas morning. Leonie doesn't say anything, just nods. I can tell her mind is elsewhere, which is not that surprising, but I also see she is starting to feel better. Uncle Oscar said she could borrow the robe indefinitely if she wants since she looks so pretty in it. So she puts it back on over her sweatpants, T-shirt, and black sequin fake Uggs, which looks kind of amazing, like she's a warrior princess.

Later that night, we wrap the present for the uncles. We use all kinds of different wrap so that it will take a long time to even figure out what it is. Since it's just the one thing, we figure we can use a lot of paper. We make a lot of noise about how cool it is so they feel like we did when they were wrapping. We hear them making punch and giggling.

* * *

In the dark, except for the Christmas tree lights inside and the twinkle of the city outside, we all squeeze around the window and sit and look out. The Coit Tower is to one side, and you can see it if you stick your head out the window. There are sparkling buildings farther away, and in the distance, we see the glow of water and bridges. Everything is red and green, all the shop lights and even stoplights. The dogs press their warm wet noses against the cold window and make foggy slobber angels on the glass. Oscar opens the window a little so they can sniff the fresh air.

From a distance, coming up the hill, is a lone man's voice singing "Angels We Have Heard on High," coming closer toward our building. Both the dogs hear him, and their ears pick up. They look down to try to see him.

When the dude is really close, he gets to the part of "Glooooooooooooooooooooooooooria! In ex-cel-sis Daaaaaaaayo!" and the dogs cock their heads to one side.

Then Sylvester yips, and The Bomb, our strange, mostly silent dog, starts *singing*. She puts her head back and howls. She just busts it out! She hollers like she's trying out for *American Idol*. Then Sylvester does too. So she does it louder. Then Leo starts howling too. Then we all do. We all howl and yip like crazy people, in wild happy abandon, because we are family, all of us: the dogs, the dude, the stars, *everyone*. . . .

The dude stops both singing and walking when we all start howling, then we hear him say judiciously, "Right on!" like he approves, and start over. He's had a little punch for Christmas too, I think. We sing the words with him this time till we get to the "Gloooooooria" part, then we howl again and so do the dogs. The Bomb sits, almost on her haunches, her head back and eyes closed in blissful pack-dom, making more noise than I have ever heard out of her before.

Who knew? She has a lovely singing voice.

And thus we are carolers for Christmas! Oscar leans his head out the window and tosses the dude a little cellophane-wrapped candy cane. "Thank you, dear!"

We hear a voice say, "My pleasure" and then footsteps clopping away, the voice now singing, "It ca-ame up-paw-on a midnight clear . . . that glor-ee-us saw-ong of old."

Eventually, finally, we at long last, get to sleep.

And are up again first thing in the morning! It's still dark! We totally can't sleep.

I think we have regressed.

The city is so quiet. It's foggy and gray, and the view outside is drifting clouds with occasional glimpses of structures. We take the dogs for a quick walk and come back and make cocoa.

It's Christmas day! Just that fact alone is enough to put me in a shiny mellow place.

Strange . . .

But *no!* I'm not overthinking anything today! After the uncles get up, we will call the moms and say Merry Christmas, but I won't think about that right now either.

Just cocoa and fog. It's awesome.

And underneath the tree are six small presents. We go get our present to the uncles and put that under there too. It's the biggest one. We resist the impulse to shake and smell our prezzies so instead we watch *It's a Wonderful Life* on TV.

It's agonizing. . . .

At long, *looooong* last the uncles finally stir. But then they get the brilliant idea we should call our moms *before* we open presents. We three look at each other.

Wait—aren't we supposed to don we now our gay apparel or some such? No? Call the moms instead? Right now? More like we better don some armor if we are calling them first.

I can see we are frankly terrified of our moms' tears. Leo grabs her phone.

"I'll go first." She dials her mother's number savagely, stabbing it with one claw.

Unsurprisingly, the phone goes to voice mail. She hangs up. Looks at us.

"How do you even get her to pay for the phone?" Beau asks sadly.

"She doesn't. It's the free one they give you and she gets one free line. I just had the idea and went and got it myself. Whatever, it's crappy. It's always off when *I* call. I don't care. So that's me." She shrugs. Puts her phone away.

Okay. Beau and I take a deep breath. Who's going to go first?

Beau takes another deep breath and plunges into the deep end. He dials.

"Hello? Hey, Mom! Merry Christmas! Yeah, we are! How are you? Good! Yeah, everyone is great. Not yet. Nah, we thought we'd call first. Uncle Frank says hi . . . uh, because maybe we *miss* you guys? Don't cry, that was supposed to be funny. Hey, we are going to start back soon . . . before school starts back up. So, Mom, listen . . . no, seriously, I'm good. Really good.

"So, listen, Mom, I've been thinking a lot, and I changed my mind about the lawsuit. Because I've learned something about one of my best friends, and if she can be that courageous, I want to be too. No, Leonie . . . well, I'll tell you later. But the point is this. Now I say: *Let's do it!* Let's sue that stupid school *and* sue Ms. Blip, okay? Because! I'm as mad as hell, and I'm not going to take this anymore! Yeah, I do know that quote . . . from Rylee. This is my life! Because maybe if Blip's in trouble personally she can grow a little respect for civil rights because she sure doesn't have any right now. Seriously, don't cry. . . . I'm good now, Mom.

"You were right. There is no way anything is going to change if there is no one to stand up and say, 'Stop it! This is my life you're ruining!' Go ahead and file, and when I get back, we'll turn a fire hose on her! We're gonna bring it! Well, yeah, not literally, but oh, what a world of whoop-ass she just opened on herself and the whole school district! I will *never* surrender! I'm going to seriously *enjoy* watching her melt down! Well, I *am* mad. But anger is a useful thing when it's constructive, right? Yeah, I *have* been listening to them a lot, because they make sense. . . . I have been hearing their stories of the olden days, and they did a lot back then! Yeah, he is cool. So is Oscar . . . Yeah . . . yeah, I do, a lot. I *am* glad I met him.

"Okay, listen, I'm going to go for now. Say hey and Merry Christmas to Matt, and we'll be back pretty soon. Before school starts. I love you too. No crying! No need to! It's all good now. . . . I'm coming *home*. Bye for now. I love you too." He hangs up, then sets his phone down on the coffee table and picks mine up.

Without a word, he hands my phone directly to me. My turn.

I dial slowly. . . .

Paul picks up.

"Hey, dude."

"Hey, Rylee! Merry Christmas! Mom! It's Rylee! You were right! She called!"

I hear my mom saying something in the background, and then she takes the phone from Paul and the next voice I hear is hers.

"Rylee?"

"Hey, Mom. Merry Christmas!"

"Oh honey! Are you okay? I'm so relieved you called! Are you in San Francisco still?"

"Yeah, it's been great. Beau's uncles are really cool, and we have been sightseeing the city and eating in restaurants and all kinds of stuff. We even got our picture in the paper!"

"What?"

"Yeah, I wasn't going to tell you till we got home, because I figured it would just flip you out, but we stopped a robbery. Well, The Bomb did."

"*What?*"

"The Bomb. Oh, right . . . that's, um, our dog. We saved her."

"*What?!*"

"Yeah . . . I kind of have a lot to tell you, I guess. I just didn't want you to freak."

"Rylee." I can hear her take a deep breath. "I don't know where to start. . . . I imagine you can tell I'm pretty mad. It was irresponsible for you to leave without telling me and make me so scared! And I hope you realize that you really left us in a bind here when you took the van. I have been on the bus trying to get to school and clinicals and Paul's karate stuff. That was pretty selfish of you."

"But I left all my money. Why didn't you just buy a new car with it?"

"Because that is a big decision for me and I don't want to make it in a hurry and the money you left wasn't enough for a van as good as ours. I babied that engine."

"Oh, but the bluebook—well . . . sorry."

"*Are* you?"

I am.

"Yes, Mom, I *am.* I didn't mean to mess stuff up for you and Paul. I felt like this was a real emergency at the time."

My mom sighs. Deeply. She is silent for a second.

"Oh, Rylee. Well, was it?"

I answer slowly, and as honestly as I can. "Yes. Not any-more. I think we are figuring it out."

I hear my mom's voice start to thaw a little.

"That's good then. I want you to come home. When are you leaving?"

"I don't know. Not yet. Soon."

"Rylee, *please*. All of you are way too young to be traipsing around the coast, and it's time you came home."

"I can't yet, Mom. But we will soon. Listen, *please* just stay calm for a little while longer. Beau is almost ready. . . . we'll for sure be back by the time school starts."

I can tell she's making a decision. She sighs again. I make her sigh a lot.

"Oh, you guys. Well, just don't wear out your welcome. They have been very nice to you, but remember: They aren't really *your* uncles. Don't presume too long on their hospitality."

Good point.

"I won't, Mom. We find a lot of things to do so we aren't in their hair."

"Or just come home. I miss you." Now her voice is starting to do the mother breakdown too.

"We will. Beau and Leo are figuring some things out, and we'll be back when we're done."

"Are you figuring some things out too?"

"Yes. I think so."

"Have you been going to Mass?"

I pause. I want to tell the truth, but I don't want to make her feel worse than I already have.

I hear her make a little choking sound. Still, I decide to tell the truth.

"No, but I will when I'm with you."

Maybe that can be the compromise for my entire life. When we are together, I'll go to please my mom, whom I love dearly.

Because when I'm a little older I will move out and then it will be time to make my own decisions. About a lot of things. And I will reflect on the values she has chosen for me and I will ponder long and hard before I reject anything this wonderful person who loves me so much has given me.

But then I *will,* if they're not right for *me.* . . .

"To thine own self be true."

Sucks to fake it. Especially for your entire life.

My mom sniffles. Then the choking sound. I've done it again.

"Rylee, do you have any idea how scared I've been? Or how much I miss you? You are my funny, sweet kid and my only girl! What would I do without you? Paul's lonesome too! Come home!"

"Mom, he's so not lonesome. He's always gone. So are you! You guys have your stuff figured out! But what about me? All I have is school and books and Facebook. And Facebook and books are fine, but school is hell! Maybe *I'm* lonesome! I am alone there so much it gets spooky! Don't get me wrong, I'm *super* glad for you! I just want us *all* good! Listen, Mama, I know we need to come home, but I got to find my way first, 'kay? Don't be mad, please?"

There is a stuttery silence while she wills herself back from crying or anger.

My mom is so giving. I can hear her thinking.

I can hear her hear me. Her silence is heavy. When she speaks, her voice is soggy.

"Oh, Rylee, honey, you're right. It's just that I was so excited to be back in school and to start earning some money again so we can do things before you guys are all grown up. You know, I want to take you traveling too, someplace besides Alaska, though it's very nice up there. I want to do fun things with you, too. It's been hard to exchange cool vacations and blow-out Christmases for the privilege of seeing you guys grow up, you know? I want to give you the stuff everybody else has, which I can't even identify, but I'll bet you and Paul

204 / *Mary McKinley*

can and . . . I just want a little more time with you, sweetheart, before you're grown and gone, without us always being so broke and anxious, so we can have fun. I know you haven't had many good times in your childhood or teens so far, but hey, it's not too late, right?"

My mom knows she has my attention. She takes a deep breath and continues.

"Here's an idea: How about I trust you as an almost adult, to make good decisions and not mess up your high school education? I will wait till you have the feeling that it's time to come back. I will not attempt a rescue like you are always accusing me of, so that when you come home, it will be because you want to, not because I guilt-tripped you into it. How's that? Did I miss anything?"

She's trying to be light so she doesn't make me feel worse, I can tell. She's being so brave it's jerking the corners of my mouth down like they're on pulleys. My throat starts to slam shut.

"Okay, Mama," I manage. "Sounds great."

"Good, sweetheart. And, Ry . . ."

"Yeah?"

"If there *is* anything I can do, you just let me know, okay? Anything that does need someone butting in, bossing you around, and giving advice, you know? It's my specialty!"

I try a laugh in honor of her awesomeness. It comes out like an underwater gurgle.

" 'Kay, Mama, I love you."

There is a small pause and then a very watery "Okay, baby. Merry Christmas. I love you too."

" 'Kay, bye." I hang up just as my nose drips on my lap.

I look up into four pairs of the sweetest, most sympathetic eyes. Six pairs, when you count the dogs.

"She says hey," I gargle. They nod. It looks wobbly through my swimming eyes.

"Your mom is awesome." Leonie looks wistful. "We could totally hear her over the phone."

"Yeah, it's always so loud it's like on speaker. Mine's kind of crappy too." I nod. I'm exhausted. I feel like I need a recharge, and it's only like noon. The uncles look at us and then each other.

They return to previously scheduled programming. It works like magic.

"No more tears! Just more cocoa!" chants Oscar. "Then prezzies!!" He bursts into a new random song. "*Good Queen Oscar looked a-round! All up in the cit-y! Scooby-doo, and la-de-da! Time to open prezzies!* Woo-hoo! Yule time, child!"

My favorite Christmas carol to date.

I love my uncle Oscar. I don't care if he's not technically my uncle.

Sometimes your soul decides who your family is, not just your DNA.

We settle around the tree and Beau is Santa. He gets my present out first. They wrapped it beautifully. It's a small box, which, when I unwrap it, contains another smaller box, also beautifully wrapped.

Inside that is a very small, perfect box that says Tiffany & Co.

I have heard of Tiffany's. Mostly from reading *Breakfast at Tiffany's*, which is a great book.

Tiffany's is very expensive. Just sayin'.

I look up, and Beau's and Leonie's eyes are huge. Beau opens his mouth at me like, "Wow!"

I open the box and take out a golden heart on a chain. It is finely wrought and glitters. The chain is so fine it's almost like an *idea* of a chain.

The uncles are like little kids. Uncle Oscar bounces as he sits on the sofa.

"Hee-hee! Do you like it? Isn't it pretty? They designed it with

us! Open it! That little catch, there almost under the hinge . . . I
know! You can barely see it! Open it!"

When I do, a cunning little device allows eight little picture
holders inside the locket to unfurl, one after another, so I can
have eight pictures of friends and loved ones, and then it en-
folds them again, all held within the beautiful heart.

"*Oh.*" It's the most perfect thing I've ever seen. I feel my
throat start to shut.

I look at the uncles.

"Wow, guys, thank you. It's so beautiful."

Uncle Oscar cackles in glee.

"It's like you are, Rylee. It's amazing how much room is in
that heart, isn't it? Just like you! See, we know you think of
yourself as so cold and heartless. You worry you're this alien-
ated, jaded, steam-punk android but really, you are one of the
most compassionate people I've ever met, and I'm *so* glad I did!
Your heart does exist, and guess what? It's huge! This little
heart is just a symbol of your heart. You are one of the most
loving people I've ever known. And I love you!!" His warm
eyes twinkle, and he blows me a kiss. He knows I cannot speak.
"Now you just sit there and think about it. And, Leonie, why
don't you go next?"

Beau hands Leo her present.

It's wrapped up in a box and then another box and then a
Tiffany's box for her too!

It's a tiny golden flute on a chain. It's as exquisite as my
heart, and when she blows it, a sweet high C sounds. It's beautiful and breathy, a little song like wind in the willows. She
stares.

The uncles chortle. "For our brave and beautiful whistle-
blower!" sings out Oscar.

"Yeah, for our gutsy Lion Heart!" adds Uncle Frank.

Oscar goes on. "We are so proud of you! If we were your
parents, we would just burst with pride! We are going to be be-

hind you every step of the way, darling, and we know a thing or two about making a stir, by this late date."

"Oh, *thank you!*" Leonie sobs out. She can't get it unfastened, and she runs over to hug the uncles on the sofa and then halfway climbs into Oscar's lap. He opens the clasp and puts it around her neck. It gleams against her creamy skin. He holds her at arm's length and admires it and her.

"You look so pretty! And, more importantly, so happy! Here: Give it a little tweet! Oh, that's so cute! See, Frankie, doesn't she look like a Botticelli? But even prettier, since you're right here in front of us! See right there? We were going to engrave it for you, sweet pea, but then we were embarrassed to admit that we didn't know your last name." Oscar makes a little "whoops" face.

"No, that's perfect!" says Leo. "Because I'm going to change my last name. I just kept forgetting to tell you guys." She looks over at Beau and me.

"You are?" I ask. News to me. "To what?"

"My real dad's last name: DuBois. I've been thinking about it. Caitiff is my stepdad's name; I just use it 'cuz my mom accidentally signed it when I started kindergarten 'cuz she was drunk and it was *her* new last name. I never said anything so it would be like hers. He never adopted me. My name is Leonie DuBois."

"Leonie Du-Bwah," Beau repeats experimentally. "It fits you! I love it!"

"I think that's a French name, Lee," I tell her. " 'Du' means 'of' and I don't know what 'Bois' means. We'll google it. But whatever, this is so cool! You're part French!" For some reason, this tickles me to no end. I like to research names and see if they mean something.

"Yeah? That's tight. My real dad's name is Ryan. Is that French too?"

"So don't know! I don't think so. I've never heard you mention him before. What else do you know about him?"

She shakes her head and shrugs. Considers.

"Um, nothing. No, wait—he fought in Bosnia and . . . I 'inherited his hair.' I just remembered. I remember my mom saying that!"

"When did you see him last?"

"Dunno. I was little." Her face starts to fall.

Leonie says that a lot in relation to her childhood. It's never about anything good.

The uncles take over. Before she can get sad.

"Well, we will figure all this out before too long, but for now let's not forget the presents! Beau, you and Leonie each open The Bomb's, and Rylee, you open Mr. Sylvester Stallone's."

Sylvester gets a giant rawhide bone thingy, which he takes off with under the desk. He's happy. I look over to see what The Bomb is getting for Christmas. She has two presents. One is a rawhide thingy, but the other present is a gift bag. Inside is a really cool red ruby collar, with "The Bomb" inlaid in glittery black beads. The tail end of the last *b* in *Bomb* has a sparkly gold thread like a lit fuse. They had it made just for her. And there's a rainbow-glitter leash as well.

"Whoa!" We are agog with the beauty of it all. "Dudes! That is *awesome!*"

We put the collar on The Bomb, who proceeds to waggle all over the place like she loves it too. Her mouth is open and laughing. She's one of those husky dogs who "smile" when they get happy.

"Oh, my! She is the prettiest dog in the world!" Uncle Oscar is delighted with our surprise.

"Now, Beau, your turn." Uncle Frank holds out the last package, which is different and lumpy.

Beau takes the present slowly.

"Thanks, guys." He looks a little uncertain. I know how he feels. It's kind of hard opening presents in front of people. He slowly unwraps the outside, and it turns into two presents, hence the lumpiness. He opens one and sure enough: Tiffany's.

It's a key chain. There is no key on it. The uncles explain.

"We also made a key for you to our apartment. Here you go. It was supposed to symbolize that you are welcome to stay here; that was before we heard what you had to say to your mom. But now I think we feel it's more appropriate than ever. We still want you to feel welcome, but if you do make Seattle home, then whenever you visit us you know you have a place to stay. Look and see what we engraved."

It says "Home" on one side and "Welcome" on the other.

"Whoa, this is awesome! It's beautiful, guys! Thanks!" He goes and gets his key to his mom's house out of his jeans and attaches both keys. They make a nice jingle.

Beau looks grateful.

"I love it, and it's crazy good timing for my new home key! And my 'home away from home' key! Thanks, dudes!"

"Oh, you're not done. Open the other one!"

Beau unwraps it and just sits looking.

It's a smartphone! He's googly-eyed. So are we. I totally admit I'd like to have one!

"Wait—how did you know the one I wanted? Omg! You guys rock! Thanks! Whoa! This is awesome!" He suddenly looks at them. "My mom, right?"

The uncles just giggle and nod. They are so delighted with themselves. Beau goes on, a little subdued.

"But we haven't gotten me one already 'cause we can't afford all that stuff right now."

"Hee-hee, that's just where we come in! It's from us—'all that stuff'! It was easy. We just added you to our phone plan, so no worries!" They grin at each other and both talk at once. "We are super handy uncles to have around because we're DINKs! Ever heard of that? It means 'Double Income, No Kids'! Hee-hee! Don't even worry, we've already asked your ma and she said fine! Go ahead, check it out. It's already charged. Now wherever you go, you will be able to see home and that's nearly as good as being there."

"Yeah, Beau, now wherever you go, there you are!" I add. He beams at us all.

"This is so amazing! You guys are the sh—I mean, *the best!* I had no idea! Wait, who should we call? Dude, let's Google-earth and see my house. Omg! This is so great! Thank you, Frankie—sorry—Frank! Thank you, Oscar!"

Uncle Frankie says gently, "You call me Frankie, Beau. It's okay." He smiles kindly. "You, too, Lee and Rylee. You're all in the clubhouse now!"

We have cocoa and cinnamon rolls for breakfast and then we give the uncles their present. They said they wanted to eat because they need to settle down; everything was just too exciting.

So we do. Sylvester walks over and smells The Bomb's new collar and she shows her teeth like, "Don't try anything, buster!" which cracks us up.

She ain't got time for that mess anymore, either!

Finally, we give the present to the uncles. They love the tricky wrapping and keep unwrapping and unwrapping till finally they get to the flier and the tickets.

"*What?*" They both look a little dazed, as they read. We can't wait anymore.

"Ahahahahahaha! It's a *balloon ride!* Are you surprised?! It's a hot air balloon and then at the end you bungee jump! It's awesome! And they take a picture and a video on the way down! Are you surprised? We looked everywhere for something you wouldn't guess!"

Now we are the ones bouncing.

"Well, darlings, you succeeded admirably! Never in a thousand years . . ." Oscar looks horrified.

They look at each other. Frankie makes a "sounds cool" face and shrugs. Oscar goes on.

"You funny bugs! Just the idea is enough to take my breath away! Even looking at the brochure might stop my heart!"

We look at him. He looks a little pale.

"Uncle Oscar, you don't have to unless you want to," I reassure him. He sort of looks like he might not.

"Oh, darlings, would you be too disappointed? I love hot air balloon rides, I just don't see the point of jumping out of one! Could I just go up and then come gently back down to the earth somehow, preferably on a red carpet?"

"Dude!" says Beau. "So funny! I thought the jumping out part would be the best! But sure, I bet you can do whatever you want."

Frankie has been reading the brochure, and he looks up with a flushed face and sparkling eyes. "This is great! How did you guys get this idea? This looks amazing!"

I answer.

"Beau saw these guys in a kiosk as we were walking around trying to think up something."

"This is too expensive for you guys to give us though."

"Nah, it's cool. They had this big sign saying 'seventy-five percent discount' because it was, like, late afternoon on Christmas Eve, and they were looking for some last-minute bank. And there we were!"

I love the look on his face. The money is not important. This is fun.

Frankie looks at Oscar, who does not appear as enthused.

"Oh, come on, honey. It'll be amazing! You know I've always wanted to bungee, and you love balloon rides. You've said so before."

"I do! They are my favorite way to travel, but I want to stay *in* them, not jump *out!* It's a perfectly good balloon!" Oscar looks askance at the shiny prospect of a dude hurtling off a basket ledge in the brochure. "That just looks worrisome to me!"

We aren't sure if our present is a success or not. I'd say it was 50 percent epic and 50 percent fail. We all look at each other furtively and let our eyes ask the question "Was this a good present?"

Oscar sees us and changes the mode.

"Well, it's not till March anyway, so I'll have lots of time to get braver! This is a wonderful idea, kids, and you are the best! I'm just so violently old." He winks at Beau when he says that.

Beau makes a face like "I have a big mouth." Oscar laughs and makes more coffee.

We cook eggs and toast. Oscar puts a little cream cheese in the scrambled eggs. I love it. So does Leo. Beau scrapes it out covertly and hides it under his toast crust.

Whatever. To each their own.

We spend Christmas evening with Oscar and Frank's friends, all of whom are "out" and none of whom are in touch with their families. The uncles call it the Annie-you-all Orphan's Christmas. Everyone brings something, and they have a giant turkey and everything is just like Norman Rockwell, if Norman Rockwell painted a Christmas dinner of drag queens. The uncles are dressed up. Frankie has an awesome tuxedo with tails and a white tie, and he has drawn a pencil mustache on his lip, but Uncle Oscar has a frothy pink gown and high heels and a scepter. (I know! But it's so awesome! He's even wearing a tiara! It's *killing* us!)

We don't bat an eye, though. When we first saw him in drag, we turned and walked quickly back into our room, closed the door, then went completely mental—hysterically laughing into our pillows, but silently, till our guts ached and we cried and peed a little. Then we wiped our noses, sedately collected ourselves, and still carefully *not* looking at each other, followed the uncles down the stairs and outside the short distance to the apartment building where the party is in full swing.

And the party! Their friends are fabulous! And extremely nice. We walk up to their friends' building where the Christmas party is happening, and the apartment we enter is huge and cool and has a big balcony. Everyone is stoked and dressed in their finest, and the drag queens have on makeup and their favorite outfits, which are different from the things they wear onstage. These are clothes from their moms and grandmas, elegant and tasteful and seriously retro. A little glitter and mostly silk.

They, of course, love us because we are young and ask questions that crack them up.

Leo asks one drag queen (who says to call her—him?—Auntie Mary) if her eyelashes were real. They stuck out like a foot and a half. Turns out they were not.

After that hysterical laughter dies down, she's the darling of the evening. The queens all love her hair and her beauty and take pictures with her. She is suddenly surrounded by any number of adoring mommies and aunties. They were so open and welcoming we totally forget they're even *in* drag and just settle down to the most astonishing Christmas ever.

And, omg, queens can *sing!* They seriously wail! Especially after the Christmas spirits go around they are a mighty chorus! It's like drag *Glee*.

One after another, impromptu, they just go up and sing. The night gets later and more lights outside go on and the lighting inside becomes glamorous, and there they are, still singing away! It's cool. It's not a performance exactly because everybody keeps talking and moving around and partying, but the people who want to hear move closer and listen.

Everyone gets a little gift bag as they come through the door. It turned out to be a sample of hair mousse and a little tube of under-eye cream left over from the Gay Pride Parade last summer. Bands of drag angels go around handing out the little bags to make sure no one is left out. Some are holding wands, which, strictly speaking, I don't think angels use. Most of the queens sashay around like they live in high heels. One of the queens cannot quite manage her heels and then goes sideways—literally. Leonie and I look away and do not notice (on purpose). We know what it's like to be laughed at.

Oscar totally works his heels, however. He walks like he wears them every day, though he doesn't. He reminds me of the guy who played Dr. Frank N. Furter in *The Rocky Horror Picture Show*. Google Tim Curry. Kind of like that. Oscar looks awesome both ways!

Everyone is very loving to him. He's very popular, more so than Frankie, even though he too has a ton of friends around him. They get separated from each other for most of the early evening, I notice.

As do we. After a while I see Beau talking to some people with Frank, but I don't know where Leo has gone, and when I finally go look, I find her getting her makeup done by some queens as she sits very still at the big vanity in the guest room. She's paying attention.

"See, sweetheart? This is a much better way to do your eyelashes. Also, let's try this color lip gloss . . . lucky strawberry blond! You don't even need makeup! *So* beautiful. Okay, now blink . . . now, blot. *Oh!* Look, Pansy, she's just perfect!"

Leonie sees herself in the mirror and beams. Her makeup is stellar and she looks lovely.

She sees me come in. I give her the thumbs-up in admiration. The queens see me.

"Hi, darling, are you next? By the way, since we haven't

met, tomorrow I'll be Patrick, but tonight I'm Auntie Nancy, and I'm very pleased to meet you! This is Aunt Pansy, but tomorrow she'll just be Doug."

"Hi. Nice to meet you. Both."

"Shall we do you next? Just a little eyeliner and a touch of blush? Here, sit, okay?"

"Do it, Rylee!" Leonie pipes in. "You'll look amazing!"

I give in and sit in the chair.

I have never had anyone do my makeup before, and the sweet, sleepy sensation of having your face brushed and your lips polished is very pleasing, I must say. You should try it, my friends. I think it might cure insomnia. Maybe even depression.

When they're done, Leonie looks at me in the mirror. We both look at me.

In amazement.

"Wow, Ry! You're hot!"

I'm so not hot. But my smoky eyes do look gigantic.

"Shut up," I say, but I'm pleased.

"*You* shut up!" she says approvingly. I grin. And can't stop. I beam at the mirror.

Beau walks in and hears her. Then he sees me.

"Shut *up!*" he says to me admiringly.

"No, *you* shut up!" I tell him so he'll shut up. We cackle.

The drag queens look worried.

"Does that mean you all like it?" Auntie Pansy asks.

"They look awesome!" Beau announces, beaming. "Seriously. Epically. Awesome!"

I think I'm going to start wearing a little eye makeup.

We go back out to the living room near where the singing is, where Oscar and Frank are finally sitting together on a sofa. We go sit beside them and listen. They are mostly through with Christmas carols and are now working on all-time gay favorites. They are not singing at the moment because they are arguing if one can or cannot sing "Small Town Boy" by Bronski Beat a capella. Turns out, whether one can or not, somebody will. Whether or not one should. Two queens start to sing it at each other, like school each other on how it should be done. We go into politely quiet hysterics, all of us, even the uncles. It sounds like when we all started howling.

After quite a few more (and less divisive) song choices, everyone starts saying Oscar should sing. Apparently our uncle Oscar is a great singing talent. He just smiles and shakes his head, and no one insists for about an hour, but then, as the party starts to grow quieter and everyone is sitting around talking in little groups, they all start asking him again and giving him requests.

"Come on, sugar! It won't be Christmas if you don't!"

"Ooo, sing it like Odetta do, darlin'!" a voice calls. "Someone grab a guitar!"

Finally, after they dim the lights real low and turn a gooseneck lamp into a spotlight for him, he gets up, dressed as Glinda the Good Witch or the Sugar Plum Fairy or whoever he's being, and walks to the impromptu stage floor beside the piano. He then proceeds to introduce an old Celtic song, which he tells us is called "She Moved Through the Fair." The guitar slowly stumbles and dissolves into discordant sobbing harmonies, kind of like *Nirvana Unplugged*. When Oscar starts to sing, his voice is so beautiful it stops conversation. It's a contralto or a high tenor or something; it is such an odd glory that it does sound like angels on high.

The party pauses to listen and is quiet when he finishes. It's a love song to dear ones, long lost but not forgotten. It's a love song and an anthem. It's stellar.

After that they get him to sing and play "Silent Night" and they sing a bunch of other carols again. Then he says he's tired and we have to go, and everyone says, "Oscar, you know you have to sing it before you can leave."

Someone else adds, "In fact, I'm not sure we can even *be* gay if you don't!"

They laugh. Someone comes to accompany him on the piano. He stands up again.

And in his crazy pink frothy dress and makeup, with his wig and his tiara, he sings us "Over the Rainbow," which is the song I suspected he'd sing, but in a way so evocative and poignant, his voice so fraught with loss and tender nostalgia, that I'm beginning to understand; that it's as if I'd never heard it before.

I look around at all the friends, sitting on the various sofas and ottomans, listening with their hearts, their eyes all shining and soft, and I see them clearly—not as the damned, not as outsiders abandoned and despised by their own kin and huddled together by necessity, but as survivors, maybe even the vanguard of the kinder, gentler future we were promised once, long ago, obviously imperfect but so often kindhearted and still striving, against great odds, to become the shining city on the hill.

I think we've put that city off long enough. I think it's a good time to build.

Oscar sings full out, his voice soaring effortlessly over the notes, over the rainbow, his eyes closed in the transcendence that is music, in the sublime, heady joy of song flight.

When it's over, we are all silent for a second, because it's too beautiful a spell to break too soon, and then we clap for him, and he curtsies and bows and holds out his arms in the long white gloves and throws us kisses.

Not much later we walk home in the cold foggy night. It's a short stroll.

Much later, after we are all in bed, I wake up and see the light of the TV.

Oscar has insomnia again. I go to investigate.

He's watching some old movie that I don't know. It's in black and white.

He sees me and signals me to come in. We sit and watch the movie with the sound almost off. I've noticed in the old movies how they just sing their fool heads off—really loud, right in each other's faces. The person not singing has no comment like, "Hello—I'm *right* here," but just looks longingly at them or off camera. All the while they're being hugged and having their ears directly yelled in.

It cracks me up. Thank gawd times change, right? Wow.

Oscar looks at me as we sit on the couch.

"Did you have a good Christmas?"

I nod. "Awesome. Did you?"

He nods. "Yep . . . best ever, maybe."

We smile at each other and watch TV for a little while longer.

"And how did you like the girls?" It takes me a second to figure out he means the drag queens.

"A *lot!* They're cool! And hilarious! I like your friends. They were really nice to Leo. And me." I blink my eyes shut to show him my makeup.

"They certainly were! You're both a hit! I'm glad you like them." He pats my hand.

"They were nice. They put makeup on me, and it was *amazing*. No one ever has before."

"You look lovely. Your mom never showed you?"

"Nah. My mom's not glam at all. She doesn't even wear makeup. She's a nurse."

Oscar snorts. "I'm sure it's not mutually exclusive."

"Well, with her it is." I shake my head judgmentally. "When she started to get gray hair, she felt so awful I said, 'Let's dye it. I'll help,' but she wouldn't."

Oscar shrugs and smiles. "Some people just don't work their fab!"

That makes me laugh, thinking about my mom. So does *not* work her fab.

I can hardly wait to see her. Even though I'm sure I'm in all kinds of trouble.

We watch an old-time actress named Jeanette MacDonald get her nose screamed into for a while. I imagine it would be like standing in a fine, hopefully minty, mist. She looks like she doesn't even mind. Acting!

We talk about the party, what everyone wore, who does drag shows and who doesn't, and how good the food was, and then he said he saw us getting giggly after we got into the punch, but since no one was driving and we didn't go hog wild he looked the other way.

I leaned my head against his shoulder in gratitude for a second when he said that. I appreciated him letting us have some punch on Christmas without giving us a bunch of grief.

I also appreciate the advice. He has a nice way of giving it.

His main thing is *never* drink and drive, which I deeply agree with and never will.

We go back to watching the old movie. The dude singing with her is one of the Canadian Mounties, with that hat like old Dudley Do-Right cartoons. He just leans right in for a nose scream on screen. I'm feeling goofy, so I dive into Uncle Oscar and fake sing directly up his nose, like one inch away, mirroring the movie, just screeching up a storm, but silently.

He totally jumps, startled, and puts his hands up to ward off my über expressive face.

"Ahhh!" He accidentally kind of yells. "Ahhh!" I accidentally kind of yell as well because I didn't expect him to jump twenty feet.

"Dang, girl, you got up in my grill!" he whispers, but loudly because he starts snort-laughing. Which makes me go off and I *blast* like a boat horn—even as I try to stifle myself. I cover my mouth with my hands. He covers my mouth with his hands too, which cracks us up harder, the only result being horrible mouth-fart sounds. Uncle Oscar shushes me, though quacking like a maniac himself. I shush him. We lol. We snuffle convulsively. We shake. We struggle to squelch ourselves, which only makes it worse. We fail. We flail. We flop. We bray.

It's not pretty.

We have almost quieted down, though still snort-grunting like truffle hogs, as we lean against the sofa backrest in a belated attempt to be chill, when Uncle Frankie staggers out of the bedroom. He has industrial bedhead.

"Could you guys keep it down? It's like five in the morning. . . . What are you even doing?"

Which we realize is the funniest thing we've ever been exposed to. We just lose it again and start flapping our little flippers and clutching each other on the couch. As he eyeballs us in squinty outrage, we honk and snorkel and cannot look at him, just trying extremely to pull our act together. It's useless. It's lost. We can't. He glares at us beadily as we weep and drool and our noses run, and then he shakes his head with deep, sleep-deprived disgust.

"Seriously, you guys have *issues*." He lurches back into the bedroom and closes the door.

After a minute Uncle Oscar wipes his eyes and turns to me. He whispers, "I'm wide awake."

"Same here."

"We should do something before we get in more trouble. I have an idea."

"Okay!" I have no idea what his idea is, but I have trust it will be awesome. We bundle up and let ourselves out of the apartment quietly. The dogs think they should go too, but we tell them no this time. We start off in a different direction than I've gone before.

The night has gotten very clear and bright. A few stars are visible, in spite of all the city lights. The air is sharp and smells like ozone. I breathe deeply and walk. Our breath is visible.

As we hill climb, we talk about Beau and all the things we think he will have to do. Same with Leonie. Uncle Oscar is sane and helpful as I speculate.

"They are both going to bring it when we get home. It's gonna be crazy. I can hardly wait to see the douche bags' faces."

"The douche bags being?"

"Blip and Ratskin."

Oscar snickers. "That sounds like a punk band from back in the day."

"A super suck crap punk band!"

"Well, remember to stay calm and not call names or do anything to merely *stir* the crazy pot . . . other than by just reminding everyone that what's going on is crazy."

"Yeah, I just hope Beau will stay calm when the fur hits the fan. And I'll be there to help. I'm worried about Leo too. I'm afraid she'll be scared."

Uncle Oscar is slowing down, even though we aren't walking very fast, since it's mostly uphill. I match my pace to his. He speaks thoughtfully.

"One thing I've noticed about our little Leonie is she brings it anyway, regardless if she's scared. Remember when you told us how she rescued The Bomb? She said she was just terrified! But still, there she was. That is the truest form of bravery. Remember, courage isn't the *absence* of fear but the mastery of it. Our little Leo will be—fine." The last parts come out in a puff.

We're starting to get winded. I wonder where we are going, but I don't even bother asking. I'm sure I'll be told to possess my soul in patience or some such. Besides, Seattle is still on my mind. I can finally articulate my concerns to an adult.

"I just wish I knew who to call to help her, you know? Like

the cops, but not the cops? I wish some team, like Amnesty International or something, could help her and arrest Ratskin—and then give him the death penalty! But not immediately, just put him into a criminally insanely hard labor twenty-four-seven for at least *two* life terms!" I feel my thermometer rising.

"Oh, my."

"And never see the face of the sun again! That *tool* . . ."

We stop to get our breath. Uncle Oscar is pretty winded now. I turn around and look back. We are uphill. The city spreads below us, scintillating in the chill air, beckoning us back. It seems like we must be near the top of somewhere.

But no. We turn and keep trudging. Uncle Oscar continues.

"I think you are going to find Leonie has more friends in her corner than you suppose. For starters, she has you. You are situated to help her, not the least reason being because you care. Think about it. Be there for her, with your thinking cap on."

We now start heading downhill, or at least it's flattening out. We breathe a bit easier as we walk on. We pause at an intersection, and Uncle Oscar holds on to the street sign to recover. A cable car approaches. The first one of the morning.

"Hey, great! I didn't know they were running this early! Let's get this!" he says unexpectedly. So we hurry and do.

We jump on. My first cable car ride. I stand as near to the doorway as I can and hang on tight. Oscar looks at me and beams. Our hair blows in the breeze. It's just like the movies.

"Where are we?" I look around. I can't tell. It's brightly lit, and the neon signs and streetlights are reflecting on the wet pavement, which shopkeepers are hosing down. The air smells like fish. There are people everywhere, mostly Asian.

"This is Chinatown. Look, right there?" Uncle Oscar points. "That's the cable car museum. Let's try to see it while you're here."

"Wow. It's like it's not even a holiday. Why is everything so busy, even on Christmas at like dawn?"

"Well, you know, it's Chinatown . . . Jake." Uncle Oscar snickers.

"Hah! I know that quote! I've seen that movie!"

"Really? You've seen *Chinatown*? Rylee, I'm impressed!"

" 'Forget it, Jake. It's Chinatown . . .' " I say, to prove it. I like movies, old and new. But only as long as they seem real. No nose singing!

We get off the cable car and start *up*hill again, for gawd's sake. I sigh and slog along behind Uncle Oscar. Maybe he's going to show me the highest place in all of San Francisco and the West Coast.

When I look up, suddenly I know where we are going. I'm not even worried when we leave the well-lit street and head up the stairs into the park.

Coit Tower is open and lit up especially for Christmas. I was hoping I'd get to climb it while I was in town. There are several people, couples and small groups, jogging and standing around in the early morning grayness.

We cross the threshold and start the stairs. A million stairs. Oh well, if my lungs explode and I croak at the top, at least there will be a beautiful view as I lay dying.

We climb.

"Oh, dear lordy . . . why did I think . . . this was . . . a good . . . idea?" Uncle Oscar is panting again. He stops.

I hold up too, and we hang on the rail and puff. We start to laugh again because we are so pathetic, which doesn't help the recovery. We climb once more. I lead. I consider the possibility that we have entered the stratosphere.

Behind me I hear Uncle Oscar moaning.

"Oh, help me, tiny baby Jesus . . . of the tiny holy newborn-size Pampers . . . ohhh . . . angels, haul me up . . . oh, lawdy, lawdy . . . oh, I'm dying back here . . . I'm wheezing . . . girl, oh, guuuuurl . . . you just . . . run ahead and throw me . . . down a rope."

When we get to the top, finally, gasping, we stagger over to the closest window to the view of the sparkling city and just gaze as we catch our breath. It is breathtaking.

It is totally worth it.

After a minute or twenty, when we can inhale quietly again, we slowly amble to the next window in the tower. Uncle Oscar resumes our earlier conversation as though no time has passed. As we stare out at the dawn's early light, he muses.

"You know, Rylee, there is something to be said for just being in the right place at the right time. Look to see what it is out there that you can do."

"Yeah, I plan to stay very close. I don't know doing what, but I have their backs."

"There will be some way for you to help, never fear. It will become clear, dearie, whether it's a big thing or just something small. But it's important for you to do it. When it comes down to it, child, we're all just cogs in the machine, but it won't run without each and every one of us."

I absorb that for a moment as we saunter clockwise from one tall stone-framed window to the next. We ponder and meander. From this elevation, the city looks like jewelry, spilled out on a huge navy-blue velvet tray. The east is faintly pink. I answer Uncle Oscar.

"That's my problem, I think. I question *everything* now. It's exhausting. And actually, that's what I'm freaking out about. . . . I'm scared I'm nothing but a pointless little cog in a pointless big machine—all of us are! I used to believe everything my mom said, but now I'm all wigged out, and every time I say anything doubtful about God and stuff I piss her off and panic my little brother. I don't mean to, but I just can't stop thinking . . . and it makes me really desperate. I feel like the bad guy. I'm so angry. I'm scared everything is a lie!"

I stop, unsteady and overheated and sad.

Uncle Oscar raises an idea.

"Darling, what if we all give poor, dear, face-palming God—and each other—a break?"

"What do you mean?"

"What if we all took a deep breath and allowed that though none of us has God's private e-mail, that's okay because sooner or later we certainly will! Or *won't!* Until then, maybe we could all be a little more relaxed?" Uncle Oscar crinkles his nose at me and faces the city. He still has traces of smudged eyeliner around his eyes. It looks cool. His cheeks are flushed. He shines so bright.

He speaks into the dawn. "Time without end? Yikes! Makes my head hurt." He shrugs cheerfully as we saunter on. "It's so big! Who cares? We don't need instructions to be kind! Do unto others, right? We are made in God's image, as I hear? Isn't that what the ardent followers are always claiming? And God is love, right?! So we *already* have the moral authority in our own hearts! Why not just reach down and let the joy out, maybe take a little time-out from everyone being so judgy and spiteful and wasting, wasting, *wasting* this time we have?"

We pause at what appears to be a wishing window, and he places a penny among some others. It's shiny and new.

I feel in my pocket, and the pebble from La Push is there. I wish on it hard and set it down among the coins.

After a second of looking thoughtfully at the pebble and the pennies, Uncle Oscar glances at me bashfully and his own voice catches, as he quotes a great man: " 'A catch in the voice, a faint sensation, as if a distant memory of falling from a great height.' It's Carl Sagan, about appreciating this fleeting moment of ours, which we have—against all odds. Have you experienced that yet, Rylee? The awe? That realization? The funny feeling we get sometimes, of goose-bumpy *recognition of something never glimpsed before*—that makes us turn our happy eyes to each other, our little hearts beating in syncopated harmony, and say, 'Are you getting this? We are here and our time is now.' The odds of us existing are astronomical! It is the marvel of us, every one of us. We *are* here! Of that alone we can be certain. That is the marvel of life: This little conscious time we share. *Make the most of it.* For me, it's the truth."

We look out at the Golden Gate Bridge stretching over the bay, shimmering like copper filigree. The light continues to grow. I nod slowly.

"Yeah, I get it . . . I think. I guess I've felt so empty and alone I started pretending to be a robot just to cope, to hang on and not be hurt, just keep going like a steam engine, but now I really want to count for *more* than just some stupid little cog in some pointless machine."

Uncle Oscar regards me in such a loving way.

"But you know what a cog is, don't you, child?" His voice is the barest whisper. Even so it echoes in the tower. Or maybe just in my head.

I shrug. He twinkles like the city as he gazes at me. Like he's filled with a wonderful secret. Over the bay the sun begins to rise.

"Why, it stands for 'child of God,' child! You didn't know that? Yes, it does! And we are! *All* of us! Every little cog is a child of God! Isn't that lucky? Each and every one!"

The next morning we all slept in till Sylvester barked at us to walk him and The Bomb. So we did.

Today is called Boxing Day, Uncle Frankie said, the day after Christmas in the UK and Canada. I've heard that. No one seems to know why, except that it doesn't have anything to do with boxers or ESPN.

We took it easy all day. Beau took pics on his smartphone so we could print them and put them into my heart locket: one of Beau, one of Leo and The Bomb and one of the uncles. In spite of my issues, that phone is awesome. Totally great pictures! It gives me an idea.

I go on Facebook and send one of Bommy to my friend Shazzie.

I love your doggy! But where have you been? she messages me back instantly. *I've been worried!!!!!! I messaged you about two days ago!*

Omg! I never thought about the fact that my Facebook friends might notice my absence! I send her a long message about what we have been up to.

Then I send her a pic . . . of me. After a minute, I hear a ping on Beau's phone.

Girlllllll!! Yer lovely! Why did you take so long?!!!!!!! I read on my page.

I beam, my eyes filled with happy tears. . . .

Later when I walk into the room where we're staying, Leo is sitting on the sofa bed, which we usually fold up during the day.

"Whatcha doing?"

"Nothing." She looks preoccupied. I can see her worried mind. Mine is too.

"Should I go away?"

"No. Stay. I'm just thinking." She has her phone out, looking at it. I can see she's been texting. Or maybe just got one.

"Is *he* at it again?" I get icy with anger. For gawd's sake, just leave her alone!

"Oh, that? Yeah, he texted like twenty million times. Rylee, don't worry! It's cool. I'm through with him! I'm deleting him!"

I look relieved as she continues.

"I'm more like thinking about when I get back. How should I do this? I'm afraid if I call CPS I might have to be a foster kid again and I will just take off again if they make me do that, and that was a mess last time. . . ." She fades out and sighs, then rubs her forehead distractedly.

I give her a second.

"Leo, how old were you when you ran away that time?"

"Thirteen."

"Well, I've been thinking about it and listen—now you're old enough to be emancipated. I looked it up. Check it out." I grab Beau's smartphone from the coffee table and navigate to where I was researching earlier. "Look, read this. There are some things we'll have to figure out for it to work, but no way do I think they are going to stick you back in foster care."

Leo snatches the phone and starts reading intently. Beau wanders in.

"Whatcha doing?"

"We are figuring out Leonie's future. It's looking so bright we gotta wear shades!"

"Cool. This phone rules."

Leonie looks up at him and over at me.

"There is some stuff I don't get. What does this mean 'an officer of the court, a member of law enforcement, a physician, or mental health care provider'? I know law enforcement is a cop. What I want to know is like Rylee said—who's the most not a cop? That's who I want to tell."

"Like your doctor," Beau suggests.

"Yeah, no . . . I don't have a doctor. I just go to whoever at the freebie clinic."

Figures. But thank God there are free clinics!

I put my hand out. By Jove, I think I might have it . . . or at least something.

"Give me back the phone. Let me try an idea."

I take the phone, go into the bathroom for privacy, and dial. When I come back out fifteen minutes later, I hand her the phone.

"My mom's name is Teresa, in case you don't know," I say as I hand her the phone. *Tell her.*

My mom is a nurse again. She is a health care professional. She will know what to do.

"Hello?" I hear my mom's wee voice coming out of the phone. "Ry? Are you still there?"

Leo takes ahold of it.

She draws a deep breath.

"Hello? Teresa? Hey. It's not Rylee. It's Leonie Cait—um— DuBois, and I would like to, um, report some abuse." She looks at me and shrugs. What to say about your whole life?

I smile encouragingly and put my hand on her shoulder. I nod my head exaggeratedly and give her a thumbs-up. Then I point for her to go in the bathroom for privacy if she wants.

Beau and I leave the vicinity. She still shuts the door behind her.

I think that worked out well.

My mom is on it! She is also determined to get Leonie's mom's attention, though Leo says good luck with that. Mom and Leo have talked twice since then, and that was the day before yesterday. And apparently there *are* other options besides going to the police.

"Something to be said for being in the right place at the right time," as my awesome Uncle Oscar observed.

And then last night . . .

We were sitting around after dinner. Beau said we would be going back to Seattle soon, in a day or so. We'd talked about it, and we wanted to get back and face the music before school was in session again, so as to be prepared.

The uncles looked sad. Seriously. Like they would miss us! Who'd a thunk?

They were so cute. They looked at each other and then Oscar shared a thought.

"You know, my dears, I've been pondering, and I think I've come up with a great solution for our quandary! You didn't know we had a quandary? A different quandary, but yes. Here's my thought: In March, during spring break, you three come back, and we will *all* go ballooning! I hereby give up my place on the terribly scary balloon you must jump from to Beau, and I will *rent us,* that is, Leonie, Rylee, and myself, unless you girls want to jump. I didn't think of that—no? Neither of you? Good! Anyway, I will rent us another nice, trustworthy balloon, from which we will float by and watch you two madmen, all the whilst taking disturbing pictures! How does that sound, chickadees? I've already made the reservations."

"Yeah! Awesome!" We think it sounds great. We think it sounds amazing!

We sit and babble about this great idea when suddenly Leonie jumps up and runs into our room. We hear her throwing stuff around and crackling paper, and then she comes out like two minutes later, with a present wrapped in the *Guardian.*

"Merry Christmas!" She hands it to Oscar and kisses his cheek.

He looks down at it and then unwraps. It's her Edward T-shirt from Forks.

"Merry Christmas, Uncle Oscar! Otherwise you wouldn't have anything from us! It will fit too, I'm pretty sure. I always have to get a large because of my boobs and then shrink it! Do you like it? Want to try it on? I only wore it once. Say yes!"

Leo is so pleased to have this gift for him.

Oscar looks over at Frankie with this look in his eyes I can't read. They telecommunicate.

Frankie micro-nods.

Oscar turns to her. His eyes are bright.

"Oh, sweetheart! That is so lovable of you and so generous! But I can't take your Edward T-shirt! Then you wouldn't have anything from *Twilight!*"

"It's cool! I want to. Besides I can always stare when Beau wears his! Please? Try it on!"

Oscar goes and puts it on. He comes back. It's tight, but he's slender so it fits just fine. Leo jumps up and down and claps her hands.

"Oh! You look so cute! Beau, take a picture of him with your phone!"

Oscar looks down at the shirt and beams.

"Well, I have to say, this is adorable, honeybee! I do really like it! Thank you, Leonie! Look at him—lil' Edward—he's as cute as an extra shiny button!"

"Sparkly even!" I interject helpfully.

"Yes, he is and I just love my new sparkly T-shirt! I might have to incorporate it into my couture for the parade."

"Yeah, maybe Captain Marvel likes *Twilight* too!" I add super brightly.

"Oh, my goodness! He might just have to!"

"We love it on you." It's a group vote. It does totally rock. The look in Leo's eyes . . .

Uncle Oscar gazes down and smiles as he smoothes his shimmery shirt.

"You know what else? This is only my second new T-shirt all year. I just realized that."

"Yeah? What was your other one?"

Oscar whispers conspiratorially. "*Harry Potter*. I have a T-shirt with wonderful Albus Dumbledore. I'm totally a fan!"

Frankie rolls his eyes and holds his hands to his heart melo-dramatically.

"In love," he mouths to us silently.

We laugh. Figures!

That was a couple days ago.

Yesterday Beau and Frankie left on the train. They are going home to Seattle a few days early so Frankie can see Gina and meet Matt. Then Beau will stay home and Frankie will return to San Francisco, and we'll all come back for the ballooning during spring break.

Leo and I are chilling for a couple more days, and then we'll drive home with The Bomb. I've talked to my mom, and she is cool with both Leo and The Bomb staying with us while they get things figured out. She has some time to help Leonie before her job starts.

In fact, knowing my mom, she will never want Leonie to leave. Or Bommy either.

When I called my mom, I told her we'd start for home soon. School starts the day after Epiphany, and I said we'd be back in Seattle by that weekend and ready to go. And we will.

But first, something happened to me.

It was yesterday afternoon, and we were down at the wharf killing time till Uncle Oscar got home from work, and people were milling around and we were enjoying the feeble sunshine. I'd sat down on one of the big benches by the water, and Leonie and The Bomb were dancing like they do, and I was laughing at them like I do, when this girl came over and sat down on the other side of the bench I was on, which of course freaked me out immediately.

The Bomb was twirling on her hind legs, and Leonie was not paying attention to what was going on, and this person was looking at me, and I could feel myself winding up, getting wrapped too tight, stressing. . . .

"Hi," she says. No attitude visible.

"Hey." I feel myself unfreeze a little.

I look over at her. She's staring at me.

This chick is good-sized. I mean, she isn't fat but she's big. Like cut. She smiles.

"I was watching you over there when you pulled that stick out of the sand and threw it to your dog."

"Yeah." I acknowledge I did do that.

"You're strong."

"Yeah, I am." I am also surly. So ready for the crap I'm about to get.

"Like how much do you weigh?"

I just look at her. Sigh deeply.

Are you kidding? After everything we've been through, that *I've* been through, to ask me that and start giving me crap again is *not* freaking on! I shut down immediately.

"Look, why don't you just bounce?" I ask wearily. "I didn't start anything with you."

She looks at me and laughs.

"No, you got it wrong! No offense. I think you are perfect!"

Now I'm worried that she's actually crazy.

"Okay. Whatever," I say. "Just go."

"Listen, have you ever heard of Roller Derby? A bunch of tough chicks all roller-skate in this indoor race? Have you ever seen one? Never? Well, do you want to?"

"We aren't even from here," I tell her to make her go away. Her face falls.

"Oh . . . dang! You're perfect. We need you! How tall are you?"

I consider not answering, but then again, why not? "Five nine."

"Wow. I bet you can totally take a charge."

"Yeah." That I can. That is one true thing.

"Do you skate?"

"Uh . . . sort of. Badly."

"It's not that hard to learn. It's mostly about heart."

I laugh.

"That I got."

Without doubt, that I got.

"Where are you from?"

"Seattle."

"Omg! Seattle?! Seattle has the *best* Roller Derby! Actually, several! You should totally go see them! You could skate with

234 / Mary McKinley

them if you tried! The Rat City Rollergirls?! Seriously! They
are epic! They are legend! They are the best!"

"Really?"

"Yeah! Omg! I can't believe you've never seen your own
Roller Derby team! Look, why don't you come see ours? We
skate tonight. We're off the hook!"

So we do. Leonie and Uncle Oscar and me.

And it looks so fun! The roller chicks are mostly about my
size, except for this little one they keep throwing forward to
make their team win. I laugh so hard I'm overheating. They are
all tall and fat, or big and buff, and most have a ton of ink.

Glamazons and rock chicks roller-skating! It's awesome.

After the derby, my new friend, whose name is Jamie, intro-
duces me around, and of course some of the roller chicks here
know some of the Rat City girls at home! We get each other's
names and plan to friend each other on Facebook so they can
introduce me.

They are really sure I would make an awesome Roller
Derby girl. I have never in my life been preapproved because of
the way I look. It's fantastic!

I am definitely going to check it out when we get home.
Jamie gave me a beaten pair of their old skates to get some practice with. I tried them on in the rink before we left, when the
track was empty. The skates are so old they fit like soft gloves,
and after falling down eleven thousand times, I'm getting the
hang of it. And you know what? I am talented! I got the need
for speed!

I got the need for speed . . . just not while driving.

So that was fun. Maybe something to make me tick!
Maybe even life changing. It feels like it.
Maybe this whole trip has been.
So okay, then I guess this is it.

I've been dreading this part, you know. It seems like all emotions ever do is make me bawl like a baby now that I actually acknowledge them. But whatever, it's actually okay. I've found that I can cry and I won't rust, you know? It's not the end of the world to have feelings. If I get knocked down, I'll just get up again. In fact, I plan on getting knocked down!

But I do feel like crying again.

So instead, let's review! What have we all learned?

Well, Beau finally figured out which way is home, Leonie got a new groove, and The Bomb is beloved. Yay! We learned not to judge a book by its cover. That nobody is perfect. That maybe "The Bomb" is a confusing name for a dog. And we learned to treat people like we want to be treated . . . the Golden Rule. The Golden Rule, guys.

And we learned to give peace a chance.

But you already knew all that, right?

Of course you did!

Hay; it's been stuffed in your little old head this whole time, *right?* It's nothing new! It's not like you get a *diploma* for realizing it! I mean, even *cobbing* to it now is a little *corny*. . . .

The other thing I want to point out is that it wouldn't have been the same trip without you.

This whole trip—it's really been Beau, Lee, The Bomb and me . . . and *you*.

I've never actually said it, but you totally had to be there too, you know? To bear witness and realize the risk we all took. So there would be a point. To tell what we've all been through and what we've seen. To spread the word. What we've learned. How we chose the right wolf.

That we're not really hurt.

And so, for that, I thank you!

With all my *heart*. Listen, friend me, okay? I'll post pictures of us in the balloon and Beau's and Frank's faces when they jump out. It'll be *hee*-larious! Just hit me up, okay? And keep in touch. I know whatever you decide to major in, you'll be *out standing* in the field!

So . . . that's my time and I'm out.

Keep your wits sharp and don't take any wooden nickels (my dad used to say that too).

See you in the funny papers!

Rusty's Retro Road Trip:
Mostly Oldies from the Eighties and Beyond

These are the tunes I listen to the most. They are generally old but cool.

I'll say what they are about/who each is for and why.

Songs for Me

"Ha Ha Ha" by Flipper:
To start things off, this is an awesome song about how everything is pathetic.

"Teenage Frankenstein" by Alice Cooper:
I'm a monster. Just ask the baboons.

"Scary Monsters (and Super Creeps)" by David Bowie:
I dedicate this to my lil' school chums.

"Cathedral" by Crosby, Stills, Nash, and Young:
A song about losing my religion.

"Mad World" by Tears for Fears:
I'm sorry to say I have felt this way most of my teens.

"All Stood Still" by Ultravox:
Because I am frozen in place. Maybe we all are.

"Kung Fu Fighting" by Carl Douglas:
Except my bro—kick on wich yer bad self!

Songs for Leonie

"Rock On" by David Essex:
For Leo, the prettiest girl I have ever seen. Turn the bass wayyyyy up!

"Hungry Like the Wolf" by Duran Duran:
Because she always is. Hungry.

"Da Da Da" by Trio:
I don't love you; you don't love me. . . . What I wish Leo would tell Ratskin.

"Tusk" by Fleetwood Mac:
Because I don't think anyone tells her they love her.

"She's Lost Control" by Joy Division:
Because Leo is outta control. Seriously.

"My Big Hands (Fall Through the Cracks)" by Talking Heads:
For Ratskin. Keep your big hands to yourself. Jerk.

"I Saved the World Today" by the Eurythmics:
For Leonie, when she saved The Bomb.

"Woman King" by Iron and Wine:
Because Leonie looks like a warrior princess in the purple silk robe.

Songs for Beau

"What Have I Done to Deserve This?" by Pet Shop Boys:
It's a question Beau asks.

"Clampdown" by the Clash:
Boy, get running! It's the best years of your life they want to steal!

"Don't Fade on Me" by Tom Petty:
For Beau, because he must stay so it does *get better!*

"Can't Find My Way Home" by Ellen McIlwaine:
Beau, even though he is home, in my opinion.

"The Town" by Macklemore:
I want the town (Seattle) to be Beau's home.

Songs for The Bomb

"Who Let the Dogs Out" by Baha Men:
Answer: Leo. And she'd do it again!

"Don't Eat the Yellow Snow" by Frank Zappa:
Watch out where the huskies go! Lol!

"I Wanna Be Your Dog" by the Stooges:
Who wouldn't want to be Leo's dog? She's sweet and kind.

"You Dropped a Bomb on Me" by the Gap Band:
Because: Duh!!!! (For us I think it's "You Dropped *The* Bomb on Me!") This one is really for Leonie, but Bommy can share it.

"Thank You" by Dido:
What The Bomb would tell Leo, if she could.

Random Songs for the Road

"Convoy" by C. W. McCall:
Because it's hilarious! They got smokeys everywhere. Lol omg! 10-4!

"I Will Follow" by U2:
Because we are running away.

"Where Did You Sleep Last Night" by Nirvana:
What our moms were wondering—mine and Beau's.

"Bela Lugosi's Dead" by Bauhaus:
For the vampires of Forks. (Also, Werewolves <3 La Push. Heh!)

***The Dark Side of the Moon* by Pink Floyd:**
I don't know, it just seems to fit, like a strange dream. . . .

Songs for the Uncles

"Same Love" by Macklemore:
For the uncles, because it is the same love.

"We're a Happy Family" by the Ramones:
Because it's hilarious! Also because we're not really hurt!

"I'm Not Like Everybody Else" by the Kinks:
Because they're not.

"She Moved Through the Fair" by Odetta:
This is almost exactly the way Uncle Oscar sang this song at the "Annie-You-All Orphan's" Christmas party.

"Angel" by Sarah McLachlan:
For Uncle Oscar because he's such an angel to Lee, especially when she's sad.

"Over the Rainbow" by Israel Kamakawiwo'ole:
A really beautiful version of this awesome old song.

Songs to Make It Better

"Make It Stop (September's Children)" by Rise Against:
Non-retro song about suicide and bullying. Make it stop. Words hurt.

"Working Class Hero" by John Lennon: We can be heroes.

"Tubthumping" by Chumbawamba:
I get knocked down—but I *get up again!* You're never gonna keep me down! This one's for all of us. (I so do not condone the cocktail list, though! Omg! Lol!)

Songs for You

"I Was Broken" by Marcus Foster:
But it's over now. (And I'm so glad!) So crazy the lyrics fit so well. It's how I feel. So, yeah. Thanks. You made it better.

See you in the funny papers!

In Remembrance

With love to the "real" Leonie: who I hope finally did rat out the real Ratskin—and come to realize her true worth.

And with so much love to my "real" Beau: 1958–1984.

As well as to all the dear ones we lost too soon, to illness and despair, that the celebration of their lives will inspire us, though bereaved, to carry on dancing.

Last words I want you to see in this book:

"Certain unalienable Rights . . . Life, Liberty and the pursuit of Happiness."